Also by Amy Carol Reeves
Ripper

To Atticus Leclair, whose creativity makes me smile.

Renegade

Renegade

AMY CAROL REEVES

flux
TM
Woodbury, Minnesota

First Edition
First Printing, 2013

Book design by Bob Gaul
Cover illustration © 2012 Dominick Finelle/The July Group
Interior map illustration © Chris Down

Flux, an imprint of Llewellyn Worldwide Ltd.

Library of Congress Cataloging-in-Publication Data
Reeves, Amy Carol.
    Renegade: a Ripper novel/Amy Carol Reeves.—First edition.
        pages cm
    Summary: "After vanquishing the Conclave, Arabella Sharp tries to focus on her medical studies but soon discovers that she and those she loves have not escaped the manipulations of the Ripper"—Provided by the publisher.
    ISBN 978-0-7387-3262-6 (alk. paper)
    1. Jack, the Ripper—Juvenile fiction. [1. Jack, the Ripper—Fiction. 2. Physicians—Fiction. 3. London (England)—History—19th century—Fiction. 4. Great Britain—History—19th century—Fiction.] I. Title.
    PZ7.R25578Re 2013
    [Fic]—dc23
                                                                2012047299

Flux
Llewellyn Worldwide Ltd.
2143 Wooddale Drive
Woodbury, MN 55125-2989
www.fluxnow.com

Acknowledgments

As always, I am so grateful to my awesome agent, Jessica Sinsheimer.

Renegade would not be in its current shape without my very insightful editor, Brian Farrey-Latz. And much thanks to Sandy Sullivan at Flux for helping me with copyedits.

Finally, I owe so much to my husband, Shawn Reeves; during the heaviest writing stages, he talked me off of very high cliffs.

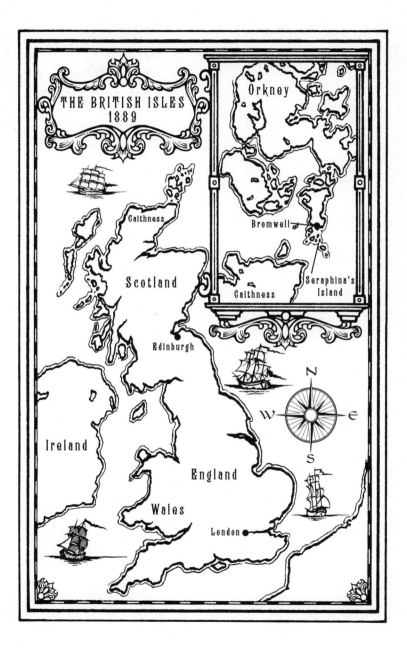

Prologue

She strayed further from her home than she had in years. Her gills pulsated with the waves as she moved along the ocean floor.

A storm raged far above her. It might have killed any human on the surface. But she slid safely along the calmer depths—her fingertips, breasts, and belly grazing the surfaces of sand and shells, her dragon-tail propelling her forward.

She paused as she felt something, anchoring herself into the sand with her claws and talons. In the watery darkness, she smiled fondly. It was a skull fragment. She had found these many times before, and she would keep it as she had the others.

Her keeper had not visited her for four months. This was a long absence, unusual. She felt a sense of trouble for him now. An intuition. When he had come to her last, in early November, he had seemed distant, distracted. She cared little for his murderous duties or his love conquests, but she worried. She remembered how agitated and distracted he had been almost twenty years ago, over that situation with that woman. She strained to remember her name. Caroline? And then jealousy pulsed within her... they had wanted the daughter.

And she hungered again as she had not in twenty years. For blood.

PART I

--- ❦ ---

"… O I wish
That I were some great princess, I would build
Far off from men a college like a man's,
And I would teach them all that men are taught;
We are twice as quick!"

—The Princess

One

Twilight was the worst time for me.

That's when the guilt seeped through my veins like an illness. Nearly every night, I was plagued with dreams about the murders I had committed. I couldn't get the images out of my mind—myself, crouched up in that hothouse tree. A knife in my mouth as I waited for Julian Bartlett. Blood from John Perkins and Marcus Brown smeared on my face and skirts. I vividly remembered the feel of the knife cutting through their flesh, tearing muscle, and hitting bone. The memories made me nauseated. In my mind, I was no better than Max as he stalked women on the streets last autumn.

But then, I always told myself, the Conclave had murdered my mother. They had planned to execute William and Simon. They would have gone on killing God knows how many innocent human beings during their immortal lives, all for the greater good.

A Posse Ad Esse.

It almost made me laugh.

That morning, as always, I went ahead and got out of bed weighted by my guilt and conflicting feelings. This guilt had become a bit of an albatross around my neck, and I didn't know how to atone for it.

As I dressed, I studied Mother's portrait. My real father, the artist Dante Gabriel Rossetti, had painted it. In my mind, it was his most daring portrait—Caroline Westfield, society belle, as a lamia, nude from her waist up. Grandmother couldn't bear seeing it, so I kept it in my closet for myself. Max had sent it to me, so it was a gift from the devil ... yet I cherished it nonetheless.

As I put on my hospital work dress and pinafore, I allowed myself to think of Max. Except for the delivery of the portrait, neither William nor Simon nor I had heard from him for over four months. But I knew he was around. Somewhere. *Au revoir*, he had signed his note. We would meet again, and when we did, it would be my blood he would want. I had killed his Conclave. The elixir and elixir formula had certainly disappeared in the fire. He had lost the means of sustaining his immortality.

I shuddered as I pinned my hair back and forced myself to mentally prepare for my day. It would be my first day returning to work at Whitechapel Hospital. I hadn't been there since returning to Grandmother's house after that terrible night with the Conclave. Then, soon after Christmas, Grandmother had fallen very ill with pneumonia. I attributed it to the stresses she had endured that autumn—our many arguments, her worry about me, my friend Mariah's death. My own guilt about how I'd bucked against her rules overwhelmed me. Yet I knew that I couldn't completely conform to her lifestyle. The boundaries must be set—at breakfast, I would tell her that I was resuming my work at the hospital. Grandmother had been feeling better; she had been stronger. In fact, I could hear her now, downstairs, fussing heartily at Ellen, her hare-brained maid.

I hurried out of my bedroom and descended the stairs, anxious to begin work at the hospital.

"Where are you going?" Grandmother asked, alarmed. She paused as she ate her eggs, staring hard at my black work dress, at the folded pinafore in my arms.

When I faced her, I saw that her complexion already seemed better. She was thinner, but not quite so pale. She would be fine now without me attending to her all day.

"I'm returning to the hospital," I said, swallowing my tea too fast and burning my throat a bit. I felt hurried as I ate.

"The murders, getting stabbed in the leg, those eviscerated women, were not enough to keep you away?"

"No, Grandmother. And there haven't been any murders for several months. I'll be fine. I must return to work. If you remember, I need to apply to medical school soon. I have not been at the hospital since October, and I need the experience."

She took a sip of tea.

I stood, wiped my mouth, and started to walk out of the dining room.

"Do you have anything else to tell me? Anything else that will further shock my system?" She asked this shrilly, without even looking at me.

As I left the dining room, I saw our very patient butler, Richard, waiting in the corridor with my coat.

I felt prickled at Grandmother's tone of voice; a thread of mischievousness coursed through my veins. Oh, why couldn't I keep my bloody mouth shut?

"Yes, in fact, I do have something else to tell you," I said as I buttoned my coat. "William Siddal and I are dining at William Morris's house on Thursday evening." William Morris and his wife, Jane Burden Morris, were Pre-Raphaelites—eccentric artists and, essentially, Grandmother's most dreaded nightmare. William had become close to them through Dante Gabriel Rossetti, his adoptive father. Gabriel had rescued William, a four-year-old orphan, from the streets and raised him as his own.

I heard the sound of her teacup smashing on the floor.

"What?" Grandmother appeared in the hallway, her eyes blazing, her back ramrod-straight. She approached me, and I saw then that she was more recovered, much healthier, than I had thought.

"You are aware that Jane Morris was William's father's mistress, are you not?" she snapped. "I had hoped, rather than believed, that you had forgotten about the Siddal boy, but now I see that I was devastatingly wrong. How can William dine with Rossetti's mistress?"

"Yes, Grandmother. I have listened to your lectures many times these past months. But you know that I am, and will continue to be, friends with William Siddal as well as with his aunt. Christina Rossetti is a dear person, and both she and William have been so kind to me. William's father's scandals are all past history, Grandmother. The family has moved on, forgotten about them. And William has told me that Jane Morris was such a mentor to him after his father's death. I have looked forward to meeting her."

Quickly, very quickly, before she could say anything else, I hurried out the door, but not before seeing a small, almost imperceptible wry smile on Richard's wrinkled face.

As she returned to her island home, she sighed angrily, frustrated at herself for her unquenchable longings, for her hunger. She hated when it arose. She had so much to keep her comfortable, and none of the daily worries, busy routines, or petty concerns that plagued the rest of the human race.

She descended the stone steps into her home in her human form, salt water dripping from her naked legs and puddling onto the cool marble floor. She passed the library. She passed the treasure room. She passed all of her half-finished portraits, which hung on the walls. She might finish one of them someday, but thus far, none seemed worth completing. She thought vaguely about how she would have to tend to the animals in the menagerie before the evening ended. Tending to the animals was perhaps her greatest duty for the Conclave. Her keeper, when he visited her island home, often brought animals to her and took others back to Robert Buck for his hothouses or experiments. As her keeper had explained, the Conclave moved their headquarters often—so often that her island menagerie was their main menagerie, the permanent home for all of Dr. Buck's animals, serpents, and birds.

Robert Buck, the great scientist, she thought wryly.

Still clutching the skull fragment, she walked the entire length of the long great hall, the center of her small but luxurious underground home. She stopped when she came to a door that opened into a narrow set of damp stone steps spiraling upward—a shortcut to another part of her small island. This staircase was merely functional— practically a cave passage up from her underground world. Outside, her island was rocky and not easy to walk upon, particularly when she was in her human form. Thus her home offered several of these hidden stairs, leading to different parts of the island, so that she did not have to walk too far to get where she wanted. Her keeper had been so thoughtful when the home was constructed.

After ascending the steps, she slid through a narrow crevice and out into the blustery evening. As she stood outside, she surveyed some small mounds of dirt. The brown spots dimpled the sandy grass that stretched the short distance between herself and the sea. The mounds would disappear eventually, when they became absorbed into the sea, spurting the bleached bones into the ocean waters.

She opened the mound nearest to her and patted the skull fragment into it. She heard it crunch against the other pieces of bone. Many of the mounds held more complete corpses, in deeper graves. She had found these dead ones in the ocean. Three infant bodies. Several women's bodies. Many men's bodies.

Hidden rocks in the area snagged so many boats.

Whenever she swam in the sea following a wreck, she felt fascinated by the faces of the drowned. She contemplated their aborted hopes. Often she found herself drawn to the dead, so she took them back with her to this place.

Almost all were dead.

Some, the stronger ones, swam to the safety of the nearby Orkney Islands' shores. She would watch their tiny forms struggle on the water's surface from the depths below.

None of them ever found her island. Not even the dead. The tides swept mostly away from where she lived; her shores and home remained shrouded under massive rocks and fog. Her keeper had picked her island well. If visible at all, it would seem to be only a jumble of sharp rock peaks, a place to be avoided. And if anyone arrived alive ... she frowned.

It was just better that they did not.

She contemplated the setting sun—golden, achingly glorious. Then she descended back into her home.

She would take a bath, a hot one. She hoped that the warmth would take away her resurgent cravings for flesh and blood.

These feelings had not arisen in so long. In the early years of her immortality, almost eighty years ago, it had been hard not to kill struggling shipwrecked victims, hapless fishermen. But she had gained better control after her first decade on this island. In fact, she hadn't killed in almost twenty years, and her keeper had warned her often that she could not—it would be devastating if she exposed herself, or them.

As she stepped into the bath, settling her naked form into the tub, the candlelight illuminated her skin. A chalice had been tattooed across her entire back. It was not small and indiscrete, as the Conclave's markings were, but large, spanning the space between her shoulders. The stem extended down her spine toward the words, *A Posse Ad Esse*.

It was her mark of Cain. She, the outcast, was a puzzling inconsistency in the modern world.

Two

I was not certain what I expected to find at Whitechapel Hospital—which was now without Julian Bartlett's and Robert Buck's leadership—but upon arriving I found it running efficiently, with more patients and workers even than before. The overwhelming atmosphere of business and urgency, always particularly strong on the first floor, hung in the air.

"Delivery. Twins," Sister Josephine snapped at me the moment I stepped into the first floor ward. I had forgotten her efficient and forceful personality, and I felt myself smile a bit as I followed her broad form to the delivery area at the back part of the ward. It was as if I had only missed one day's work, as opposed to four months.

"I'm not terribly worried," Josephine added quickly, the silver cross around her neck swinging ferociously as I hurried behind her to the curtained delivery area. "She delivered a large child last year with no difficulty. Still... twins can be complicated." She bit her lip.

"Of course," I replied as we went behind the curtain. I had only seen two sets of twins delivered at Whitechapel Hospital in which both infants emerged healthily and without incident. But upon observing the patient and seeing that she was of a proper age to deliver—thirty-one—and apparently physically healthy—of good weight, with most of her teeth—my fears abated a bit. Her name was Fanny Brunson. As I read through Simon's neatly written notes on her medical history, I saw that Josephine was indeed correct—the woman's last delivery had been an easy one, and her child healthy.

I felt warmed when William stepped behind the curtain to aid in the delivery. Not wanting to agitate Grandmother during her illness, I had not invited William to our house. I had only seen him at stolen moments. We had had brief conversations at agreed-upon times while I walked her pug, Jupe, around our Kensington neighborhood. I did get to visit him once, when I escaped Grandmother's home long enough to call upon Christina. But as it was high time for Grandmother to accept him as part of my life, I'd told him to come to the house for tea, on Thursday, before we left for the Morris household.

"Back in the land of the living, Abbie?" William asked with an arched eyebrow.

As I talked to him, I felt struck, once again, by his dark handsomeness—despite having known him for months now and even saving his life. Yet I hadn't seen him at the hospital in so long … and I couldn't help but ponder, for a moment, how he looked like a portrait model rather than an overworked physician in an impoverished East End hospital.

As we talked, Simon entered the delivery area and I immediately felt a dull ache in my gut. Simon had visited Grandmother and me several times since Christmas, but he knew that I loved William. And I knew this was painful for him—particularly since he and William were far from friends. Even though they now directed Whitechapel Hospital together, I could sense the tension between them, and suspected that their working relationship was probably often difficult.

Josephine and the other nurses had left to locate supplies, leaving William, Simon, and me alone momentarily. William rinsed his hands in a lime chloride solution and began studying Simon's notes from Fanny's previous delivery.

"I have this one, Simon. But I think the nursery might need a Sunday School teacher. Or perhaps an exorcist, if those infants don't stop squalling."

Simon's lips remained in a thin, tight line. With his pale, handsome face, tall thin figure, and curly blond hair, he, like William, looked out of place. He seemed too ethereal, too lovely, to work in this place where we all smelled like carbolic acid, blood, and urine by the end of the day.

"This is a twin delivery, William. It would be wise to have two attending physicians."

"Yes, yes," William said irritably. "But you see, Miss…" He peeked at the woman's chart. "Fanny Brunson has delivered a ten-pound child last year with ease. Twins, I am convinced, will not be a problem. And I have the excellent Miss Arabella Sharp—the future physician, bare-knuckle boxer, and skilled knife thrower—here, so I think everything should go swimmingly."

I was about to come to Simon's defense when a nurse entered with a tray of instruments.

Simon, his expression cool, nodded and left. The curtain rippled sharply behind him.

The infants came out with ease, but when Miss Brunson didn't expel the placenta, I saw William's brows furrow. He was a capable physician, but I'd worked with him long enough in deliveries and surgeries to know that he did not handle stress well. He grew impatient too quickly.

"Damn!" he cursed, then began to try to pull the placenta out himself. He should have known better than to try that.

"No, William," I whispered, so that Fanny would not hear us. She was exhausted after all the pushing and seemed to pay no attention to us. Nonetheless, I did not want to alarm her. "We should be patient, even if it takes time. I don't want her to bleed more, and there's an increased risk for puerperal fever if you pull the placenta out."

Fanny moaned as her contractions began again, and William's agitation increased even more. I remembered how agitated and depressed he had become when a young girl died after the caesarean he had performed upon her.

After several minutes, I decided that Fanny Brunson should be checked. I cleaned my hands and stepped in front of William, feeling inside her.

Simon must have heard William's loud cursing because he suddenly stepped into the curtained delivery area. "Aren't things going *swimmingly?*"

Before William could retort, I felt something and smiled. Both William and Simon quieted and stared at me. "Triplets."

When I finally had a break in the afternoon, I made my way up to the fourth floor to find a few stolen moments with William. I discovered that much was left unchanged since Dr. Bartlett and Dr. Buck had been there. The floor was still poorly lit, shadowed and stuffy. I tried to swallow my feelings of fear, of disgust—memories of the murders. Nonetheless, I felt myself tremble a bit as I walked down the fourth floor corridor.

"William," I said, knocking on the door that had once been the door to Robert Buck's office. This was the office closest to the stairs. The door was already slightly ajar as I stepped inside. Although no one was in it, I saw that Simon now used the office. His desk had only a single book on it. I saw its title: *Neurypnology.* From the description under the title, it appeared to be a book on hypnosis and mesmerism, specifically something called hypnotherapy. *Curious.* I'd heard of hypnosis but did not know much about it, and I wondered what Simon's interest in it was. As I glanced about the room, I saw medical books, theology books, and several

Greek Bibles lining the bookshelves. Robert Buck's taxidermied owl still peered down from a high shelf behind the desk. I felt the hairs on my neck prickle a bit.

Quickly, I continued to the end of the hall, to where Dr. Bartlett's office had been. William must have claimed that office for himself. I saw William's medical books, notebooks with his handwriting, and pens scattered about the desk. Julian Bartlett's small pedestal with the skull, that curious skull covered with pen-scratched notes, remained in the corner of the room. Again I felt myself unsettled. Wondering where William could be, I turned and saw that the large doors to the laboratory were slightly ajar.

Like the offices, the laboratory seemed very much the same. In spite of the fact that I wanted to erase the memory of the Conclave from my mind, I felt somewhat glad to see Dr. Buck's specimens still lining the shelves. All of his odd creatures in formaldehyde had always intrigued me. It was such an incredible collection. I let my eyes linger on the baby sting rays, the small sharks. A case of exotic insects. I frowned, suddenly remembering the more gruesome specimens he had kept in cases at the Montgomery Street house—the shrunken heads, the hair.

The pharmacy door in the laboratory was wide open, all of the medicines and herbal bottles stacked neatly as usual. William always insisted that it be kept orderly. I went into the side room with the tub. I hoped, as I opened the door to it, that William had had the decency to remove the picture—that little painting of the goblet with the Conclave's phrase across it: *A Posse Ad Esse*.

I entered the room.

No. The painting was still there, facing me.

Don't be foolish, Abbie, I heard myself say. *Face your fears.*
Walking over to the picture, I reached out. Gingerly, I
touched it.

I hadn't had a vision since the autumn. But the moment
my fingers touched the cheap wood frame of the painting,
one came upon me like an electric current. I saw bubbles in
the greenish depths of water somewhere. A creature, dragonlike, with a tail. Claws. In the murky water, I saw the creature's scaly haunches, thick and muscular like a lioness's, as
my nostrils became overwhelmed with the smell of fish, of
seaweed. The monster had hair, long hazelnut hair billow-
ing out like burnt gold threads in the water. I saw the swift,
fleshy movement of breasts.

I gasped, and the vision left me almost as soon as it
appeared.

I stood there, shaking and reeling. Dizzied. I immediately thought of Rossetti's portrait of my mother. But this
creature was certainly not my mother. The hair was different; I felt sure it was not her painted image come to life. But
the being in the vision nevertheless seemed to be the mythological lamia—the exact creature Mother had portrayed.

Lamias were in fairy tales, in myths, in Rossetti's painting. They did not exist. Yet all of my visions, so far, had been
of true events, of actual people.

The vision was baffling enough, but new thoughts now
began to enter my mind. *Why did Max give me the portrait?
Is there some kind of message in it?*

I felt hands upon my shoulders, then around my face. I whipped around.

"William! You frightened me."

But before I could say another word, his lips were upon mine. During the few times this year when I had met with William, it had always been in public places where we had very little time or opportunity for intimacy. Thus now, alone with William, uninterrupted, the disturbing vision melted from my consciousness as I surrendered myself to the kiss.

I fell deeper into the kiss, a melting heat building inside me. It had been too long since we had touched like this. My desire became almost overwhelming. Somehow, William untied my stained work pinafore, letting it slide away from my dress onto the floor. Then in a single movement he plucked the pins from my hair, and I felt it fall heavy around my shoulders.

My thoughts and senses became frenzied as I felt his fingers wrapped in the locks of my hair. His lips moved softly down my cheek, my neck, to the top button of my dress, which he began to unbutton. Vaguely, I thought I should be using better sense; still, in spite of this, I heard myself groan, softly.

Only Simon's footsteps entering the laboratory pulled me from my thoughts. The door to this closet was still open slightly. I hoped that he hadn't heard us.

He had.

The footsteps stopped abruptly just inside the laboratory. After a three-second pause, as I tried to quiet my breathing,

I heard him turn and exit. In another moment, I heard the door of his office shut. Hard.

"William…" I pushed him away from me, blushing as I pinned back my hair and tied my pinafore back on.

He sighed, his face flushed. He ran his fingers through his hair.

"I'm sorry," I stuttered. "I know we haven't had much time alone, but this is…" I felt my cheeks grow fiery. "Moving far too swiftly to be rational."

He smirked. Unrepentant. I smiled and kissed him lightly.

"I need to return to work."

"Yes." He sighed again. Loudly this time. "I've got paperwork in my office." He pulled his pocket watch out and groaned. "And an old friend of ours, Inspector Abberline, will be paying Simon and me a visit this afternoon."

I had finished putting the last pin in my hair and tying my pinafore. "Why?"

William shrugged. "Actually, I'm not precisely certain. Perhaps about the Ripper murders. Still unsolved in his mind."

"Perhaps. But almost four months have elapsed since then." I felt an odd mix of amusement and pity, thinking of how the hard-working Inspector would never solve this case. Simultaneously, I also felt my general uneasiness—Max was still out there. Somewhere.

"Abberline came here a few times in January," William said. "But we haven't seen him lately. The timing is odd…" His voice drained off a bit. As we left the laboratory, he whispered, "So you still haven't heard from Max since the portrait delivery?"

"No."

He lowered his voice to a whisper. "And you have had no more... visions?"

Josephine reached the top of the stairs in a fluster, wanting to speak to William about something. I felt relieved. The vision of the lamia made no sense. It did not seem to fit with the Conclave's history, or with my experiences with them. And yet, I had seen it when I touched the painting. But I felt ridiculous telling William about it now. So I welcomed Josephine's interruption.

As they proceeded down the corridor to his office, I paused at Simon's door—still shut. He was in there; I saw the lamplight stream out from under the door. I almost knocked. Oddly, I felt the urge to talk to him, before William, about the vision. I loved William, fiercely. Too fiercely. I bit my lip; certainly I loved him heedlessly. I felt myself blush, remembering how heated I'd become just now. But though I loved William, I knew I would feel more comfortable discussing the vision with Simon. I thought of how understanding he had been toward me when I first told him about my visions. Thinking of the book on his desk about hypnotherapy, I knew that Simon had more understanding of the mind's mysteries, of the esoteric.

But then I remembered hearing Simon's footsteps in the laboratory, knowing that he knew I was in there with William. I didn't love Simon, and yet, I admired him so intensely... his compassion, even his guarded nature intrigued me. He was so lovely and enigmatic, and I often wanted to peek behind the veil of his thoughts. But I considered how sharply he had shut his office door. And the ache within me intensified, so I only paused, then continued to the stairs.

Three

On Thursday, William arrived promptly in the early evening for tea. I was hoping to kindly ease Grandmother into becoming comfortable with William, to seeing that he was not a laudanum-addicted rake like Dante Gabriel Rossetti had been. But the moment the three of us sat down in the parlor, I began to feel that I'd been wrong in assuming that this was a good idea.

Grandmother held Jupe tightly on her lap as she took tea with us, and her warmth toward William was more like an Arctic chill. I watched the clock—watched it tick away at an agonizingly slow pace. We only had fifteen more minutes to endure with her before we would depart for dinner at the Morris household. Grandmother kept asking William prying questions about his family. About his Italian relatives, the Polidoris. About his aunt, Christina Rossetti, and how she dealt with the "notoriety" of her great-uncle, John Polidori, the physician and vampire-book writer, and the scandals of her brother,

Gabriel. I blushed in embarrassment and anger for Grandmother; it was beneath even her to be so rude. Yet William exceeded all my expectations in his patience with her, answering each time pleasantly and calmly.

The moment I had the opportunity, I changed the subject back to the present, to Whitechapel Hospital.

"William and Simon have the hospital functioning quite properly," I said, stirring my tea.

Grandmother sighed. "Julian Bartlett's death in that fire was so tragic. He was such a skilled physician, so charitable. And such a gentleman."

William and I exchanged glances quickly. Although Grandmother knew of the fatal house fire on Montgomery Street, she, like everyone else in London, thought the house had burned to the ground in a grievous accident. Fortunately, the fire had spread so rapidly, the flames had been so hot, that there was little but ashes left of the bodies of Julian Bartlett and his housemates—their cause of death appeared to be from the fire only.

If Grandmother only knew the truth behind Julian Bartlett's "charitable" nature, about his feelings toward my mother. The silence in the room seemed roaring, but I did not know what to say as my thoughts turned again to Mother's murder, back in Ireland. It had happened less than a year ago, but in some ways it felt like a lifetime.

William spoke first, setting his teacup down lightly in its saucer. "Yes, yes. It was tragic. Terrible. He was a wise instructor, and Simon and I are grateful to have had his guidance."

Mercifully, the clock finally chimed six o'clock. Time to leave.

William and I walked arm in arm after the carriage let us out in the Hammersmith area. I had remained rather quiet during the ride. I felt bothered by Grandmother's assumptions about William and his unstable family. I contemplated the numerous times before and during her illness that Grandmother had lectured me about them. She could not tell me anything that I did not already know; in actuality, I knew far more about the Rossetti family's "falls" and eccentricities than she did. The fact remained, though, that I loved William. He did not seem to possess the same weaknesses as his father. For all of his failings, shortcomings, and faults, Gabriel Rossetti had been a good adoptive father to William. I frowned. Although Gabriel was my biological father, I had never met him.

As we walked, I noticed fondly the patches of daffodils just beginning to brighten gray-tinged London. The moon was a brilliant thumbprint in the sky. Still, the spring evening seemed extraordinarily chilly, and I clutched the collar of my coat tighter at my throat.

The sound of determined footsteps behind us startled me from my reveries, and I felt William tense beside me. I sucked in my breath and glanced behind us: a man in a coat, probably a solicitor or accountant on his way home from work, cast a bored glance in our direction before turning down a side street.

My fears spilled out in a whisper. "Max can't be far, William. I know that he hasn't given up. He's lost the Conclave and the elixir. He cannot be immortal without it."

Although I knew that the Conclave was gone, whenever I looked at my mother's portrait I felt the nagging sense that Max, the surviving member, must have had some reason to keep William, Simon, and me alive. He still needed something from us—or from me. I shook my head, desperate to dispel the thoughts. And now there was that odd vision of a lamia that had come to me when I'd touched the picture in the laboratory.

The evening chill had spread to my bones.

"With the exception of Max, the Conclave is no more, Abbie," William said. "Simon and I have searched every crevice in the laboratory and offices at the hospital, and we went back to search the rubbish in the house ashes as well. They have left no secrets. Even my father's notes and Polidori's papers burned in the flames."

"William, you say 'with the exception of Max' as if he's just a minor detail," I pointed out. "He's the most dangerous one of the group. I don't wish to be too alarming, but wherever he is, he has not given up."

We were approaching the Morris's doorstep.

"Have you had any more … " William's voice was barely audible.

"Visions … " I finished his sentence. I'd already decided that I was not yet ready to tell William of my latest vision. It seemed too out of place, too bizarre. I had to tell Simon first.

An unsettling feeling crept over me.

Quickly, I dropped my voice even lower: "Do Jane and

William Morris know of the Conclave? None of the other Pre-Raphaelites, except for your father and Christina, knew of their existence. Am I correct?"

William shook his head. "My father was extraordinarily careful with the secret. Besides, Jane and William Morris are still alive, are they not?" He smiled darkly.

It was a good point.

I did not find Jane Burden Morris to be as extraordinary as William had portrayed her. It was true that her flaming red hair, made famous in her days as a portrait model, had only grayed a little, and she walked with the posture and strength of a much younger woman. She seemed well-read and articulate. But I became disappointed with her during dinner; her aura of conceit came out forcefully, and I failed to see why she dazzled William so.

Also, I did not like the way she gazed upon me. Her expression, I sensed, was not entirely friendly. I knew that my mother, another muse for Gabriel, would have been Jane's romantic rival; I sensed that she suspected or perhaps knew the truth of my parentage.

The chill between Jane and her husband felt icy and overbearing. Her string of lovers in her long-loveless marriage had made him apathetic, even bitter toward her. Although the couple conversed comfortably, reminiscing on the past, Morris said next to nothing else. When he retired to bed as soon as he'd finished eating, I thought William and

I would depart soon as well. However, William seemed in no hurry to leave, and I quickly found myself, William, and Jane sitting in the study with tea.

"Do you remember your father's pet wombats?" Jane asked William.

"How could I forget them? Those beasts had better places at the dinner table than I did."

During dinner, I had begun to feel rising irritation as Jane and William discussed Gabriel and the other Pre-Raphaelites, some of whom were still living. Though I had wanted to hear such stories, I sensed that Jane was determined to make me feel like an outsider. So by the time we were sitting in the study, I had stopped trying to participate in the conversation. Instead, I scanned the walls, which displayed many of Morris's sketches. Several were of buildings, often crumbling cathedrals. The bookcases were filled with volumes on subjects ranging from art, to architecture, to radical politics. William had once told me that while Jane was shut out from posh London circles due to her romantic affairs, Morris had been ousted as a result of his political beliefs.

I turned my attention back to William, where he sat by Jane across from me in the small parlor. I sighed in irritation, thinking that Jane's politically controversial husband seemed marginally more interesting than Jane herself.

The sigh was too audible. William looked at me sharply.

At that moment, a realization came upon me with the force of a storm wind. I scrutinized the scene before me slowly, carefully. I watched Jane Morris's hand rest on William's shoulder. It was a maternal gesture... but not *entirely* maternal.

The truth suddenly became quite clear.

William instantly looked uncomfortable when he saw my expression.

I sat up in my seat suddenly, nearly slamming my teacup down in its saucer.

How could I have missed this?

Mentor. Friend in the years following Gabriel's death.

"Arabella, are you unwell?" Jane asked.

"Abbie!" William stood up and rushed toward me.

"We must leave," I replied curtly. "Thank you for dinner, but it is time for me to go home."

It was near ten o'clock when we abruptly left, and the night had gone from chilly to cold. A volcano of emotion erupted within me. Grandmother's warnings about the Pre-Raphaelites and their bohemian lifestyle flashed through my mind. Now, though, I actually gave weight to her words.

"Abbie…what is the matter?" William asked. He could see that I was furious.

I ignored him and kept walking, too hurt and furious to speak.

After several blocks, I stopped and faced him. I could see my breath puff out in the air.

"You never told me."

He knew exactly to what I referred. Nevertheless, he stood silent, bewildered as to what he might say in these circumstances. I glared back at him for several more seconds. Then he spoke: "I did not think it was necessary. Why should I have told you? It was in the past."

"Tell me everything. Now."

He looked baffled. "You cannot expect...."

"No, wait," I said quickly. "Don't."

I turned, walking quickly away from him, then stopped, facing him again. "No, do—I mean, not the details."

"It was a few years after my father's death. Both Jane and I grieved for him. I was nineteen, busy in my studies at Oxford. But I was lonely. I had only my aunt when I returned home."

My imagination became overwhelmed with images that I did not want to see. My mother had been far from conventional, and she had, unlike the manner of most mothers, never hesitated to tell me about basic life matters such as lovemaking.

"She's old enough to be your mother!" I spat out. "And she was your father's mistress. That's revolting, William."

"She was more experienced than I was at the time in such matters. You must understand, I was young—"

"Enough!" I yelled, cutting him off. "I'm going home." I turned and began walking away. The tears warmed my face.

William rushed after me, panicked now.

"She is the only one I have been with." He paused, blushing. "Other than Isabella, a friend's sister, just after I returned to London from Oxford."

"What?"

"But it was a brief affair. I had not yet met you."

I had not even known William for an entire year, I reminded myself. I began to wonder if I had been mad for plunging headfirst into a relationship with a Rossetti. William's unconventional deflowering bothered me. I worried that he might be more like his father than I had thought. And I could not stand the fact that he had known others in a way he had not known me. But then, how could I have been so naïve as to think that he had not? He was, after all, a man. Isabella, whomever she was, was forgivable. But the other affair . . . with his father's married mistress . . . It seemed too much like something Gabriel Rossetti himself would do; it was so unorthodox, so bizarre. Furthermore, I felt such a jealousy toward Jane Morris. William had adored Jane almost as a mother, but now I knew that she had been more than that to him.

He laid his hand on my arm.

I shook him away. The shock of what I had discovered was still too much. I trembled in rage.

"I do not care how your father and his friends lived. I do not care even how my mother lived. But I am not going to remain with you only to end up, in thirty years, as Jane and William Morris are now."

William looked as if I had struck him. "Why would you think we would be like that?"

Incensed, I continued, "But you have esteemed her so much in the past to me. And she is not only part of your past but part of your family's history, beloved by your father. I can never be her, or live up to who you think she is, and you cannot love her or anyone else if you are going to be with me."

"Abbie," he replied softly. "Why would you think that my history with Jane would have any bearing upon us now?"

I did not know how to answer that question, so I said instead, "You certainly seemed to feel fondness for her tonight."

He sighed. "Jane is still a dear friend, a friend only. I will never see her again if it will make you feel better."

"But you have known her that way. You have done what we have not…"

William looked almost amused. "Abbie, I was nineteen years old at the time. And I am a man, after all."

It was the wrong answer. I flashed him a disgusted look before turning and running away from him to catch my own hansom cab. The exertion of running was somewhat soothing. Once I had left him and was safely in a carriage, my heart thudded within me on the ride back to Kensington. My thoughts remained shocked and scattered.

I let myself into Grandmother's house, tearful, flushed, and perspiring. I flung off my coat myself, without waiting for Richard to take it. I hoped Grandmother was in bed, as I knew I looked and felt disarrayed.

"Abbie!" I heard my name shouted from outside.

William had followed me and was forcing himself through the front door just as Richard attempted to close it.

Hearing Grandmother's and Ellen's alarmed voices, I ran immediately to my right, to the parlor. William, close behind me, slammed the parlor door behind us. He was no longer panicked; he seemed angry.

"Abbie, you are being irrational. I am not Simon St. John. I never was."

"No you are not," I said, walking away from him toward the fireplace. When I turned to face him again, his expression was stony, unreadable. I blushed, ashamed of my desire to hurt him. But my anger, my jealousy, felt overwhelming. I had thought that he was mine alone, and that he had always been meant for me. It was a selfish—and even then I knew, a foolish—thought.

Also, new fears about William and his future constancy crept into my consciousness. Everything seemed irreparable.

"What we had together, William, must end," I whispered. "Do not come back here again."

He stayed where he was, near the door. He did not move toward me. "There has and never will be anyone that I love but you."

I heard a step in the hallway, and I knew that Richard waited out there.

"How can this be about trust, Abbie?" William continued. "Can you tell me, honestly, that you have not withheld anything about your past life from me? About your earlier years, before you met me?"

Roddy. My friend Roddy. I felt startled. I had never told William about Roddy. But that was different. Although I had begun to have stirrings for Roddy, I didn't have a sexual secret. I pulled my mind away from that terrible day when I lost Roddy—that day I hardly allowed myself to think of.

"It doesn't matter, William. But I can assure you that I have never been with anyone in that manner. And certainly, I have never slept with anyone who had been my parent's lover! Who does that, William?"

No response.

My head throbbed. I touched my temples with my fingertips. "This night has to end," I whispered. "Please leave."

"Abbie, please, I will not let you go." William seemed desperate as he started to cross the room toward me.

I felt furious. "Not *let* me?" I exclaimed. "I am not yours to keep!"

Before I could stop myself, I grabbed a porcelain shepherdess off the mantelpiece and hurled it toward him. William ducked just in time, and it smashed into the wall behind him.

Richard flung the parlor door open, concerned at how the argument had escalated.

"Goodbye, Abbie." William straightened. He could not say more. But he remained where he was.

"Goodbye, William," I said.

Richard cleared his throat, signaling to William that it was time for him to leave.

William bowed very slightly and left.

As I left the parlor, I felt a silly and awkward urge to hug Richard. But I held myself back; it seemed inappropriate. I had grown quite fond of Richard in the past year. I felt more endeared to him, most of the time, than to anyone else in the house.

I rushed past Grandmother and Ellen, who both stared wide-eyed and silent at the foot of the stairs. I knew they must have heard the argument, seen William storm past.

I could hardly believe what I had done, or the angry emotions that had exploded between William and myself. But what I knew for certain was that whatever had happened, it had emerged from my own entry into a swift and foolhardy relationship in which I let my feelings overrule good sense.

Still, in spite of all this, my heart felt as if it bled.

The hunger continued to rise inside of her; it was becoming unbearable. She thought perhaps vigorous swimming would ease it, so after feeding the animals one evening, she went into the water. But instead of swimming out to sea, she felt drawn toward shore, where villagers and fishermen would be. She knew that she should not do this, particularly in her hungry state, but she could not help herself. She was a hunter, drawn to prey—and there was flesh, beating hearts, on the shore. Perhaps if she could see these humans, hear their beating hearts, her appetite would be satisfied a bit, and she could return to her island home and feed on her normal meal of fish, bread, and vegetables.

She pulsed through the salty sea into shallower waters. The air was foggy, dusty, the waters gray, but her vision remained sharp and clear. She saw the stingrays, some small, some beautifully large, gliding along the bottoms below her. She saw pieces of old fishing boats covered in moss and barnacles, pieces of paddles. Old torn fishing nets pulsing in the depths.

When she broke the surface, in a small lagoon shrouded by mossy rocks, she heard voices nearby.

"Are ye insane, man?" a youth's voice shouted. She eased

up against the hard rock. Two young men, no more than eighteen years old, swam along the shores nearby.

"Only as insane as ye! Gie out haur wi' me!"

Through the foggy blanket, she could barely make out their figures, splashing each other, wrestling in the surf.

She pulled herself under again, watching them from beneath the shallow surface. The youths had stripped all their clothes off, and she saw their pale naked bodies swimming and diving in the cold shallow waters just offshore, the depth no greater than ten feet.

She felt almost proud of herself, lingering here, not rushing forward to kill them. Perhaps this was all that she needed to ease her cravings for a bit.

But even as she watched the boys swimming, she remembered being a child and stealing gingerbread one afternoon. The spicy, sweet aroma had beckoned her to the kitchen— where she was normally not allowed to go. It had been close to dinnertime and she knew that she would receive a slap on her wrist from the cook for even trying to eat the bread. She still remembered how watching the bread had done no good; as the cook stirred a stew over the fire on the far side of the kitchen, she had pulled a large hunk from the bread and run to her room.

Even as this thought crossed her mind, a scarlet cloud burst out from the leg of one of the boys.

The venom flowed in her mouth, and her stomach growled.

No.

No.

She could not let this happen.

She clutched at the rocky wall behind her, trying to hold herself back, until her own clawed fingers bled.

The boy broke the surface, shouted in pain.

"Well, haury up mate, ye don' want to bring th' sharks."

The other boy moaned in pain as they headed quickly toward shore.

She couldn't hold her hunger anymore. In a frenzy, she swam toward them, suddenly regaining control just as they stepped onto the rocky shore. Her hesitation, and their speed, was what saved them.

Quickly, before she could pursue them onto land, she turned away and swam back to her island. The venom still flowed heavily in her mouth; she knew that her appetite for humans was intensifying even more.

When I reached my room, I locked the door behind me. Hearing no footsteps on the stairs, I gave a silent prayer of thanks that Grandmother had not followed me. My legs wobbled and I leaned against the door, sliding down until I sat on the floor. It was then that I gave myself free reign to cry.

As I sat there, in the darkness of my room, I felt too weak to even go to my bed. Wiping my face with my sleeve, I leaned my head back against the door and let myself think of Roddy—of that terrible day when he had died and I had almost drowned. Only now could I allow the pieces of that day, like driftwood, to fit together in my mind. Mother's death, and the truth behind her death, had been difficult enough for me to face…

When Mother and I had moved to the outskirts of Dublin for her governess position on the Edgeworths' estate, Roddy had quickly established himself as my best friend. I squinted through tears in the shadows of my bedroom, remembering his face so vividly. I could almost see him, like it was a photograph in my mind. He was tanned, freckled, the son of a blacksmith. He'd had taken pity on me the first time I had been ruthlessly bullied by the local children; I was only ten years old at the time, and Mother and I had only recently moved into our small house on the estate. Because Roddy had an uncle who was a boxer in Stepney, even at ten years old he harbored a fierce obsession with fighting, particularly bare-knuckle boxing. It had been Roddy who had taught me how to fight and knife throw. I was never as skilled at fighting as he was, but within a year I surpassed him at knife-throwing.

I wiped a tear from my eyes. Seven years. Seven years he had been my friend. We were so close. Then Mother's seizures—which I now knew were her psychic visions—intensified.

"Can you tell me, honestly, that you have not withheld anything about your past life from me?"

William's words stung me now.

There was no possible way I could tell William about Roddy. I had barely allowed myself to think of Roddy during these past months. I wiped the tears from my eyes and took a deep breath as I remembered how our friendship evolved after we both turned sixteen. Something almost imperceptible had grown between us, and neither of us knew how to accommodate its presence. Our friendly touches had become awkward. Part of me wanted to embrace these feelings, and part of me wanted to ignore them; a large part of me wished for our old endearing relationship where we were nothing more than friends.

During those years, Roddy had stopped by our cottage at the edge of the Edgeworths' estate nearly every day, most often in the late afternoons after he finished his work in his father's shop. But after Mother was diagnosed with dysentery, I had to care for her, and I feared that he would catch the illness. At least we all *thought* she had had dysentery—I clenched my fists so tightly that my fingernails cut into my palms. Max, I now knew, had murdered her—most probably poisoned her.

The pain she had endured... I shut my mind against the thought.

I heard the grandfather clock strike eleven, but I could not even consider trying to sleep. I thought about how awful I had felt upon learning that the Conclave executed her, of how that knowledge had driven me to kill. That night at the Montgomery Street house, I became a different person... murderous. I wanted nothing more than to kill each and every one of them. And ever since that night last autumn, I had been forced to rewrite, reassess, my last days with my mother in Dublin. And now I was finally allowing myself to think of my last day with Roddy, of his fate and the mysterious circumstances under which my life had been saved.

The day Mother's illness came upon her, she had been giving the Edgeworth children their lessons. One of Sir Edgeworth's servants brought her back to our cottage and laid her in bed. Fear gripped me as throughout the day as her fever increased and she began vomiting. Then, by the late afternoon, her excrement became bloody. Roddy stayed with me until Sir Edgeworth's physician arrived, and then he had to return to his work in the blacksmith shop.

"Dysentery," the physician announced dryly after examining Mother. He stood, rubbed his nose, and put his stethoscope back in his bag. "I've recently seen a couple cases in the city. I will inform Sir Edgeworth that she should not be around his family for the time being. She is highly contagious."

"But what about her? Will my mother recover?"

He had only shrugged wearily before leaving.

The moment he left, I felt a terrible worry and then the beginning of an aching loneliness.

I cursed quietly through my tears, unable to imagine life without her. I loved her and could not even begin to comprehend the possibility of her death. I had always wondered why she had fled London—why we never went back. She had told me essentially nothing about her previous life there; all I knew was that London was the place where her estranged mother lived. She rarely discussed Jacque Sharp, my father—at least, the man I had *thought* was my father.

The evening she fell ill, the storm winds and rains slammed loudly against the cottage's shutters. Roddy had come that night; I still remember him standing on the doorstep, soaking wet, the strong lingering smells of metals and of smoke from the shop upon him.

"Roddy," I said quickly. "You shouldn't be here. It's dysentery. She's contagious."

"I don't care," he said. "Yer know I never git sick anyway. How is she? How are ye?"

Unable to answer him, I had left him momentarily to check on her. When I reached her room, she lay amid the blankets, her face still flushed with fever, but she slept soundly. Quietly, I turned down the lamp and left the room, pulling the bedroom door almost closed.

Roddy and I talked late into the night. I still remembered how, when he took his cap off in the low light of our tiny, dim parlor, his blond curls were so bright against his dark tan; he was already burnt brown, although it was not even the middle point of summer.

In spite of our newfound awkwardness, I let my emotions go just before he left that night, embracing him and crying. I tried to keep the sound of my sobbing down, and I spoke in croaking whispers so that Mother would not hear me.

Now, I heard Ellen's footsteps in the hallway outside my door, proceeding down the hall toward the servant stairs as she retired to bed for the night. All candles and lamplight were out in the house, and I was enshrouded in complete darkness. I rested my forehead upon my bent knees and put my hands against my now tear-swollen face.

That night, after Roddy left, I quietly pushed open the door to the bedroom and was surprised to see Mother out of bed, staring out the window toward Sir Edgeworth's forest, which stretched beyond the back of our cottage. Her hand had been pressed hard and flat against the pane.

She didn't hear me. It was as if she was in a trance. I began panicking, hoping that another of her seizures—psychic visions, I later discovered—wasn't about to start. I led her back to bed and then, when I turned to shut the drapes, I froze, startled. Lightning cracked, illuminating the sky, and in that instant I thought I saw a figure at the edge of the woods, watching us. I blinked and the figure was gone.

I had always assumed that it must have been one of Sir Edgeworth's servants, on some night errand. I had also wondered whether I might be mistaken—that there had been no one there at all. Now, I knew that it was most likely Max—he was waiting for Mother to die. Waiting for me. Watching me, even then...

Mother was no better the next morning.

I had been up throughout the night with her as her illness worsened. By dawn her lips were dry, cracked, and purple shadows stood out in deep half-moons under her eyes. Periods of sleep, and then violent illness, continued in cycles all day. I took brief naps and ate only a little. That night, as the night before, I didn't sleep.

I must have fallen asleep at dawn sometime the next morning, because I awoke, startled, to find her sitting up in the bed beside me. Her face was still pale and hollow, but she seemed very conscious. Not at all delirious or trancelike.

"Mother!" I said, as I jolted myself from the bonds of my sleep.

"Shhh..." She hushed me.

I sat up, facing her. "You're feeling better."

She said nothing, but looked at me sadly. There was something veiled, very thoughtful, behind her eyes, and now I would sell my soul to be able to know what she was thinking in that moment.

I couldn't believe she would die. I knew she would recover. Soon. That our life would continue as it had. But then my hope sank when she spoke, her voice weak, hoarse.

"I am making arrangements. Do not worry."

My panic returned. "What arrangements? What are you saying?"

"Shhhh..." She hushed me again, this time putting her finger hard against my lips.

We said nothing more on the matter.

By noon, she finally fell asleep. She slept for most of the afternoon, and I felt a twinge of hope. The house stank, and for the first time I noticed how stuffy and oppressive it seemed. I opened every window, letting the breeze flow through.

As I stood in the parlor eating a piece of bread with jam, Roddy knocked on the door.

"Ab. Papa let me leave early to see yer. How is Mrs. Sharp?"

I shrugged.

"The same?"

I nodded. "She's sleeping now."

"Let's go on a walk, Ab. Yer need ter git oyt of 'ere for a few minutes. We'll just walk in the forest..."

"No. I can't leave her."

"Abbie. I want you to go." Mother's voice startled both

of us. She stood in the bedroom doorway, holding onto the doorframe for support.

"No, you're still very ill."

"You have been in here too long," she said. "You must take a break. You need some fresh air."

There was an intensity in her voice that made me think she wanted me to leave, wanted me to leave her alone in the house. After a few more minutes of persuasion, both from her and from Roddy, I finally agreed to take a short walk with him.

After we left the house, we walked into the forest. The day was bright, very warm. Birds shrieked from the surrounding trees, and a firm breeze rattled through dewed leaves—still wet from a light rain. In spite of the lovely weather, I felt my worry about Mother, my desire to be with her, like a lingering weight pressing upon me. This didn't escape Roddy's notice; cautiously he reached for my hand, and as we walked, I let him hold it.

We went a long distance in silence, taking a rough trail that we had never taken. The trail curved sharply in several places, and I could not see where it ended. We walked for over an hour; I knew that we were on a far part of the property that I had never visited.

The woods stopped abruptly, opening into a clearing. Amid the long grasses and wild rose bushes I saw a small graveyard of only ten markers. The stones had been bleached nearly white by the sun. Almost directly beside the graves was a large pond. A deer, which had been drinking from the water, saw us and fled into the brush of the surrounding forest.

Roddy crouched down and cleared brambles off of a tiny grave.

I knelt beside him and tried to focus on the letters, but they had all worn away. The sun beat upon us and the day felt warmer than when we had set out. I was very aware of his body next to mine, and I felt dizzy. I stood, the weakness almost overpowering me. I felt nauseated and regretted taking such a long walk after eating and drinking almost nothing for two days. We had been gone over an hour, and I was becoming anxious to get back to Mother.

"Are ye all right?" Roddy asked, standing and steadying me.

"Yes. I think…I think I just walked too far. I need to get back to her."

Suddenly a branch cracked loudly.

We realized that we were not alone. Three young men, the oldest of them about twenty, stood at the edge of the clearing.

I knew immediately who they were and what they wanted. They were young vagabonds, robbers out to prey on Dubliners in the country. Sir Edgeworth had warned me once of these gangs roaming through the woods, threatening people for money or jewelry.

Without a word, all three of the young men began walking toward us, breaking apart as if they meant to surround us. One pulled out a knife, and I felt certain that the others were armed, too.

Roddy almost imperceptibly waved his hand at me, a signal that I should stay near him.

"We don't 'ave anythin'," he said to the group.

"Nathin'?" the leader replied. "I don't believe yer."

"We'll leave if yer wish, but we 'ave nothing to give yer."

At that point they surrounded us, and I knew that they had no intention of letting us go. "I tink we'll fend oyt for ourselves," one of them said. He nodded at the other two.

They searched Roddy first. He held his arms out, letting them search him without confrontation.

My fear and outrage mounted as one of the group put his hands on my waist. He pulled my hair away from the back of my neck.

"Let 'er go," Roddy said.

"Naw."

Tensing, I tried to remember the technique Roddy had taught me for disengaging a grip—sharp elbow to the upper chest, twist right, and run. I felt weak, sluggish, but nonetheless, after summoning some strength, I caught Roddy's eye so that he knew what I was going to do, twisted, and then bludgeoned the young man hard in the chest with my elbow so that he fell back.

Roddy and I ran fast toward the woods before the other two could grab us. But then I felt a vise-grip on my arm as one of the boys grabbed me and pulled me back toward the direction of the pond.

The boy holding me pressed a knife blade sharply against my back as I struggled against him. Coming to my aid, Roddy pummeled another one of the boys to the ground and delivered hard blows to his face. The other gang member pulled out a knife and advanced toward Roddy.

"Roddy, run! He has a knife!"

I struggled against my captor, but he pressed the knife only harder into my back.

Roddy and the other boy fell to the ground, rolling toward the pond.

"Let me go!" I screamed, kicking my captor hard in the knees. But he pressed the knife so hard into my back that I felt it break through the fabric of my dress and draw blood. As I screamed in pain and tried to break away, I knew that Roddy wouldn't have a chance against two of them.

The boy Roddy had beaten stood up, furious, his nose bleeding. I watched in horror, unbelieving, as the other boy pinned Roddy down just long enough for the bleeding thug to stab him several times in the abdomen.

"Noooooo!!!"

Everything in my vision spun, and I only vaguely wondered if my captor would stab me. All I could think about was getting to Roddy.

I screamed again as I watched the two boys hoist Roddy up and throw him out into the pond.

"No! No! Let me go!!!" I screamed.

Inexplicably, the gang leader did let me go, pushing me to the ground. After stumbling over my skirts, I ran wildly toward the pond.

"What aboyt 'er?" I heard one of them ask the others.

"Leave 'er!" was the reply as the three vagabonds ran toward the woods. "I'm certain ye killed 'im. We 'av to git out of 'ere! Now!"

"Roddy! Roddy!" I screamed as I jumped into the pond. I was soon waist-deep, desperately pushing away the tangles of lily pads and weeds. Roddy's body floated facedown, not far from me. But then the water was over my head, and, although I knew how to swim, I was still wearing my boots, and all of my skirts weighed me down. Even so, I could almost reach Roddy's body. Then my fingertips touched his shoulder, and I shuddered at how limp he was.

Just before I could pull him toward me and get his face above the water, my foot became entangled in something—twine from a fishing net, or perhaps a weed. I tried to jerk myself free, but could not. After taking a deep gulp of air, I dived underneath the surface. My ankle was caught by a thick, heavy piece of vine that would not break, and I could not free myself. I struggled with the vine until my lungs felt as if they were on fire. But when I attempted to surface, I saw Roddy floating almost directly above me, his lifeless eyes gazing down. The sunlight broke down through the pond's surface above Roddy's body, and I saw clearly the scarlet-tinged water surrounding me.

All of the air in my lungs escaped in my underwater scream. Frenzied, I sucked in a tremendous amount of water. I reached upward toward Roddy's body, choking, not able to believe that he was dead, that I was about to die. Light flickered at the periphery of my vision, and then all became blackness.

I never understood exactly how I came to be saved, but I had sometimes wondered if one of the vagabonds, feeling a wave of guilt, had returned to pull me out. All I knew was that after feeling a sharp and sudden tug on the vine ensnaring my ankle, an arm locked around my waist and pulled me to the surface. I reeled in and out of consciousness, seeing and sensing nothing clearly. My body limp, I was dragged to the hot ground on the bank of the pond. My lungs were so clogged with water that I could not breathe, even though the burning sensation had stopped. I felt no pain then, simply heaviness.

Suddenly there was an awful tingling, and then pain erupted in my chest. As a great spasm overtook my body, I rolled to my side and vomited. Fits of coughing and wheezing overwhelmed me for several minutes.

When the coughing ceased, I was too exhausted to move. I opened my eyes to see who had saved me only to find myself alone. Bullfrogs croaked around the pond, fireflies flickered in the forest brush. I tried to sit up, still thinking of Roddy, but my dress was like a great weight sucking upon me. I turned toward the pond, only to see his body still floating. Then I fainted.

Somehow, in the fringes of my consciousness, I became aware of someone carrying me. I felt branches, leaves, thistles, scratching my face, twisting about my hair. I had, at that time, no idea who carried me. Perhaps it was one of the Edgeworths' servants. I tried to open my eyes, to bring myself to my senses—but then I would remember that my best friend was dead.

Roddy was dead.

I vaguely wondered if someone had also retrieved Roddy's body from the pond. But it wouldn't matter. Nothing would bring him back as my flesh-and-blood friend again.

Then I smelled the odors of illness, and I knew I had been taken back in our cottage. I felt myself laid down in the bed, next to Mother, and I heard her scream. Once again, I struggled, fought to become fully conscious, to hear and see what was going on around me. But my body stayed locked, and I knew I was on the brink of losing consciousness again.

Mother was arguing violently with someone, a man, and I felt her grip my body as I lay beside her. I had always wondered why she'd argued with Sir Edgeworth's servant, someone who it seemed had saved me and brought me back to her. Her anger had never made sense to me.

I heard someone else's voice in the room, but I was fading fast and soon succumbed to the sweet sleep of unconsciousness.

When I awoke, it was sometime during the night. All was dark except for a couple of candles lit on the stand beside our bed. I felt Mother's cool hand stroking my face. When I looked up at her, her face was grayish, frightfully grayish.

"Mother…" I said, crying, feeling a childish need to be comforted in spite of her illness. "Roddy…"

"It was a terrible accident, Arabella. Let's not speak of it now."

As my eyes adjusted to the darkness, I saw that she was lying beside me.

"Who brought me back?" I had asked. "Why were you arguing with him?"

She turned even paler than she already was.

"A servant found you. Brought you home. But I argued with no one."

I felt certain that I had heard her arguing.

"Go to sleep, Abbie."

She stayed beside me that night, and died in her sleep.

As I pried myself away from those memories, to where I still lay curled on the floor of my bedroom, I stuffed my fist in my mouth to prevent anyone from hearing me cry.

Roddy. Revisiting the tragedy of losing him was like reopening a wound. But now that I knew how intensely the Conclave had pursued Mother and me, the pieces of those last Dublin days made more sense. It seemed that Max had not only killed my mother, but had probably also saved me—that it had been him who had pulled me from the pond and brought me to her. This explained why she had been fearfully angry, seeing him carrying me.

I wondered what Mother's relationship with Max had been like. And why had she wanted me to leave the cottage so badly, when she encouraged me to walk with Roddy? I had always assumed that she was finishing arrangements, sending information to Sir Edgeworth about my grandmother, about her whereabouts. Now I wondered if she'd met with Max; perhaps she had begged him—futilely—to let me alone.

A coldness crept over my flesh and I rose, crawling into bed while still in my clothes. I would probably never know the details of that day. But I acknowledged, with near certainty now, that it had been Max who saved me from drowning.

I would still kill him.

I couldn't remember ever feeling so hopeless before. So alone. William was not who I had thought he was ... I had lost Roddy, Mother, and now him.

I tried, fruitlessly, to sleep.

Four

Her porcelain soap dish shattered onto the marble floor as her monstrous form burst into being.

Once again, she had hoped that a hot bath would relax her—take her thoughts away from those young men swimming, away from all her desperate and bloody memories, from her increasing hunger for human flesh. But it did not. The transformation always began like a stirring, a heat deep inside her, coursing through her bones, muscles, skin until she could no longer contain it.

In the candlelight, she pondered her monster body in the mirror. She still resembled a woman—her long hazelnut hair unchanged, her breasts still free upon her chest. But her skin had taken on a pale greenish color, and light green scales covered her arms. They became denser and coarser toward her hands and claws and from her waist downward, completely covering her legs and the tops of her feet. Her lower legs and feet did not resemble human shape at all—they were the legs of a dragon, muscular, with talons for tearing. Her tail, thick and heavy, hung over the tub, dripping large water puddles on the floor around the pieces of the soap dish.

With her webbed fingers, she retracted her claws and gingerly touched the gill slits on her neck.

The most predatory part of her was not her claws, feet, or even venomous fangs. It was her eyes. Slitted, coarse, serpentine, they were sharper, more keen, than her human eyes had been. Her transformation could happen at will, of course. But at times, to her despair, it came even when she did not will it, when the anger or bloodlust became too much. And right now, she felt a brewing restlessness. The venom dripped in her mouth as she remembered her last kill, almost two decades before.

Since then, she had had such an excellent record. Her keeper had been away from her longer than usual that time, too; it had been the point just before she had learned about Caroline Westfield. At that time, his long absence had spurred her restlessness, her jealousy, and she had darted through the waters to work off her hunger.

It was then that she had found the young man—alive but unconscious, his body looped over a piece of driftwood. She had been proud of herself, suppressing her hunger long enough to save him. It was January, and he would not have lasted long in the frigid waters.

Taking care to keep his head above the surface, she had taken him to her island. In her human form, she cared for him, removing his wet clothes, preparing a meal for him for when he awoke. She had thought at the time that he would never even have to know who she was. Her keeper was to visit her that night. He could take the young man safely back to the mainland.

She watched the man as he slept in her bed—he was youthful, not much past boyhood, with dark hair and an olive complexion. The wrecked ship in the distance appeared French; she wondered why he had been traveling in these waters, and she felt curious about him. When he stirred, her heart pounded.

He grunted, turned. When he had opened his eyes, he struggled to focus. Then, just as he seemed to see her, his confusion appeared to clear. Though she had never seen this strange young man before, he looked at her with a sort of affectionate familiarity. Her feelings warmed.

He reached out toward her. "Sophie ... "

He thought she was someone else—his lover, or perhaps his wife; some woman named Sophie. *He belonged to someone else.* This should not have surprised her. But to hear the endearing, affectionate words, spoken for someone else when she had done so much for him, when she had saved his life ...

It was too much. The transformation had happened almost against her will. His end came quickly. And her too-long fast from human blood had made her gorge on it.

Her keeper arrived on the island, and he walked in upon her.

She looked up. Blood on her face. She was caught, the naughty girl in the pantry, one hand in the jar of jam.

His eyes had glinted in amusement, and he shook his head. She felt infinite relief at the mild reproach.

"Effie... Effie," was all that he had said.

Five

I did not in fact sleep that night. Instead, I lay in bed so angry, so sad, and thought about my argument with William. I felt physically ill, and even vomited into my washbasin once. I did not understand the anger that spiraled up within me. I had not thought of myself as naïve. Ever. Why had I never suspected the affair? I think I felt more threatened by Jane than I would have any other woman because of his great esteem for her.

Furthermore, I could not forget about the personalities in the Rossetti's artistic circle. The family was erratic, libertine. Christina was very religious, but even she had her eccentricities, such as offering housing to women "friends"—typically former prostitutes—who were struggling to make a living at respectable jobs. William had been raised within this circle of writers and painters. The feelings I felt for him I had never felt before, for anyone else; my changing relationship with Roddy had not had any of the intensity marking my feelings for William. I could not imagine, I could not even comprehend, the heartache I would feel if William tired of me, if he fell in love with someone else—the possibility of that pain was too much. I thought fearfully of what might have happened in the laboratory closet if we hadn't been interrupted by Simon. That had been such poor, poor judgment on my part.

"Unstable," "bohemian," Grandmother had said of his family, so many times.

In the darkness of my bedroom I rolled over, clutched my pillow tight against my chest.

What if Grandmother's words were true? Too much was at stake. Apart from the heartbreak, I needed clarity of mind to begin my application to London Medical School for Women. I could not allow this kind of drama to get in the way of that.

At some point, in the early hours of the morning, I finally fell asleep, my mind cluttered with all of my fiery, frantic thoughts. I began dreaming almost immediately. I was in Highgate Cemetery—it was early morning. A blanket of wet chill settled around me, and I felt goose bumps rise up on my arms. Morning sun broke through dark rainclouds. I felt briefly disoriented, as ravens screamed from the tops of tombs and a thick fog obliterated some of my vision. The path that I stood upon, the small path winding between tombs, seemed familiar. Déjà vu swept over me, and I wondered if I stood near the Rossetti family plot.

I heard the tremble of a breath nearby before realizing why this particular place felt familiar. A branch cracked.

I turned.

"Mariah!"

My voice came out broken, stunned. And then I swallowed a scream. Before I could speak again, I saw that my friend's eyes focused not on me, but behind me.

At someone else, in the direction from which I had just turned.

Her mouth twitched up, almost imperceptibly.

I heard a step in the gravel behind me and then, to my deep horror, a chuckle. I realized I was trapped. A mouse about to be devoured.

"No! No!" I screamed, sitting up in bed. I saw streaks of morning grayness seeping in from between the drawn drapes. Rain began to thud against the window panes.

Just a dream. Just a dream.

But it seemed so much like the visions I had experienced in the autumn—the visions that showed me the murders.

And Mariah was dead. At peace. In the grave. She could not be walking about Highgate Cemetery in flesh and blood.

Nonetheless, I got out of bed and, still shaking, splashed water from my washbasin against my face.

Just a dream.

Just a dream.

The previous night had been so awful, so painful for me. I needed to go to work. I needed occupation, to be busy, to start applying to medical school or I would lose my mind. Quickly, I put on my work dress. I shouldn't let what happened with William cause me such mental anguish. Besides, I wanted to see Simon. I needed to see Simon.

When I was almost dressed, I heard the rustle of a skirt in the hallway and froze. I did not want to see Grandmother. I felt my cheeks burn, knowing that she had heard part of my argument with William. She would come into my room feeling vindicated.

Her firm knock sounded at the door before she entered. I took a deep breath and braced myself for her words.

With her eagle-eye gaze, she surveyed my work dress.

"Oh ... " She sighed, infinitely disappointed. "You are returning to the hospital, even after last evening?"

"Why shouldn't I?" I stood at my mirror, brushing my hair back to the base of my neck. I tried to secure the hair combs, but my fingers trembled and shook. I felt in very poor control of my emotions.

Grandmother crossed the room quickly, in only a few strides. Then, taking the hairbrush, she stood behind me, so close that I could smell the scent of her lavender soap. I kept my eyes downward, afraid to meet her gaze. I knew my eyes were red, bloodshot. I felt as if I was on the verge of crying again.

Gently, firmly, she removed the brush from my hand and took the sloppily arranged combs from my hair. I felt it fall down, loose upon my back. Heavy. Thick. It was my mother's hair.

Without a word, Grandmother placed the combs between her teeth as she brushed and brushed my hair in great strong strokes. She pulled it back, swooping it over my ears and securing it in a neat knot at the nape of my neck. She stuck the combs in hard, her movements efficient. As if she could steady me from my spiraling misery. The combs pressed into my scalp. If an earthquake struck Whitechapel Hospital while I worked, my hair would stay in place.

I stood facing the mirror, my eyes downward, my back toward her, humiliated, trying to hide my quivering lip.

"Arabella," she said, placing her hands on my shoulders. "Do you think I feel any pleasure in being proved correct? Do you think I desired this?"

I felt my shoulders stiffen. Of course she had desired my separation from William. She stood rigid before me, but her voice was so kind that I half-believed her. At least I believed that she hadn't wanted me to be hurt.

"I heard the argument," she said.

Fresh tears welled up. My pain felt like an open wound.

"He's gone, Grandmother. It won't work..." I bit my lip as the tears came out again. *Don't discuss this with her, Abbie*, I advised myself. But in that moment I felt so vulnerable.

Her expression softened a bit. "Arabella, even more than I wanted William Siddal to go away..."

I felt a flush of anger come over my face, and she paused before continuing.

"Even more than that, I wanted you to be happy. You were not happy with the life I would have had for you. I understand that." She stopped, as if the words she was about to say tasted bad. "So I want you to make your own path."

She began to push the loose curls of hair away from my temple. Her expression softened a bit; I knew she was thinking of my mother.

"Perhaps you should stay away from the hospital for a while now. Or..." She paused. I knew she did not want to say what she was going to say. Her nose wrinkled the slightest bit. "You might perhaps work at another hospital. That is, if you still plan to go to medical school."

In spite of her words, I hardened myself. I was still speaking to Lady Charlotte Westfield.

"I do still plan to go." I turned to leave my room. I could only endure so much, and a discussion with Grandmother at this hour in the morning was not what I desired.

She stood where she was, but she cleared her throat loudly. "Arabella, he will be there. You do not want your heart to be broken twice. You must guard it."

I paused in the doorway. She was correct. I knew William would be there. But I couldn't mope around here in Kensington all day like an invalid. The patients were still at Whitechapel, and William and Simon needed my help now as much as any other time. And I wanted to see Simon. I would need strength to deal with William—I still couldn't bear what I had learned about him, and I feared, too much, the implications it might have for our future if we remained together.

I left Grandmother's house without saying a word.

Life had to go on. Nonetheless, my heart was broken.

Six

Fortunately, the morning was busy, and I did not have to work with William. I knew he was there, for I heard his name shouted a few times, and once, in my peripheral vision, I saw him running across the first floor ward to the delivery area.

I spent most my time working in the nursery, which was more chaotic than usual. We had no fewer than twenty-five infants, including the triplets who had been born earlier in the week. Although we had no actual emergencies in the nursery, an eye infection had spread among many of the infants. I was also trying to teach one of our newest nurses, a very young and incompetent girl named Emily, how to cut the strips of cloths we would need to wash out the infants' eyes.

"There," I said, holding down the cloth as she cut it with a pair of scissors. "But don't cut the strips too large. We need to use a different one for each infant, to stop the spread of the infection." I was feeling impatient with Emily, as she had already spilled a large jar of expensive herbs and almost dropped a baby boy as she bathed him.

I looked up, through the partially ajar nursery door, when I heard William's name shouted. It was then that I saw him running toward the delivery room.

"Owwwww!" I screamed, feeling hot searing pain in my palm. I looked down and saw blood running from a puncture wound.

"Oops," Emily murmured quietly.

I should have been kind, told her that we all make mistakes, but my patience had run thin. Grabbing a cloth to cover the wound, I left the nursery, sharply telling Nurse Josephine on my way out not to leave Emily alone with the infants as she was too much of a hazard to them.

I ascended the stairs to the third floor surgery room where I knew we were well-stocked in bandages. The door was shut but not locked, and when I opened it, I saw one of our patients sitting in a chair in the middle of the room, her back toward me. Simon sat in a chair at her side. He had his long legs crossed in front of him and was writing quickly in a notebook. Laying one finger over his lips, he motioned for me to come in but to remain silent.

As I walked into the room, still clutching my bleeding hand, I saw that the patient—who looked to be near fifty, with deep paunches under her eyes and graying black hair— sat staring at a long crack in the wall. She seemed altogether engulfed in a trance. I watched, fascinated, for a few seconds, almost forgetting my pain, until Simon's voice broke through the silence.

"We are finished now, Miss Jordan."

The glazed look in her eyes left quickly, and she just seemed a bit dazed. A nurse from the hallway came in to lead the woman out, and Simon finished writing something in his notebook.

He stood, collecting his notes, and glanced down at my hand. "It appears as if you have a problem, Abbie."

I had nearly forgotten about the wound.

"What was happening?" I asked, more interested in what I had just seen.

But Simon had already crossed the room and taken the wrapped cloth off of my hand to examine the wound.

"Scissors?" he asked.

"Yes," I replied. The bleeding had mostly stopped.

"Nurse Emily?"

I smiled a bit. "Who else? I'm just happy there's someone here clumsier than myself. I can clean and bandage this..."

But Simon had already opened a cabinet and taken out a jar of carbolic acid and some cloth bandages. He took my hand in his and began cleaning the wound carefully. His long pale fingers felt cool and soothing, diminishing the stinging of the area as he cleaned it.

"You asked about what I was just doing," he said quietly.

"Yes."

"Hypnotherapy, Abbie." He wrapped and bandaged my palm tightly in what seemed like a single movement, and then threw away the cut pieces of cloth and the bloodied rag.

"Hypnotism?" I remembered the books I had found

in his office. I knew only a little about hypnotism, but it seemed like such an odd practice.

Simon must have seen the perplexed look on my face. "It's actually an extraordinary scientific process that utilizes parts of the brain otherwise dormant while suppressing most other parts of the nervous system. Two years ago, I learned about its use in medical therapy, and then a few weeks ago, I attended a lecture on the matter in Oxford. I am trying..." He smiled a bit. "Well, *experimenting* with using the treatment on some of our most persistent alcoholics and nymphomaniacs."

"And does it work?" I asked, my interest piqued.

He shrugged. "I am only just beginning the treatments with two patients. This is a learning process for me too."

My hand was bandaged, and all the materials had been put away. Simon towered tall above me, considering me with his cool gaze. I wondered if he knew about what had happened between William and me.

There was a long silence between us.

"Abbie, do you need a cup of tea?"

As I drank tea with Simon in his office, I thought again how much I appreciated his steadiness, his calmness. There was something so reliable about him. Although a physician with a medical degree from Oxford, he had recently completed his seminary degree as well. I felt a pang of jealousy and envy—degrees were so easy for men to attain. Whenever we discussed my medical studies, I knew that my options were more limited.

"So, I suppose Oxford is not a possibility for medical school?" I asked wryly, although I already knew the answer.

Simon set down his teacup and drummed his long, graceful fingers. He took a deep breath. "As of now. But London Medical School for Women is quite excellent. I have met Dr. Elizabeth Garrett Anderson, a physician and a founder of the institution. She is a good person and an extraordinary physician."

I had heard of her. Dr. Anderson was a powerful force in the medical world—she had broken down so many barriers. She had even created a hospital for impoverished women, called the New Hospital for Women, which was very similar to Whitechapel Hospital. And yet I could not study medicine at Oxford itself. The institution still refused to grant women degrees.

I swallowed hard. The hot tea burned the back of my throat, but I said nothing.

"There are women finding ways to make the system work to their advantage," Simon said quietly.

"I know." Oddly, I felt agitated. Simon could be so caring, but elusive. I wondered how he felt about me now... a few months ago, I had refused his marriage proposal. My conflicted thoughts rose within me and, before I could stop myself, I asked, "Where is William?"

I regretted the question the moment it came out of my mouth.

Simon peered at me for a full three seconds, his ice-blue eyes unreadable. I wondered, in voyeuristic guilt, if he still loved me. Once again, I wondered if he knew of my falling out with William. I felt certain he did. Simon had uncanny discernment. And William was terrible at controlling his emotions.

"William has been hard at work on the second floor this morning," Simon replied, looking away and drumming his fingers once again on his desk. "We have been overburdened there lately."

"Oh." I took another sip of tea, wishing that I had not brought William up. An inexplicable tension, an invisible wall, rose up between Simon and me. Then I felt myself blush, remembering how Simon had walked into the laboratory during my impassioned moment with William.

After a few more moments of silent awkwardness, Simon chuckled. "We have been seeing an old friend here lately."

I looked sharply at him, perplexed.

"Inspector Abberline."

"What? I knew he had a meeting with William ... " I stopped myself awkwardly, lowered my voice. "Is he still trying to find ...?"

It seemed almost foolish to call the Whitechapel murderer by his more well-known name, Jack the Ripper, when Simon and I both knew his true identity.

"No," Simon replied. "I think everyone believes the Ripper to be either dead or gone—after all, there have been no more murders since the autumn."

He set down his teacup. "This latest case is slightly more mundane. Apparently there has been a rash of grave robbings."

I widened my eyes a little, remembering my dream about Highgate Cemetery. About Mariah. But that had nothing to do with grave robbing.

"We try to make sure that all the corpses we receive for study here are attained from reputable suppliers, but, as you know, it is nearly impossible to be absolutely certain. Most, even the stolen ones, are from paupers' graves—with very little security or attentive family survivors. Two weeks ago, however, one of the bodies we received was the sixteen-year-old son of a Member of Parliament."

"Uh-oh," I heard myself murmur.

"Precisely." Simon chuckled. "I would never have known, but one of our medical students recognized the boy. Apart from the horror of having to return the body, which we had already begun to dissect, to the still-grieving family ... "

I sucked in my breath.

"Yes, it was awful for the boy's family and a disgrace for the hospital. Abberline has used the incident to interrogate our business practices here."

"Well, he probably still thinks that the Ripper works here," I said.

Simon merely smiled. "He might try to corner you."

"I think I can manage him," I said quickly, not wanting to remember my past interactions with Abberline, particularly that terrible evening at Scotland Yard when he had tried to blackmail me.

I poured another cup of tea. Swallowed. "Simon..."

He leaned forward, concerned. "Have you seen him? Max?"

"No. I haven't." I paused. I had a sudden desperate urge to tell Simon about Roddy's death, and how I felt sure it was Max who had saved me, but I could not. I could not discuss that day with anyone—at least not for a long time yet. I then decided it would be best to simply tell Simon what he should know now.

"I had another vision," I said.

Simon leaned across the desk, attentive.

Quickly, I told him about the vision of the lamia brought on by the painting in the laboratory. While Simon had not yet seen the portrait of my mother as a lamia, I had told both him and William about it and he could understand my comparison.

"It's quite bizarre," I said. "The creature was not my mother—Mother had red hair, like mine. And although Gabriel painted the portrait, Christina mentioned once that my mother had given directions for how it was to be done. It's unlike anything else that Gabriel ever created." I bit my lip; it was always hard talking about this. "Mother told me nothing about her past with the Conclave. But I'm wondering if there is some sort of message to me, from her, in the painting."

Simon remained silent. His eyes veiled.

I chuckled a bit. "Of course, this all seems like foolishness. Lamias only exist in stories. The creature in my vision cannot be real."

Once again, I had all of Simon's attention, and yet he seemed maddeningly unreadable. So I continued. "And then, last night, I had a vivid nightmare about Mariah. I was in Highgate Cemetery, and she was alive. And someone was behind me."

I smiled even as I felt a tear prick my eye. "Perhaps, after all the psychic excitement we've gone through, I have finally gone batty, but..."

My voice came out as a croak.

"Something is happening, Simon. I'm fearful. There's a reason we haven't seen Max yet. A reason that he hasn't killed us by now."

Simon's light face seemed to shine a bit in the dim office. He started to speak, but at that moment I heard footsteps ascending the stairs, walking quickly past Simon's office.

William. His office door at the end of the hall closed loudly.

Simon's lips pressed together tightly; I felt my own face crumple a bit in distress and realized that I couldn't talk about this anymore.

I looked down at my nearly empty teacup, feeling terribly awkward again. Why couldn't I control my emotions any better?

"Excuse me." I stood and left abruptly, descending the stairs and returning to my work in the nursery.

Later that day, I returned to the fourth floor to restock the pharmacy closet. As I put the bottles on the shelves in the darkness, I felt a firm grip on my wrist.

I turned around to meet William's gaze, and I gasped sharply. He kept the viselike grip, leading me silently to his office. Against my will, I followed, promising myself that at all costs, I would be guarded.

William's office felt warm and muggy, even though the spring day outside was chilly and sunless.

Pushing me back against the closed door, he pressed his forehead against my own. His skin felt scalding upon my skin. His curls tickled my cheeks.

"I am nearly physically ill," he murmured.

I trembled, caught up in the spell of his warmth, of having him close to me. I recalled vomiting the previous night. Although I said nothing, I understood our shared malaise.

He put both of his hands on my cheeks.

I wanted to surrender. But I felt too bewildered, confused, angry, sad.

Scared.

I pulled away a little.

"Abbie," William continued. "I do not understand why something I did before I met you matters so much."

My bewilderment rose. Although I didn't listen to her advice most of the time, in this matter, I could not ignore Grandmother's words. *I could not.* They echoed in my mind, echoed too closely my own heart's trepidation. I was inexperienced in love relationships. And William could be so ... volatile. Good sense dictated that I should pull away. I removed his hands from my face and stepped away.

A tear slid down my cheek. "I'm scared, William."

His eyes shined, perplexed. "I have never hurt you. I have never been untrue."

"What if you tire of me?" I asked. "What if you become distracted? I have never felt this way about anyone. *Anyone.*"

"Abbie, I am not my father." He saw my troubled expression. "Yes"—he ran his fingers nervously through his hair—

"I followed him in that one regard. But please, Abbie, no one is perfect. Trust rather in the person I am now. I do not want to be Dante Gabriel Rossetti. I am more constant than that."

He pulled me back to him and kissed me.

Blood rushed to my head, and I, incapacitated, kissed him back.

Somewhere in the distance, I heard Simon's office door shut and his steely steps going toward the staircase.

Be guarded, Abbie.

"But there is no guarantee of your constancy," I said firmly, finally pushing him away from me.

William sighed. "No, there is not."

He pulled away and I saw a realization wash over his expression like a wave rushing over sand.

We stared at each other, unable to proceed. A cord had been severed that could not be repaired.

Unbelievably, I saw his dark eyes fill with tears before he turned his head to walk to the window, to stare at the dirty, busy street far below. He squinted and shielded his face with his hands as if he had a headache.

"Goodbye, William," I said.

"Goodbye."

He did not even turn around.

Seven

After the bath, she went outside in her monstrous form to rest upon one of her favorite tall craggy peaks on the island. She couldn't stop thinking of that last kill. Immediately after she'd killed the French boy, so many years ago, her keeper had disposed of the body and returned to her in the menagerie. She was feeding one of the dodo birds; Robert Buck had been trying to breed the two birds with no success for some time. All the animals in the large underground room—indeed, it was larger than the entire house itself—were dear pets to her. They were the only living beings she saw most of her days. She made toys for the monkeys and allowed the numerous parrots and other birds to fly free from their cages on many days. She even allowed her particular favorite, the Bengal tiger Petey, to wander in her own quarters. The tiger had been a man-eater in India when the Conclave had captured him thirty years before. They had made him—like the other birds and animals of the menagerie, and like she herself—immortal with the elixir.

Still, in spite of the tiger's violent past, with her he was tame as a kitten.

Though she tried to tend to the animals only when in her human form, the few times she had transformed inside the menagerie the animals never cowered from her. They knew that she would never harm them.

This was probably the reason her keeper was always safe around the tiger, and around her. She smiled to herself. Even though her keeper was human in form, his heart seemed half-beast itself.

"Effie," Max had said when he'd entered the menagerie after burying the boy. Her keeper was the only person who ever made a nickname from her full name, Seraphina. "My dear, dear Effie." He hauled several bags of birdseed down the steps from outside and into the menagerie. That time, as now, he had been gone for too many months, but when he returned he brought her an abundance of new supplies, more food for herself and the animals. "You had such a lovely record—you had become almost tame since your early days here."

"It was reckless of me." Seraphina bit her lip. "I didn't want to kill this one. But I was … " She struggled for the right words. "Overcome."

"That happens to me quite often," Max had said as he fed Petey.

She swept the floor. With pride she thought of how Max had told her that most menageries reeked of animal wastes and smells. Hers had no odors other than the incense she burned twice a day. Her menagerie was a place of beauty, the floors the same marble as the rest of the house. She took care to hang her unfinished portraits on these walls also. Animals needed beauty in their environment as much as humans. This she believed as she would a religious creed.

"I have much to tell you of our affairs in the world," Max had said later, as they took their dinner in the house. They ate on the floor in front of the fire in the library, reclined on pillows.

Seraphina took a sip of wine. "Affairs." She smiled. "I have no interest in your affairs."

"Effie, you know I am always yours." She could still remember how his eyes had glinted green, that evening in the firelight.

She did know. She always knew this. Whatever he did in the rest of the world, he always returned to her. Her lover. Her companion. He knew her—he had seen her transformation many times and it made no difference to him. Still, she was well aware that there was only so much he could offer her. Max was a libertine, free from the laws of love and constancy. He was loyal to no one—except to the Conclave. And she secretly believed that he did their bidding only because of the power it bestowed on him, the immortality they gave him every year in that ceremony.

As she had sat there with him on the floor, their empty dinner dishes now set aside, she'd thought of how Max made certain that she had enough activity to entertain herself. He brought her painting supplies, and books on nearly every subject to fill her library. He worked with her extensively to try to control her transformations. But mastering the monstrous part of herself was still impossible. Until she could keep the transformation from happening, or until

Robert found a cure, she would always be confined to this island and the surrounding waters. And yet she still had no knowledge of the world, about how it had changed since she had been banished to this place near the turn of the century... 1810. That year seemed engraved upon her mind.

As if to compensate for her isolation, Max had kept her updated on the Conclave's activities and accomplishments. He showed her sketches of the hospital that Julian Bartlett planned to establish in East End London. He once showed her pictures of their large and sprawling house on Montgomery Street, as well as their other homes in the Alps, in Scotland, and in the wilderness of the American West. Then, after the astronomer John Herschel described his discovery of photography to the Royal Society in London, the Conclave directed Max to take up the art, to document their life and work: their houses, Robert Buck's specimens, places around the world that they visited. Max would often practice his photography at the island, taking pictures of the sea, the rocky paths. He often photographed her body, both in its nude human form and its monstrous one. He arranged all the photographs neatly in books, and Seraphina looked through them obsessively in his absences. For her, the photographs of the Conclave's activities were nothing less than rows and rows of glimpses into the outside world.

On the evening of that day that she killed the boy, long after dinner while Max was out securing his boat from the impending storm, Seraphina stayed in the library and flipped through his latest photographs: the beaches, jungles, one of Julian Bartlett with midwives in Africa. Then she stopped at a photograph of a red-headed woman.

The photograph was out of place—this was not a picture documenting the Conclave's travels. Rather, it was of a woman with long hair, loose down her back, painting in a garden. The woman appeared to have no idea that she was being photographed; she was biting her lip in intense concentration, and the image was fuzzied from her movement.

Seraphina knew that Max had other lovers, but he was thoughtless, ruthless, and had never cared at all for them. Why had this picture been taken with such apparent care, and been made part of the Conclave's documented history?

At that moment, Max had entered the library. His black curls were wet, tousled from the wind and rain, and he brought with him the smell of salt, of wood.

"Who is she?" she had asked sharply, pointing to the photograph.

Max lit a cigar and considered Seraphina through a cloud of smoke.

"Caroline Westfield."

"Is she one of your ... conquests?"

Max smiled brilliantly. "Not yet." He sat on the sofa near Seraphina and gazed distractedly at the ceiling. "She means more than that to us. To Julian."

Seraphina cocked her head. Perplexed.

"Does she know?" She held her breath. "About the Conclave ... "

"We are planning to tell her."

Seraphina's heart stopped. "You are offering her the elixir, then?"

"Yes," Max said, peering carefully at Seraphina. He looked at her steadily: "We need another physician this time, a female one. And she has many talents…" His voice dwindled a bit.

Seraphina laughed, bitterly.

"After four hundred years, a woman in your ranks."

"You are in our ranks," Max said.

"As a pet."

"You are invaluable," he said, with a strange mixture of affection and irritation.

"Take me with you," she begged suddenly. She felt desperate this time, as she had been so many times in the past.

His green eyes flashed at her. They could go from blue to the exact color of the seagreen ocean that she swam in, and then back to blue. Wearily he answered her plea: "We have talked of this already. You know that is impossible. You could expose us all. You nearly did at one point, remember."

She always tried not to remember that time. "But I am better at controlling it," she said weakly.

"Seriously, love?" Max smiled widely in the candlelight. A mere few hours earlier he had been cleaning up the blood and gore from the French boy.

She chuckled in spite of herself.

"Robert is working on a cure, Effie."

He has been for over half a century, she thought bitterly. With every passing decade, she despaired that she would always be like this. And though she never said anything to Max, she questioned how hard, truly, Robert Buck was working on a cure. After all, the Conclave needed her; they needed her to care for their many animals, to guard their wealth.

She feared she would always be as she was now.

Wearily, she had changed the subject, but her mind kept returning to that redheaded woman—Caroline.

Max reclined a bit, leaning back upon her. He stared up at the ceiling as he smoked, deep in concentration. Seraphina felt her jealously flare up. A woman in the Conclave... but a woman who could travel and study with them, who would see more of the world than she had. Seraphina always felt like a child, pushing against the glass walls of a fabulous world that she could not venture into.

Petey roared in his cage, only seconds before lightning cracked in the sky outside. The tiger always roared before the fiercest storms, and that night there was a terrible one.

She leaned over, curling into Max. She wondered where his thoughts were. She knew that he had mental powers and physical powers that others did not—psychic abilities, the ability to climb down walls, defy gravity. The elixir had had this odd effect upon him, and he was almost as mythical as she was. She wished now that she had his mental powers, that she could see his visions, that his thoughts would slip out toward her mind like water. He had shared so much with her. Now he seemed distracted, and she was interested in his sealed-away thoughts. She wondered if he thought of Caroline; she wanted him to be hers alone. Only hers.

"How long are you staying?" she had asked, letting her gown slip away a bit from her shoulders.

She had his attention in that instant.

He ran his hand along her back, along her tattoo, which was only slightly raised in scar tissue and ink. She had requested that her tattoo be drawn larger than those on the other Conclave members, that it cover her entire back. She had embraced her position within the Conclave with sorrow and relish. At first, she had thought the immortality would be a gift, giving her power she had not had in her mortal life, but eventually realized that she had not only become their pet, but their slave. She had not seen the other Conclave members since they had made her immortal, after...she rarely allowed herself to think about that time.

Also, she couldn't think of how Robert Buck, and especially Julian Bartlett, had abandoned her. For years now, Max had been the one to supply her, to bring her a yearly dose of the elixir. She took her elixir with him, without ceremony, when he came to inject a concentrated formula into all of the animals.

"Only two nights," Max had said finally. "I must leave the following morning."

She had stood, the fire and storm sounds roaring. She pulled the ribbon that held her gown together, letting it fall to the floor.

His stays were too short. Always too short.

It stormed. For two nights and an entire day. On the morning he left, the storm finally moved eastward—away from her world.

Often over the years, from the tall craggy peak where she now rested, she would watch him row away from her island. Now, sunlight broke through a crack in the black storm clouds and she stretched her back in the beam. Shiny. Indestructible. Dense. As she coiled her tail, Seraphina's thoughts turned to her old life—to the days before the transformations, before her life had fallen into this beautiful placid ruin.

Reflecting on her human life could be too painful. It was

only here, in her monster form, that she could allow herself to think of the time before she became an immortal freak.

That life, in most respects, had been one of ease. Her father was the wealthiest Scotsman on the island, her family's estate just outside the nearest Orkney isle seaside town of Bromwell. She thought now of how many lives had started and ended while she lived out her decades on her island home, just across the waters from Bromwell. She had been forbidden by the Conclave from going there. Still, she often wondered about her father's mansion, whether it was empty, overgrown with weeds and ivy like the castles and Roman ruins scattered about the isles. Perhaps another family, unafraid of ghosts and shadows, had moved into it, repainting and refurnishing the halls and galleries.

Her childhood...

She had been so curious as a child, wandering the estate daily with her governess. Usually it was just herself and the governess—they had a loch very close to the house, and she had loved taking long walks along the water's edge in the summers. The waters were often still and slate black, shiny, by late afternoon. She was always thrilled to see her father's carriage on the estate's long driveway. And now, despite her eternal eighteen-year-old form, she felt perplexed at that girlish thrill; as best she could remember, her strong, distant father had said less than a hundred words to her in her whole life. A merchant, Joseph Umphrey spent most of his time on business in London, in Edinburgh, or even overseas. She remembered bursting through the front doors on the days of his return, and seeing his hard profile as he sat warming his feet by the fire. She would run to him then, but it was always the same—he would distractedly rumple her hair, his eyes on the fire. As she chattered, he only nodded, his thoughts far away. When her governess took her upstairs to bed, there was always a gift, some expensive gown or doll, something exquisite he had brought back to her from his travels.

She had often wondered why he didn't care about her more, why he never wanted to look upon her. She wondered sometimes whether it was because her mother died giving birth to her. She wondered if her father hated her, his only child, for this reason. But then she had no idea whether or not he even loved her mother; the only thing she knew about her was that she was dead, that her name had been Lucy, and that there was a portrait of her hanging in the main gallery. But even the portrait couldn't reveal to her anything specific about her mama—in the portrait, Lucy Umphrey had ordinary pretty features and an ordinary pretty smile; she wore silks and taffetas and held her small Pekingese in front of a faux pastoral background landscape. She seemed so expressionless, so vague. Whether this was the work of an unskilled artist or whether her mother was unremarkable, Seraphina would never know.

She had had no other relatives. All her grandparents or cousins were either dead or they lived too far away to see; she often thought bitterly that her life underground, as a monster, seemed so similar, too similar, to her earlier life— isolated, secluded. Even though she was unrelentingly curious about the outside world, she was unable to participate in it, to be part of it. She was simply given beautiful things to placate her.

Then there was her childhood skin condition. She remembered screaming in pain when the eczema was at its worst—itchy, scale-like hives, whitish and red splotches. It had been terrible. By the time she was ten she wore long sleeves all the time, even on warm days, just to cover her arms; her arms, especially, had had the pigment altered from all the outbreaks. Anything could bring on an outbreak—a new dress or food, a change in the weather. The skin condition returned often, and became increasingly severe.

Even now, with the disease gone, she could vividly remember the hot, burning pain. Her governesses had brought physician after physician to help her. She had been soaked in so many medicinal baths; she had taken so many herbs and bitter tonics. One physician had even tried bleeding her. She still remembered her childhood terror as he cut into her arm and began draining the "poisonous blood" into a small bowl. That hadn't helped her at all. She had merely fainted from the loss of blood.

She had taken up painting at the age of thirteen, and painted landscapes rich with the eyebright and orchids around the loch. At that time she had been able to finish the paintings, and they were coherent, organized ... unlike most of her portraits now, which were darker, mostly faces from her memories. And although she had painted hundreds of them, she couldn't finish a single one. But during her mortal days, the loch in autumn under the setting sun, crimson over the waters, had caught her eye and been her favorite scene to paint. Even during her worst eczema episodes, she could almost forget her pain as she painted.

She thought of those last few years of her mortal life, when she had dreamt of becoming an artist; she thought of her doomed engagement, of Dr. Buck's first treatments upon her, and then the first transformation...

Now, as she had so many times over the years, she thought about how hard it was to accept what she had become. She looked out in the direction of Bromwell—although she could not see it through the fogs and mists—and allowed herself to think of those early years. When Max had left her that time, twenty years ago, she had been disturbed by thoughts of Caroline; and now, once again alone with her memories, Seraphina remembered Max's very last visit in November—that awful visit when she had learned of the Conclave's interest in Caroline's daughter, Arabella.

As she thought of his November visit, her slitted, serpentine eyes narrowed in the evening darkness; she heard the idiot calling of sea gulls on the north shore of her island, and smelled, with her keen senses, the smell of a fisherman somewhere, perhaps a mile away. She repressed her urges with a low guttural growl. But she knew that if Max did not return to her soon, she could not repress the rising urge to hunt.

Eight

Dinner with Grandmother that evening was a silent event. I felt so terrible it was nearly impossible even to engage in small talk with her. Fortunately, she asked nothing and said nothing about William.

On the staircase landing, on the way to my room, I met Richard.

"Miss Arabella," he said, handing me a note. "This arrived in the mail earlier today. I thought I would hand it directly to you, so that it isn't"—he lowered his voice and cast his eyes to the parlor where Grandmother sat reading—"lost."

My heart quickened. If Richard had the discretion to protect the note from Grandmother's eyes and Ellen's hands, it had to be from William, or perhaps from his aunt.

"Thank you, Richard." I smiled, seeing Christina's name on the outside.

Always the professional butler, Richard only nodded. As I hurried up the stairs to my bedroom to read the note, I thought warmly of how kind and reliable Richard had been to me since I'd arrived in Kensington last year. I remembered what Simon had said when I'd worried about Grandmother's safety on that terrible night when we pursued the Conclave. I remembered Simon's cryptic words: "You should know your butler better." And then I had seen Simon try to hand Richard money, as if in payment for something. Yet with all that had happened since then, I had forgotten to ask Simon about Richard.

Once in my room, I tore the note open.

Abbie, please do arrive at the house on Monday evening at eight o'clock. I have a proposal to make. —Christina Rossetti

My spirits rose a little. Christina volunteered in another London hospital for the poor. Perhaps she knew someone who might offer me advice regarding my professional studies. That had to be the case. But I also felt a wave of anxiety as I wondered if this might be some sort of attempt on her part to reconcile William and myself. I did not know how much he confided to her of his romantic peccadilloes.

I wondered if Christina knew about William's history with Jane Burden Morris—after all, Jane was an old acquaintance of Christina's too.

I bit my lip as the angry thoughts surged again.

I returned to Whitechapel Hospital on Monday after a mostly sleepless weekend. Fortunately, upon returning, I discovered that I was too busy to think of William much. Mostly I worked alongside of Simon, or kept myself in the nursery. But when necessary, William and I worked together with detached cordiality.

By nightfall, when I arrived at Christina's home, I felt exhausted.

"Abbie!" Christina exclaimed when she opened the door. Each time I saw her, I felt surprised by her smallness—it seemed so at odds with her personality. Christina pulled me inside and helped me take off my coat.

I cast a discrete glance around me, hoping that William was not at home. He had still been at the hospital when I had left.

"William is not here," Christina said quietly. "He is still at the hospital."

"I..."

"It is all right," Christina replied. "This will pass. Whatever it is, William can be quite an ass..."

Then she peered into my face.

"Oh dear," she whispered. "You and William truly did have it out."

"Did William not tell you?" I asked quietly.

She shook her head. "William has told me none of the details, and—well, he can be so moody anyway. But..." She put her hand over her mouth and looked troubled. "I had no idea that there was a—split." She paused. "Do you want..."

"No," I said quickly. "Thank you, but I don't wish to talk about it."

I inhaled deeply, clearing my head. I could not keep dwelling on this melodrama.

Christina took me to the parlor. All of her rescued animals ran or flew, in a frenzy, about the room. This was a typical scene. I seated myself on an upholstered chair that had dove feathers stuck to the back.

"Abbie," Christina said cheerfully as she thrust a cup of tea into my hand. "At work today I met Dr. Elizabeth Garrett Anderson."

"The physician," I said stupidly, stunned.

"The very one. She works in several hospitals for the poor around London; she is a member of the British Medical Association." Christina frowned. "Since she became a member they have closed membership for women, and as you might already know, she has, in recent years, established a hospital for women, not too very different from Whitechapel Hospital." Christina sat on the couch. "I have told her much about you, how remarkable you are, how you plan to attend medical school, how I am certain you will get an excellent endorsement from Whitechapel Hospital."

My heart beat quickly. Pounding, in fact.

"She would like for you to begin working at New Hospital, her charity hospital. She would like to meet you, and if all goes well, she said that she can direct your studies until you apply to London Medical School for Women and take your examinations. She has assured me that it is highly possible for you to be ready to attend medical school in the autumn."

"When am I to begin?" I asked, just as a puppy knocked over my teacup.

"Bad, Flush!" Christina exclaimed, chastising the dog while taking him into her arms. "I found him in an alley yesterday—he has yet to learn his house manners."

None of Christina's rescued animals had "house" manners

except Hugo, William's Great Dane, who was sleeping peacefully on the floor at my feet.

"She said that you may begin immediately," Christina said as she struggled to maintain a grip on the puppy. "If you wish, you can begin tomorrow morning. It will be good training for medical school. I know it's not Oxford, but the London Medical School for Women has an excellent reputation."

I couldn't believe it. This would be such a remarkable opportunity. To work and study alongside Elizabeth Garrett Anderson. I looked into the fireplace, flames roaring from it in great gold billows, and I considered the looming portrait of William's great-uncle John Polidori. The man had been a vampire-book writer as well as a personal physician for Lord Byron. The concept of a female physician was essentially nonexistent during Polidori's lifetime.

The front door opened suddenly.

I feared it was William, and I rose quickly to get my coat. I had hoped that I might leave before he came home. I felt great relief when I saw that it was only a neighbor, returning a borrowed bag of sugar.

It was nearly ten thirty as I made my way back toward Kensington. I told Christina that I would take a hansom cab. I knew I had to hurry to reach Kensington; it was so late. I very well might hear a lecture. Grandmother knew that she had very little control over my comings and goings, but nonetheless I tried, out of respect for her, not to stay out very late. As the carriage rolled out of Torrington Square, I stared out the window. The night was chilly and foggy; a damp mist had settled in the air, creating bright halo circles around the streetlamps. Emotionally, I felt almost ill—I still couldn't find it in my heart to forgive William, to understand what he'd done with Jane Morris; it was too revolting.

When the carriage had traveled a few blocks and was about to turn west onto Marylebone Road, toward Kensington, the persistent cry of a child caught my attention, bringing me away from my reflections. The street was relatively empty, but I saw a woman wearing a dark cloak. As the hood blew aside, I saw her long curly hair falling loose down her back. She was walking northwards, toward the Highgate area, and she carried in her arms a child of about two years of age. At first, I saw nothing particularly remarkable about the two figures. Then the baby's tear-stained face, wisps of blond hair blowing about, peered at me over the woman's shoulder.

I froze as I recognized the child—she was one of the children who lived on the first floor of Whitechapel Hospital. Her name was Christabel. The woman, whose face I could still not see, paused in her walk. The moment the cab turned onto Marylebone, she half-turned her face in my direction so that I could see her profile and the small curve of a smile.

The woman's face made my heart quicken; I remembered my nightmare.

Mariah.

But it couldn't be. Mariah was dead.

The situation was peculiar. The carriage progressed west,

and after a few moments of indecision, which I spent trying to tell myself that the woman might be Christabel's mother, I called to the driver to stop. I paid him and hurried back, attempting to follow the woman and child. They were no longer in my sight, but I could hear the child's cries far ahead.

They had been walking swiftly, and it was a while before I reached Swains Lane, just in front of the Highgate Cemetery gates, and saw them again. I stopped, out of breath from my hurried pace, my corset tight around my chest like a vise. I then saw the woman more clearly, and heard myself gasp. Somehow, as she had walked ahead of me in the darkness of the streets, she had shed her cloak and shoes. Now she stood still, holding the child and wearing only a white gauzy dress or nightgown, even outdoors in the chilly air. She turned and met my eyes before disappearing through the open gates, with Christabel. Two thoughts struck me at once:

The gates should not be open at this time of night.

Mariah. She looks like Mariah.

I wondered once again if the woman might be the child's mother, discharged from the hospital. But Whitechapel Hospital was quite a few miles from Torrington Square, a bit far to walk with a baby on a cold evening. Furthermore, I could not recall Christabel's mother's face. Perhaps the child was one of the orphans that Simon was keeping at the hospital, not having the heart to send them to the orphanage. The nightmare of seeing Mariah kept surfacing in my mind, and I tried to push away these darker thoughts.

The white dress. The curly hair.

Once again, I told myself that Mariah was dead. To see her walking here would be an impossibility.

Quickly, following the baby's cries, I entered the cemetery.

It was all darkness once I walked through the gates—the great canopies of trees that kept the place dark, even on the brightest days, now shrouded the cemetery in blackness. Not even the streetlights could break through the leaves. Only a few strong moonbeams spilt whitish-gray spots on some of the gravestones. Gradually, my eyes adjusted a little to the darkness, and I started to follow one of the maze-like paths in the direction of the child's cries.

The bushes at my left rustled. I saw a flash of white. But whether it was moonlight or the white of the woman's dress, I could not tell. The child continued to cry, from far ahead on the path. My blood froze when I heard a giggle from behind some tombs nearby in the darkness.

I heard the mendacious undertone of the giggle, and I sensed that I was being watched—by more than one person.

Max! My heart pounded as I looked around. I half-expected to see some shadow creeping down a tall monument. Of course—he had lured me here to kill me. I could fight him, but I had no weapon, no knife.

Get the child and leave, I told myself.

As I continued quickly down the path, not familiar with this portion of the cemetery, a tree branch scraped my face. It was painful; my cheek burned.

The child's cries seemed closer, and I breathed a sigh of relief when I came around a sharp twist to the path.

A moonbeam illuminated Christabel, seated alone on a stone bench near a grave. She was still crying, barefoot and confused.

There was no sign of the woman anywhere.

"Chrissy," I said, trying to sound calm and unworried as I lifted her into my arms. "Come with me."

I almost screamed when the bushes beside me rustled.

"Abbie," I heard whispered from the darkness behind me. The voice was soft, breathy. And if I had not heard my name spoken, I might have thought it was a rush of wind through the leaves. The hair on my neck rose.

Christabel continued crying as I put her face into my neck and began running back toward the entrance of the graveyard.

I stopped, frozen, when I saw a figure blocking the path ahead. It was not Max, but a woman. She was not the dark-haired woman I had seen earlier—this one was older, around forty years of age. She wore a heavy wool black dress. Her blond hair was pulled back into a knot at the back of her head. She looked dignified, attractive, as if she might have been one of Grandmother's guests at a cribbage game.

But I did not continue forward. I stayed where I was.

The woman walked toward me, sharp leaf shadows cutting across her white face . . . her mouth smeared with blood.

The giggle from behind me rang out.

They were closing in on me.

I ran down a path to my right, praying that it would take me to the entrance.

It did. I saw the open gates ahead.

A man stood in front of the gates. When he saw me, he began walking toward me. He was tall, older. He wore some kind of uniform, probably a constable's.

"Help!" I yelled, running toward him. He turned to me.

It was then that I saw a thick drop of blood slide down his chin.

I sprinted, panicked now, down yet another path, my heart pounded vigorously. I had no idea what I was going to do. Christabel screamed in my arms. The tombs and monuments offered many hiding places, but they were useless to me if the child continued to cry.

I heard crashing through the branches behind me.

I had to face my pursuers. I had to fight them, even though I knew now that I had at least three pursuers. Yet I had no idea how to defend myself with the child in my arms. So I continued running, deeper into the cemetery. We would be trapped soon.

I felt my elbow grasped in a painful tight grip.

Nearly dropping Christabel, I swung around to kick the person away.

"No!" I yelled loudly.

I felt both relief and shock when I saw it was William. I had found him unexpectedly once before, last year; I knew that he often walked around London, even late at night after work, when he was agitated. The Highgate area was one of his favored routes.

"What the bloody hell are you doing here?" he said, panting, looking quickly at myself and then at Christabel.

"Did you see them?" I asked rapidly. I heard no noise now. Saw no one.

"Who?" William said, staring at me as if I was crazy. "And why do you have one of the hospital's children with you?"

"We have to get out of here!" I said, ignoring him and running in the direction of the entrance.

I saw and heard nothing unusual as we left the cemetery. There was no sign of the man or the two women. When we stepped out onto the street, William shut the gates behind us.

My heart still raced. I clutched Christabel closer.

"What is happening here?" he demanded

"Never mind! We need to get away from here. Fast. Now." I kept imagining a white bloody hand reaching out, through the cemetery bushes, from behind the tombs.

William and I walked several blocks in irritated silence. When I finally faced him, as I fumbled to take off my own coat and wrap it around the child—she was shivering violently in the wet night air—William spoke, incredulous and furious.

"You never answered my question. How did she get here?" He pointed angrily at Christabel. She still heaved with sobs and clutched me as she sucked her thumb.

I told him what happened. I fought to control my breathing—I felt such panic, it came out in sharp clips. "It was Mariah, I am almost certain. I saw blood on the other woman's mouth and on the man's mouth. They"—a chill ran through me—"were not like living people."

William still looked incredulous.

"I don't know what you saw, Abbie. But what you are describing to me—insane murderers, vampires, walking dead, whatever—seems impossible. However, someone might have tried to kidnap the child. This is serious. I will return her, talk to Josephine, try to determine what precisely occurred.

I'll alert Scotland Yard if necessary. But the rest of your story, Abbie, is simply not possible."

I stared at him, unbelieving. William seemed cold, detached. He was looking at me as if I were a madwoman. And how could he say this after having seen the horror, the seeming impossibility, of that murderous group of immortals known as the Conclave?

Still, I kept my voice calm. "I'm not sure if you heard me, William. I am not a hysteric; neither do I suffer from an overactive imagination. You should know me better than that. I do not comprehend all that I saw, but I saw it, nonetheless. It was quite bizarre."

William's dark eyes flashed indecisively for one instant, but out of surprise, concern, or confusion I could not tell. Then his gaze narrowed. "Abbie, this is not rational thinking."

"What are you saying?" I hissed. "After all that we have been through! I didn't see Max, but apart from what happened in there, I know that he is likely still around. Somewhere. It is not as if we have nothing to fear."

My mind scrambled. I was trying to make sense of what did not make sense. My nightmare of Mariah ... what I had seen tonight ... the vision of the lamia. None of it appeared to be connected to Max or the Conclave. And yet ... somehow it felt centered around me. I seemed to have been lured here, tonight.

Then another thought arose. Perhaps I truly was mad? After all, William had not seen my pursuers. Yet someone had brought Christabel here; she was in my arms. Although why had they seemed to disappear once William showed up? My head pounded.

Christabel had now fallen asleep on my shoulder. I held her against my chest, draping my coat around her.

William said nothing. His look now was sharp, reproachful. I had never before felt such a distance between us.

"Are you saying that you do not believe me?" I asked.

He paused. "Yes, in fact, I am. I do not believe that you are intentionally embellishing or lying. I do believe that you saw whoever took the child enter the graveyard; you became confused in the darkness. Your mind played tricks. It happens, Abbie. There was no one in there. I've had a difficult day at the hospital, and ... " He ran his fingers through his hair, then looked away, agitated. "I was out walking. It was when I passed the West cemetery entrance that I heard you cry out. I saw no walking dead, no blood-smeared faces."

I felt incensed, confused.

"Max has probably gone abroad," William added. "You know how he is. He has probably forgotten about us by now ... "

Astonished, I sincerely hoped that he was merely trying to annoy me, that he was being cruel because of our falling out. Max was brutal, relentless, and William's seeming oblivion to this went beyond foolishness. I feared for William. My mind raced. Our history with the Conclave, my lamia vision, what I had just seen in the graveyard—something must connect all of this. I felt as if I was missing something directly in front of me.

William took Christabel from me. "Let me escort you home, and then I'll take the child back to the hospital and deal with this matter."

"I can find another carriage myself."

"It is late."

"Do not follow me."

I turned around quickly so that he could not see the hot tears stinging my eyes.

Nine

Rain poured in great sheets outside my window the next morning. I stood, already dressed, and prepared to start my work at New Hospital. Although it was springtime, I felt a blanket of terror descending upon me. It felt thick and unrelenting. Reason could not persuade me that I had not fallen into a web, into some terrible game.

I jumped as a sharp hand squeezed my shoulder.

"I am sorry, Miss Arabella. I did not mean to scare you." Ellen's voice came out raspy, dramatic, her bulbous eyes rapidly searched my own. I had seen that look on Ellen's face many times. She was greedily searching for a listener for her gossip.

I needed an umbrella. I focused on locating my umbrella in my closet so that I could leave. I was in no mood to listen to Ellen's chatter.

"You have not heard yet, Miss?" she exclaimed in a sharp whisper as I pulled the umbrella out from behind a pair of boots.

"I have not yet been out of my room, Ellen."

"Do not tell Lady Westfield that I'm talking to you about this. She has forbidden me from speaking of it—awful nonsense, she called it. But I thought you should know, since you're goin' out and all."

"What is it, Ellen?" I sighed wearily.

"The word on the street is all about them two murders in Highgate Cemetery last night."

"What?"

"Shhh! Remember, the missus threatened to sack me if I talk'd about it anymore in 'er house."

"Tell me what happened," I demanded in a whispered hiss.

"They were murdered. Eat'n! Their throats ripped out. Their insides chewed all up. Devoured."

Now that Ellen had my full attention, she relished in the drama of her story.

"It was grave-robbers, resurrectionists, what were murdered, low sorts from what I've heard. Two men—they were found this mornin', and the 'hol Highgate neighborhood is risen up, scar'd and angry."

I felt nearly overwhelmed now, remembering the blood-smeared beings from the night before. Nonetheless, I tried to remain composed.

"It sounds, rather, as if a lion escaped from the zoological gardens."

"No, it's cannibals in London! And I, for one, am feared for my life." Her eyes widened even further.

"Grandmother is correct, Ellen. You should not speak of such nonsense."

Silencing Ellen as she began to protest, I told her to tell Grandmother that I would now be working at New Hospital instead of Whitechapel Hospital. I certainly did not feel like discussing anything with Grandmother. As I descended the stairs toward the front door, I heard the clatter of Grandmother's knife and fork striking against her china plate. But I left without speaking a word to her. I resolved to send a note to Simon later today, letting him know about my decision.

Before going to New Hospital, I decided to ride through Swains Lane. After last night, and the news from Ellen, I was determined to visit Mariah's grave site to see if it was undisturbed.

That was, if I could get past the curious crowds. It was no later than six o'clock in the morning, and in spite of the rain, a small but crushing group of journalists and others stood outside Highgate Cemetery. Constables were working hard to barricade the entrance.

There would be no possibility of penetrating through the pressing crowd, but I watched as a small group of medics arrived, stretchers and medical bags of supplies in hand. The bodies must not have been removed yet. I wondered if Dr. George Bagster Phillips, the mortuary surgeon, would be performing the autopsies on the bodies as he had done for the Ripper case.

Quickly throwing aside my umbrella and pulling my cloak's hood up with purpose, I attached myself to the six medical workers who had just exited their carriages and were confronting the small crowd. I quickly told one of the nearby constables blocking the gate that I was from the mortuary; he looked at my black dress and pinafore, typical nurse's attire, and nodded. I was, after all, a hospital worker, and under the circumstances, no one questioned me further.

The inside of the cemetery seemed almost as crowded as the outside. Constables seemed to be everywhere as I moved forward with the tiny cluster of medical workers.

We were ushered toward the tombs in the Egyptian Avenue section. They stood out from the foliage around them, giant, chalky. A small path split off from the main one; it was the path leading to Mariah's grave. But at the point when I might have easily slipped unnoticed in that direction, I decided to press on with the main group, toward the spot where the bodies lay. I could not shun this opportunity to see firsthand what had happened the night before.

The first sign of violence in the scene was a bloodied handprint, rust-brown in the rain. The print stood midway up a looming, tall grave shaped like an angel. The granite being held a sword in one hand; the angel's other arm was outstretched, the palm upward in an inviting gesture of protection and peace. It was as if the fleeing body-thief, in desperation or perhaps in panicked repentance for disturbing the dead, had appealed to the useless stone being.

Almost immediately after passing the blood-stained tombstone, I came upon the murder scene. A photographer was taking the crime photos—blinding all around him with great white flashes. Some of the medical workers stood by with the stretchers; others, and a few constables, held umbrellas over the bodies. Every single one of us covered our noses with handkerchiefs. The slaughterhouse odor, even in the rain, was overwhelming. Even with the cloth over my nose, I felt my stomach convulse a couple of times.

Dr. Phillips crouched over the two corpses to begin his initial medical examination. I listened, averting my eyes from the bodies—ragged wounds at their throats, open caverns in their stomachs.

"Two males—one early twenties, other late forties. Possible relatives," I heard a familiar voice saying to the crouching Phillips.

Abberline! I pulled my hood further around my face. I did not want the Inspector to see me. He would know that I did not belong with these forensic workers. And I did not wish to speak to him, particularly given my experiences with him in the past.

But for the moment, at least, Abberline knelt near Phillips, all his attention consumed in the scene before him. His voice came out loud and gravely. "One source has already identified them as a father and son, Felix and Thaddeus Cruncher—though I would like to verify this further. We will make efforts to locate families later today. A cemetery worker discovered the pair at four thirty this morning."

"The stage of rigor mortis shows me that they have been lying here all night," Phillips said in dry assertion. "Death occurred sometime between eight o'clock and ten at night."

I stepped a few feet away, worried that Abberline might decide to look up and see me. Furthermore, I needed the distance, as the smell suddenly seemed more pungent. The tiny flies swarmed even amid the rain, and their buzzing roared unrelenting in my ears.

I heard Abberline point out the "bite marks" on the throats and chests.

There was a long silence and I heard Phillips give a tremendous sniff. Without seeing his expression, I could not decide if the sound came from boredom or deep reflection.

"Have you located the kidneys, livers, and hearts of the victims, Abberline?" Phillips asked suddenly.

"No, we have not."

"When I perform the autopsies, I'll determine whether more organs are missing. All of these wounds appear to have been made by human teeth, nails, and hands. I see no evidence of any knife cuts."

"So the attacker was human?" Abberline asked.

"Most certainly," Phillips said. Out of the corner of my eye, I saw him, with a small pair of tweezers, place something in a small jar held by an assistant. Using a small cloth strip, he began swabbing at one of the wounds on the younger victim.

"Abberline," Phillips said, peering closer into the wound, "at least two attackers were involved here. Do a thorough check of the nearby asylums for missing persons. I doubt that your men will locate the organs."

A throat cleared. "Why is that?" Abberline asked.

"Because I am surmising that the organs have been consumed," Phillips said, standing and wiping his hands upon a nearby rag. From the tone of his voice, he might as well have been answering a question about the type of tea brand he preferred.

"Guess we won't have to worry about watchin' out for

them resurrection men around here no more," one constable near me whispered to another.

Consumed. I felt the strangest mixtures of emotion. Horror, at the thought that I had been in the cemetery possibly mere minutes after these murders occurred, overwhelmed me. That I had been pursued by the murderers, that they had somehow managed to take one of our children from the orphanage. It was an impossible but apparently real atrocity. What was this? Who were those bloodstained people who pursued me last night? Oddly, also I felt a bit of stark, dark amusement at how quickly Ellen had attained accurate information about the murders.

When I had seen and heard enough, I turned toward Mariah's grave. I had to see it before I left. As I walked, I kept looking behind me to make certain that I was not being followed. I hoped that Abberline hadn't seen me here; if he had, he would certainly want to speak to me.

Then, as I rounded a corner near Mariah's grave, I was startled to see a man, in a very long coat, smoking a pipe as he leaned against a tombstone. He nodded politely at me, and I nodded back. I had never seen him before—I assumed he might work with Dr. Phillips, an assistant perhaps. He was probably somewhere in his forties, and he had a very distinct face—sunburned—and shocking ash-blond hair that was almost white. He watched me as I passed, and I heard him lightly hit his pipe against a nearby tomb to knock out the ash.

I continued on my way.

I found the place. The simple front of the granite marker

seemed unmolested, reading only *Mariah Anne Crawford 1869–1889.*

But as I surveyed the surrounding dirt, I could not determine if the ground had been disturbed at all. Someone, probably a groundskeeper, had spread gravel all around the grave. And since Mariah had been dead only a few months, grass had not yet had much of an opportunity to cover the ground.

I knelt in front of the marker, the tiny white rocks crunching under my kneecaps. I felt an overwhelming, almost hot emotion surge through me as I recalled Mariah. I remembered the look in her eyes, panic and determination to survive, before she fell to her death. After such violence she deserved peace, and if my darkest suppositions were correct—that she was somehow the woman I had seen the night before with the child—she was clearly not at peace. She must be returned to the grave.

A lone morning moth landed onto my skirt.

I contemplated the philosophical concept of Ockham's razor: that the most probable theory or explanation for something was also typically the simplest explanation. Of course, the Conclave and their history had not represented the simplest explanation behind the Whitechapel murders, and it had been the true one. But I struggled not to apply my outrageous suspicions—that it was re-animated corpses who were responsible—to this case. No, it seemed more likely to be some sort of cult, perhaps a cannibal blood-cult, or escaped lunatics as Phillips had suggested. Still, my other theory persisted like a clinging cobweb on my skin.

The moth flew away and I stood, leaving that place.

I made it out of the cemetery, pushing my way past the dwindling crowd at the front gates. It was already nine o'clock. I would have liked to have been at New Hospital by now. As I walked a few blocks from the graveyard, I saw that the sidewalks were already very busy, crowded with hurried people.

The moment I focused on locating a hansom cab, I heard a voice behind me.

"Miss Sharp."

I felt my shoulders tense. I thought I had escaped him.

I turned to see Inspector Abberline looming above me. Bristling, I remembered how heavy-handed he had been with me during his Ripper investigation; in fact, I felt my insides burn as I thought of how he had practically blackmailed me in an attempt to find evidence against William or Simon.

Blast. Every single carriage passing me was occupied.

"Certainly you have a few moments ... "

"I'm trying to go to work," I said quickly. *Please God send me an available carriage.* The streets were always full of available carriages. Of course, this would be the one instance where I could not secure one immediately.

"I can take you in my own carriage to the hospital. You can save your fare."

"No."

Ahhh ... I spotted a hansom cab coming in my direction.

"Miss Sharp. I'll get to the point. What were you doing just now at the murder scene?"

Bloody hell. Someone else had reached the cab before I could, and I watched as the carriage turned the opposite direction from where I needed to go.

I shrugged at Abberline. "I was on my way to work, and I was curious. Half of London was already at the gates, and my uniform allowed me to get past."

"Are you still working at Whitechapel Hospital?"

"That is none of your concern, Inspector."

"You are rather out of the way of Whitechapel, are you not?"

Another available carriage approached.

"If you'll excuse me," I said, stepping toward the cab as it came closer.

"Miss Sharp!" This time he grabbed my elbow in a firm grip.

"Inspector," I hissed at him angrily. "Let go of me." This was impertinent. Low, even for him.

He bent close to my face and I smelled his odor of orange tea, of cigars, of his stale office where he spent far too many hours. "Can you tell me if this means anything to you?"

He held out a notebook. It contained a sketch of the chalice, with *A Posse Ad Esse* written around the symbol.

My blood froze in my veins. "Where did you see that?"

"Does it mean something to you?" he asked, suddenly more interested. His brows pushed together.

Jerking my arm away from his grip, I stepped into the carriage.

His eyes narrowed. "What do you know, Arabella Sharp?"

I felt my gut twitch a bit.

"Good day," I said, slamming the carriage door. Once inside, I felt my hands trembling violently. I took several deep breaths. How much did Abberline know? I shuddered, knowing that if he investigated much further in this direction—he would be a dead man.

Ten

Seraphina dashed her easel against the wall. She hissed, and her heartbeat tripled. She knew she had to get control before a transformation came on. She did not want to split apart the gown she wore, nor one of her last remaining painting bibs.

A dark oil-paint droplet slid down the partially finished face on her wrecked canvas like a black tear. She had been painting her keeper's face. But, as with so many other portraits, she had lost the inclination to finish it.

Where was he? He had been gone too long.

She paced in worried agitation; this was his longest absence from her. It had now been almost five months with no word from him. She uttered a guttural growl somewhere deep inside, not believing that he could leave her alone this long—he knew how restless she became. He hadn't been away this long since the Conclave's experience with Caroline. And now, there was that daughter...In Seraphina's loneliest times, she waited like an eager child for him to bring her blossoms of news and images from the world of humanity. This restlessness was dangerous for her. Max knew this.

Yet again, she wondered if Robert Buck still sought a cure. She always felt like Robert and the others never forgave her for coming into being, and for the troubles she had caused for them in those early days.

She tossed aside her paint-stained bib and strode to the menagerie. It was time to feed the animals.

While she gave the herbivores their bins of grain, the carnivores their rodents, or rabbits, or chilled meats, she struggled with the suffocating sensation that she had been abandoned—that something was wrong. And she couldn't forget the fierce argument that she had had with her keeper before he left her last.

In the same way that she could sniff whale migrations approaching her region, which incited her to chase the young gray seals to safer waters; in the same way that she, while floating in the ocean depths, could extend her webbed fingertips ahead, predicting in the currents the coming of cooler waters, she felt—she sensed—that something was amiss. Her hunger for human blood could be satiated as long as Max continued to connect her to the outside world through his visits. But now she felt her hunger rising.

She tossed four struggling rats at her Komodo dragon. He ate them whole, in about four minutes.

The women.

Max had never again talked about Caroline, after the Conclave had offered Caroline the elixir those many years ago, except to tell her that Caroline had refused their offer.

Seraphina knew what this meant for the woman. The Conclave's offer hadn't really been a choice from the start.

Seraphina considered her last conversation with Max, that cold evening this past November. He had brought the animals and birds from the Conclave's London home to her, along with more food and supplies.

"Tell me what's happening…" she had said, after helping him unload the crates and supplies. She remembered the cold feeling inside her as the wind whipped at her hair. They had struggled to bring the animals inside, especially the caged spider monkeys, who were panicked amid the stormy blasts.

Max had said nothing. But instinct, the best part of her part-beast existence, rose immediately. She lowered her voice. "It's another woman, isn't it? You have made the offer to another woman?"

He had smiled, and his eyes—so feral, like her own— glistened leopard-like. He wiped some sea spray off her brow. "Yes."

Seraphina growled. "But you know that the last one didn't end well. You had to kill her, did you not?"

"We did. Eventually. But this is her daughter. Same gifts as the mother, in fact. Extraordinarily psychic. With the elixir, she'll likely be like me."

Seraphina felt the burning jealousy rising within her. Caroline and now her daughter—these women could share her keeper's gifts, his mind. They had powers that she would never have. She would always only be his pet. The useful, dutiful pet of the Conclave. She tried to repress her memories of her mortal life, a life when her hopes and ambitions had been as wide as the seas.

"When did you ask her?" she hissed.

"The Conclave made the offer to her a few nights back. She'll accept." He smiled cryptically in the darkness of her great hall. "I'm not anticipating any problems. We have some leverage, and she truly cannot refuse us."

Seraphina did not know what possessed her. But her rage was too much. She growled and flung herself at him. Her transformation began. She felt the venom flow into her fangs, her nails become longer, sharper. She had never done this—in the entire eighty years that he had been her caretaker, she had never transformed to attack him.

Within a second, he had her pinned against the cold wall, her back pressed painfully against the marble. He had his hand on her throat, cutting off her blood supply and air. Possibly because of this, her transformation ceased midway. Several of her half-finished portraits collapsed around them. His eyes blazed in anger, and the pain was crushing, both in her throat and the back of her head. She became dizzied and feared she would lose consciousness.

"What is this, Effie? You would bite the hand that feeds you?"

The clatter of the portraits must have disturbed the animals. She heard the monkeys squealing from the menagerie. Petey roared from his cage.

The pain in her lungs became intolerable. She gagged, tried to remove his grip, but it was too tight. He glared at her, only pressed her harder against the wall. The beast within her fought to come out; it rose to the surface in hideous bubbles. If he did not release her, and she could not transform, she felt as if she might die.

"Please," she croaked. "Please, let me go." She began to see flickering lights in her peripheral vision.

She knew he was the Conclave's assassin. That he had horrible means of carrying out their will. But he had never attacked her like this. She hated and loved him in that moment, and she wept. He had never abused her in this way, and yet ... yet ... she had never attacked him in this way, either. Even amid her pain, she felt a flush of shame rise within her.

"Remember," he whispered in the darkness, his face inches from hers, "the only reason you are still alive is because of me." Then he flung her to the floor and she exploded into her beast form, splitting her gown to pieces. She felt herself cry, and curled into a ball. Feelings of abandonment overwhelmed her rage and anger, and she fainted.

She had awoken, in human form, where she had fallen—on the floor of the great hall in the main part of her home. Her keeper must have released Petey from his cage, for the tiger was curled near her, his warm tongue licking her face. Sunlight shone down the main stone steps of her home in a great white stream. The stone door to that stairwell had been pulled away. He was preparing to leave her.

Seraphina had sat up, wiped her eyes, and moaned. The back of her head throbbed and her neck ached. Then the sunstream darkened and she saw Max looming above her. He smiled and kneeled down beside her. His smile was affectionate but not kind, and certainly not repentant. It was a distracted smile. He had a scent for that new woman, and he desired to return to London in haste, to return to the newest Conclave member.

"Effie." Carefully, he had lifted her naked form and carried her back to the bedroom. He laid her on the bed.

"You are leaving?" she asked amid her tears.

"For now," he said, covering her with the blankets—pale green silk sheets like the waters around her island.

She had been silent, biting her lip. If she asked, he might answer her.

"What is her name? The girl? You can tell me her name, at least."

He looked down at her, his eyes glinting. Casually, he ran his fingers through her long hair, playing with her locks, his fingers gently wiping away the perspiration about her face.

"Arabella Sharp."

"She looks like her mother?" Seraphina wanted an image in her head. An image of the woman who would be with the Conclave in their travels, in their work. Who still had the potential to do remarkable things.

"Exactly," he said. "Same blood-red hair."

Seraphina sighed and rolled over in bed. She would be silent now.

"Goodbye, Effie." He bent, kissing her cheek. She had heard him leave her room, ascend the stone steps. Then, when he closed the door, darkness enshrouded her once again.

That was the last time she had seen him, back in the cold, windy autumn.

Returning her thoughts to the present, she watched the Komodo dragon roll lethargically in his enclosure. She hissed again, her rage surfacing. Who *was* this girl? Who was Arabella, that she could make Max neglect his duties to her, Seraphina, his only constant love. She pictured the girl as her mother in the photograph—the curly long hair, the dark eyes. She imagined Arabella Sharp alongside Robert Buck on his journeys in the Amazon and the Congo, collecting specimens. She pictured her alongside Julian Bartlett in his London hospital. That had been her dream—to be one of them. That had been her dream before everything went terribly wrong.

She thought of how she had wrecked her painting. She could not control her rumblings any longer and, in a fit of rage, she burst out, ruining yet another gown. The bloodlust was too much. Her desires were as uncontainable as salty sea spray.

She leapt into the water and swam away.

To search for answers.

To eat.

Eleven

I felt myself tremble all the way to New Hospital. Where would Abberline have seen the Conclave's symbol? I wondered if he had seen it in the rubbish of the Montgomery Street house. I wondered briefly if he had seen it on the Conclave members' corpses after the fire. But the bodies had been charred almost beyond recognition by the time the fire was put out. In fact, the *Times* had stated that the morgue couldn't confirm the identities of the men inside the house. Scotland Yard had simply made the assumption that they were Bartlett, Buck, Perkins, and Brown, and the newspapers never indicated that foul play was involved.

I tried to repress these thoughts when I arrived at New Hospital. Unfortunately, I didn't meet Dr. Elizabeth Garrett Anderson until later in the day. But the time flew by as I worked alongside two very young physicians in the prenatal unit, Doctors Hettie Davis and Rachel Carmichael, who had been expecting me.

When I finally met Dr. Anderson, she was on her way to examine a young boy. "I do apologize for not being available earlier. I have been so busy," she told me. She was very tall and thin and wore spectacles, and had her brown hair, which was streaked with gray, pulled tightly back in a knot away from her face.

She walked quickly down the halls of New Hospital, and I nearly had to run to keep up with her. "You are of special interest to me, Abbie Sharp," she continued, "having been mentored by Dr. Bartlett and Dr. Buck. Their hospital is very similar to ours, and my students and I have attended some of Dr. Bartlett's seminars. He is extraordinarily brilliant." Her face shadowed a bit and she shook her head. "That fire ... such a tragedy. They had done such great things for the Whitechapel district."

I averted my eyes; we were rapidly approaching another ward.

"But, nonetheless, now you have Dr. Siddal and Dr. St. John. I haven't been to Whitechapel Hospital since they took charge, but I know that Dr. St. John is especially competent. He was recently here inquiring about some of our vaccination practices. Ahhh ... " she said as we entered the next ward, where a little boy waited for us with his mother. "It is young Nicholas." Her eyes sparked a bit in my direction. "Abbie, you may take this one if you would like."

"No! I don't want her to touch me!" the blond child screamed immediately after bloodying my nose. "I only want Dr. Anderson."

I fought tears as well as a burning desire to curse. The kick, unbelievably forceful for a four-year-old, caused the whole middle section of my face to feel as if it were on fire. The boy had dealt the blow just as I had attempted to listen to his heart with a stethoscope.

Dr. Anderson calmly handed me a tissue.

Dr. Davis, who had just entered the room, stood against a wall and tried to look concerned but I saw that she was repressing amusement. Her look made me wonder if the little fiend had ever injured her.

After I wiped the blood away, Dr. Anderson examined my nose briefly. "Not broken, merely bloodied. It will be sore for a day at least. It will bruise."

I blushed, embarrassed. Although we had several children at Whitechapel Hospital, I had just exhibited what very little experience I had in pediatric care. Mostly, I had cared for women and newborns.

Nicholas screamed at his mother when she chided him for his bad behavior.

"Shhhh … hush, Nicholas," Dr. Anderson said, taking the stethoscope from my hands and kneeling so that she was eye-level with the boy. "You have hurt Miss Sharp very badly."

"I dun care," he retorted, glaring at me.

"I said hush." Dr. Anderson firmly placed the stethoscope upon his chest.

He quieted as she listened to his heartbeat.

"Abbie," Dr. Anderson said, "come here." She shot a dragon-gaze at Nicholas. "You remain still, my young man."

When I listened through the stethoscope, I heard a tiny whistling sound amidst the regular strong beat of the little boy's heart.

"Heart murmur," Dr. Anderson said, standing. "It's a small leak, brought about by a tiny hole in the heart valves. Specifically, this one is a mild systolic heart murmur. I have every hope that it will close on its own before he turns seven."

She looked reassuringly at the mother. "Still, we will monitor it nonetheless."

Almost immediately after we left Nicholas, I had to rush to a delivery with Dr. Davis.

Though that particular delivery went smoothly, we had three more that were rather complicated. One of the mothers truly was only a girl—thirteen. The baby came out stillborn. But we were mainly relieved that the girl survived the birth.

Before the last delivery of the day, our throats parched, Dr. Davis, Dr. Carmichael, a medical student named Anna, and I escaped for a few minutes to drink some water. As small talk commenced, my ears pricked when the conversation turned to the murders in Highgate Cemetery.

"The police think it is an escaped lunatic," Dr. Carmichael said excitedly

Anna chuckled. "Are we certain it's not our very own Tillie from ward four?"

Some laughter, as Rachel explained to me that Tillie was an absolutely insane former prostitute in her eighties who essentially lived at the hospital.

"Well, at least this will slow up the body thieves," Dr. Davis remarked, smiling.

"Whitechapel Hospital will lose all their suppliers," Anna said quickly.

The scandal with the Member of Parliament's son must be quite public by now, I thought. A silent awkwardness set in as they all remembered that I had worked at Whitechapel Hospital.

Dr. Davis was the first one to break the silence: "Apologies, Miss Sharp. We all forgot."

"It's fine." I actually cared very little. We all knew that this sort of thing might happen at any hospital.

"Dr. Anderson has told us that Whitechapel Hospital is similar to New Hospital. Is that true?" Dr. Davis asked.

"Very true. Have you never visited?" I asked, looking at all three of them.

"Never," Dr. Davis replied. Anna and Dr. Carmichael both shook their heads.

"But we spoke to Dr. Bartlett once at a dinner party at Dr. Anderson's home," Dr. Davis said. She cast a smiling glance cast toward the others. "And a few of his young physicians, specifically a Dr. St. John, was there. Did you happen to work with him?"

"The pale one?" Dr. Carmichael nearly cut Dr. Davis off. "Yes, he's quite handsome, but Hettie, you should give up on him. He's pale as a marble statue and cold as one too. I had to deal with him when he met with Dr. Anderson to discuss some new ways of organizing our delivery room. He's not merely a physician—he has a seminary degree. Trust me, the poor man is all work and godliness."

I smiled a little, thinking of Simon-the-enigma.

"Well then the other one, the dark haired one, he seemed more human, did he not?" Dr. Davis asked Anna.

William. My heart began pounding and I felt my possessive instincts rise. Then I felt foolish, hating my pettiness, my jealousy. I should not care so much.

"Oh, not much more," Anna replied. "But he seemed mysterious, intense. And he seemed to think of women more than Dr. St. John."

I became dizzy. Had I become consumed, addicted to William, the same way that all other women were? Love was perhaps a grand game of bees and nectar to him, and I myself had almost been swept away.

"Yes, I know which one you are speaking of," Dr. Carmichael said, giggling. "Those eyes—fiery green. I felt almost as if I could not move when he looked at me. But he wasn't a physician, Hettie. He was some eccentric nephew of Dr. Bartlett's."

Only a small sense of relief overcame me as I realized that they were not speaking of William. I remembered, suddenly, vividly, seeing Max at the Conclave's home. At that point, at Dr. Bartlett's dinner party, I hadn't known him, and I had been struck by his arresting gaze. As I recalled how he had terrorized me thereafter, a fresh wave of nausea swept over me. The dizziness remained.

Control, control, I reminded myself, feeling their eyes upon me. I took a great gulp of my water, which was now warm.

"Excuse me," I said evenly, taking a deep breath as I left the room.

That evening, Grandmother was only marginally happier that I was working at New Hospital rather than Whitechapel Hospital. Although she would prefer for me not to work at all, to abandon my desire to attend London Medical School for Women, she knew better than to push the matter. She was, I imagined bitterly, particularly happy that I no longer worked alongside William Siddal.

"But your nose, Arabella. It is hideous. You look like a common hooligan who has been in a street fight."

I sighed and ate my roast beef. I had eaten very little all day and felt absolutely famished. Every muscle in my legs ached and I just wanted to crawl into bed. When I'd first arrived home from work, Richard had winced a bit when he opened the door, and only then had I seen my reflection in the entranceway mirror. My nose was dark, purplish, swollen, and the purple had spread a bit to my cheeks like a stain.

"I'll be certain to have Ellen bring you some ice before bed. You simply must take down that swelling, otherwise everyone will think you are the Elephant Man's sister." She spoke in a clipped voice about her day, about her cribbage game with Lady Violet and Lady Catherine, and I struggled to stay awake.

Apart from my exhaustion, I knew that I had to speak to Simon about the murders, about what had happened with Abberline—about how the Inspector knew about the symbol. But by the time I had reached Kensington after work and stopped by Simon's home, it was almost dinner time. His maid told me that he would be staying late at the hospital, and that he might be home the next morning.

The rest of the week continued, where I worked to exhaustion all hours of the day. I stopped by Simon's house on Thursday night, but he was once again at the hospital. He seemed to be there all the time lately.

But then, at the end of the week, on Friday night, I had another nightmare—and it was then that Max returned to me.

Part II

"No doubt we seem a kind of monster to you."

—*The Princess*

Twelve

It'll be raining soon. Pourin' down. Best to hurry up and get these in while we can, before we get steeped," Donnie shouted as the swollen storm clouds above began to rumble.

Donnie and the other two fishermen pulled in the last of their nets. It had been a slow night for them. Disappointing catches. Unpredictable currents. Nonetheless, they had caught a respectable number of cod.

After anchoring their boat, they walked along the rocky beach, toward the path to the nearby town of Bromwell.

"Good e'enin. Have to be gettin' home," Donnie said. His home was located not far from the beach, on the fringe of town. As the oldest of the fishermen, at twenty-nine, he was the only one married, and therefore not able to go with the others for a pint at the pub. "Don' ye stay out too late!" he said before taking leave of them. "Early morn agin tomorrow."

"Aye, we won't," Franklin and John assured him. They had become used to these long days on the boat. It wasn't even summer, and yet their skin was already burnt from the hours out on the ocean, under the blazing sun.

Soon the rain Donnie had predicted began, and a full-blown, late March lightning storm flashed through the sky. Franklin and John began running, taking a shortcut to town that led through a small forest near the beach. Yet Franklin paused, despite the rain. Something in his peripheral vision had caught his attention. He'd seen it in the white flash of the lightning... on the wet rocks of the shoreline, just beyond the trees.

He peered through the black branches. *No. It couldn't be...*

Lightning flashed again through the sky, and the young man's eyes widened.

A creature, feminine and monstrous, sat on one of the rocks. Her skin, slick and scaly, shone in the lit-up sky. He saw her breasts, and how the talons of her dragon-feet rested on the rock. Fear and fascination almost overwhelmed him, particularly when he saw that her eyes were upon him, watching him.

Then the flash of lightning was over, yet he couldn't stop staring at the rocky place.

The lightning flash came again.

She was gone.

"What is it, man?" John asked him. "Ye look as if you've seen a spirit."

"Nay, not a ghost." Franklin still couldn't peel his eyes from the spot.

"Selkie?" John chuckled.

"Nay." Franklin laughed nervously—everyone in Orkney knew of the selkie legends. It was a common bedtime story: seals turning into beautiful women on certain nights of the year. But this was no seal. All he could think about was her breasts. And her talons.

He hoped that his eyes had been playing tricks on him, and that he had not actually seen that creature. He'd never believed those old bedtime stories, the old myths. And yet he had been so certain. He wondered vaguely if he was going batty.

"Will ye bide on me?" John asked, running toward the shore and disappearing behind some rocks, near where Frank had thought that he'd seen the creature.

"Be quick, man—it's start'n to pour," Franklin shouted after him, frustrated that John couldn't wait to use the pub lavy. He felt vaguely uneasy, and moved under a copse of trees closer to shore. He pulled his jacket up over his head for some protection from the pelting rain. When, after about a quarter of an hour, John still hadn't returned, Franklin felt annoyed.

And concerned.

"John!" Franklin yelled above the thunder. "John!" He cupped his hands around his mouth.

No answer.

A fear rose within him that he wanted to ignore. The fear made him feel foolish. Why did he give credence to the bedtime stories? The night was chilly, but he felt perspiration on his forehead.

"Don't be stupid," he muttered out loud to himself,

embarrassed by his rising fear. "John!" he shouted again, although through the rain, his shouts would not carry far.

Finally, Franklin walked to the shore, easing his way toward the enormous pile of rocks where John had disappeared. When he reached the mound, he stopped, horrified.

That woman-creature—that lamia, that carnivorous selkie, whatever she was—crouched before him, her body hunched over something on the dark muddy sand. In a flash of lightning, he saw her wet hair draped across her scaly belly like a nut-gold blanket. She had long, greenish, scaled arms that became increasingly scaly and bloodstained toward the claws. There was something mythical, something hypnotic about her terrible beauty. And even as he saw her fangs, even as her bloody lips curled away from them in a snarl, he felt mesmerized by her form. He could not move.

Franklin felt only vague horror at her crouch as she inched toward him, her movement that of a predator over a prey. Her greenish serpentine eyes slitted, dilated, and then focused upon him.

The instinct to run rose within him, and yet he could not, even as she came closer. He felt arrested by her gaze. The rain had lightened, and some sort of eerie calm settled around them. Her blood-stained face became less startling; he heard the echoes of the fairy tales his gran had told him in a sweet, soothing voice. These stories were not terrible; they were of fairies, of elves, and would lull him, make him warm. Cocooned. Secure.

The creature was almost upon him. In fact, he could smell her scent of saltwater and blood.

Stupidly he muttered, "Selkie?"

"Oh no, my lad, much worse."

Her voice was old, layered. He thought of aged wine.

There was only a little pain.

Thirteen

The dream started out lovely. I was swimming some-where in the depths of the ocean, seeing creatures I had never seen before—seals, stingrays, porpoises—and craggy underwater caves and caverns. It felt both soothing and exhil-arating. But I had an uncanny sense of déjà vu, and, remem-bering my vision of the lamia, I stretched my body out in the water. I saw talons instead of fingernails; my breast and entire body had grown and were covered in scales. My hair swirled in the water, hazelnut and long. Buttery gold. But I was not me. I was some sort of creature—the mythical lamia.

"Abbie."

My heart pounded as I heard Max's voice in my head.

"Abbie."

His voice came out sharp and clear. I hadn't heard it in months, and intuitively, I knew that this was more than a nightmare.

Wake up. Wake up. I willed myself desperately to wake up.

When I finally awoke, I found myself drenched in sweat and I couldn't catch my breath. My chest felt as if it was seizing upon itself. Pulling apart my bed curtains, I sat up and saw that it was near daybreak.

Max. He was somewhere, summoning me. He had to be behind the dreams of the lamia. But it didn't make sense.

I forced myself to be calm, to deal only with one issue at a time. I felt certain that Max had spoken to me, sent me a vision, and I had to warn William and Simon that he had returned to us.

On my way out, I told Richard, who had just taken Jupe outside, that I had to be at work early that morning. He looked at me curiously. I usually didn't work on Saturdays, but I hurried away before he could ask me any questions. I practically ran to Simon's house, hoping that his mother was away at her seaside place and that his sisters were not at home. I wanted to speak to Simon alone.

A pert young maid in a crisp dress answered the door. I hadn't seen her at the St. John's residence before. The other servants knew who I was, but she looked up and down my work dress and pinafore with distaste.

"I must speak to Dr. St. John."

She did not open the door fully. "He is at breakfast ... "

I pushed past her.

"Miss!" she shouted behind me.

Quickly, I found my way to the dining room where Simon sat eating alone, already dressed for work at Whitechapel Hospital.

"Abbie," he said, standing, alarmed. I thought I must look terrible. Ill, perhaps. I felt panicked.

"He's returned," I whispered.

"You must sit down." He lead me quickly to a chair in the dining room. "You are pale. You must eat something."

After another servant brought in breakfast, Simon shut all the doors. I was almost annoyed by his considerate, practiced attention. I was in no mood to eat, and sipped nothing but some tea. I told him about my nightmare, about hearing Max's voice last night loud and clear in my head. Then I told him about what I saw that night in Highgate Cemetery, about that woman with the uncanny resemblance to Mariah, about the strange figures. I also told him about my exchange with Abberline where he showed me the sketch of the Conclave's symbol.

Simon was silent for a few moments. Sunlight began to flood the breakfast room; it was almost blinding upon the pale daisy wallpaper as it glinted off the mirrors. I heard a great clatter; a servant somewhere must have dropped a bundle of silverware. It felt odd, discussing such unbelievable matters in ordered, comfortable Kensington.

"I would have spoken to you sooner," I said quickly. "But I worked so many hours at New Hospital this week, and I assumed that William had at least told you about the stolen child."

"He did not. Of course, on that night, I was not at the hospital. But he should have told me the next day." Simon's extraordinarily pale face flushed, almost pink in anger. "You should know, Abbie, that immediately after … " He cut himself off, unable to proceed.

"After William and I parted ways." Speaking it plainly to Simon saddened me, but it needed to be said.

He cleared his throat. "Yes. And ever since you left us, William has been extraordinarily... irresponsible. On Wednesday, when he arrived at work, I suspected that he had been drinking too much. He has been working late hours this week, it's true, but he's also been arriving far too late in the morning. This Thursday, he didn't arrive until almost noon. And if, as it seems, a child was taken from our ward, that is a serious security issue. I have heard nothing about this matter, and I must confront him regarding this issue."

I knew the weight of the word "confront" in an interaction between William and Simon. But why hadn't William said anything to Simon? That did indeed seem negligent—"extraordinarily irresponsible," as Simon had put it.

I bit my lip before taking a long sip of tea. "The children have to be safe."

Simon said nothing. He was silent, deep in thought, his blond brows furrowed.

"What do we do about all of this?" I asked. I could make no sense of any of it, and I felt as if something terrible was being played out. That Max was somehow behind it. And I felt like he was reeling me in, pulling me toward him. But it all seemed so indecipherable, and I was at a loss about how to react.

Simon sat quietly, thoughtfully, for a few seconds. Then his blond eyebrows drew together and he said, "In terms of Inspector Abberline, I am not terribly concerned with his knowledge of the symbol. It is, after all, on that painting in the laboratory closet. Furthermore, it is not unlikely that he saw it on one of the Conclave member's arms. What does matter, however, is that he does not learn of its significance. And it seems that he has not."

"If he does," I said bleakly, "he is a dead man."

"Undoubtedly."

"These Highgate Cemetery murders and the Ripper murders might be unconnected," I surmised. "The cannibalism could have been committed by a random crazed lunatic. That woman might have merely looked like Mariah. Perhaps I am jumping to conclusions."

"And perhaps you are not." Simon picked up the morning edition of the *Times*, turning it over so that I could see the headline:

More cannibalism and murder in Brompton Cemetery.

Fourteen

On the way to New Hospital that day, I felt stunned. Three more resurrection men had been murdered and cannibalized, in Brompton Cemetery in Southwest London, the night before. The murders were almost identical in nature to those that had occurred in Highgate Cemetery. My dream of the lamia—Max's voice in the dream—these murders—I had no specific evidence that they were connected, yet I felt great unease. Nothing made sense, and it was maddening. Simon and I had agreed to be on guard, to communicate everything to each other from that point forward. I feared for William's safety, but Simon assured me that he would relay to William everything that happened.

Even though it was Saturday, Simon was going to work as well. Although I was not expected at New Hospital, the last thing I felt like doing was returning to Kensington and doing nothing.

"Abbie, be extraordinarily careful. I'll call upon you soon," Simon said as we took our leave.

"Of course."

But he held my arm a moment longer, his level gaze half-serious, half-amused. I loved the way Simon could communicate so well with his expression. I could tell he was remembering how foolhardy I'd been last autumn, when I'd traveled to Whitechapel Hospital by myself at night.

I smiled a little. "Of course, Simon. I'll be very careful."

He said nothing, but I knew he was not reassured.

I returned to Grandmother's house in the late afternoon, my arms heavy with medical and anatomy books. I had spent the entire day following Dr. Davis around the wards, aiding her in deliveries and prenatal exams, but before I left, Dr. Anderson met with me briefly to give me the books. They would help me study for my examinations in the fall.

When I walked through the door, Richard met me with a note. Once again, I felt warmly toward him for safeguarding all of my mail. "Thank you, Richard," I said, my heart skipping a beat when I saw that the message was from William. I tore it open as soon as I reached the privacy of my bedroom.

The note contained only three words: *I believe you.*

Grandmother, fortunately, was at Lady Violet's home for the evening. She wouldn't be back until late. I felt grateful for this, as it saved me from having to argue with her about going out again. Swiftly, I washed my face and removed my work pinafore, but I didn't even bother changing out of my work dress.

Just before leaving, I paused at my bedroom door.

"Be extraordinarily careful," Simon had said.

I flew to my closet and opened the trunk where I kept many of Mother's things. The lamia portrait hung upon the closet wall, above the trunk. In spite of my hurry, I had to pause to stare at it. In the dim light of my bedroom, in that moment, I began to see it differently.

The painting had a stark beauty to it. More than in any of Rossetti's other works, there was something raw, more than mythical, about it. Gabriel had taken great care to make Mother look human as well as monstrous, and I thought his depiction of her was nothing less than brilliant. A bleakness marked her features, under the haze of sunlight. Her face seemed tragic. Sand was smeared among her hands, and wiry green seaweed dangled from her red locks like bold tendrils.

What are you trying to tell me, Mother?

Lamias did not exist. They were mythical creatures. And yet, in my dream and in my vision, I had seen one with hazelnut hair—very different from my mother's flaming red hair. But my mother's body in the portrait, her talons and exposed breasts, bore such a close resemblance to the beast. And I had seen the impossible already—a Conclave of immortals. Furthermore, *Max* had sent me the portrait. He'd wanted me to see it for some reason; that meant he must be behind my visions of the lamia. But then again, the visions might not have been accurate. My visions during the Ripper murders had proved true, but Max might be trying to confuse me now, for some reason. He was, after all, an assassin. And he had never revealed to me that he had killed my mother—thus I knew he was also a liar.

As I rifled through the trunk of her belongings, I located my bowie knife. I'd never told anyone, not even William or Simon, that I'd kept it after that fateful night. Personally, I wasn't certain *why* I'd kept it—upon discovering that the Conclave had killed my mother, I'd become so infuriated that I myself had turned murderous. The deaths of those four men haunted me even now.

Once alone, I had washed all the dried blood off the knife obsessively, so that now it shone. It was as if I could make it clean again. As if I could make myself clean. And yet I couldn't discard it. The knife had saved my life. My favorite sport of knife throwing in Dublin had made me comfortable with knives. The smaller blades were easier to throw, but with my fear, my adrenaline, this one had served me so well that night. It was more lethal.

Although it frightened me a bit that I'd saved the knife, still I could not let it go. Perhaps I shouldn't let it go. The last, most dangerous Conclave member was still alive, beckoning me toward him in a bewildering web.

I put the knife inside my boot and left Grandmother's house.

On the carriage ride to William's home, I reflected upon his note: *I believe you.*

Thoughts flooded me ... that I had been foolish for leaving him, that I needed to forgive him. I half-wished that these new feelings would drown out my other trepidations and fears regarding William's character and constancy.

As the carriage approached, I saw that nearly all of the lights in the Rossetti house were on.

I knocked on the door. William answered it. My hopes sank. He opened the door only a few inches and his expression seemed defensive, angry. He was visibly drunk. Although Simon suspected that he had been drinking too much, I had never seen William overindulge. It was entirely out of character.

"Might I come in?" I asked.

He opened the door wide, and with one dramatic arm swoop, ushered me in.

As I stood in the foyer, I heard voices and giggling from the parlor.

"Who is it?" asked one of the voices.

A female voice. And not Christina's.

I stepped around the corner, ahead of William, into the parlor.

Amid all of Christina's rescued animals, on the couch sat two identical-looking women. They had to be at least a decade older than me, but they giggled like girls. The women dressed with expensive flamboyance—red silks and taffetas that were entirely too much for an evening visit. By the look of their flushed faces and tossed ringlets, they were inebriated, too, sipping generously from large glasses of champagne held in their pale, elegant fingers.

Both suppressed giggles as they observed my disheveled appearance and work dress.

"And who is she?" one asked William. He stood quietly behind me, pouring himself another glass of gin.

"One of your aunt's 'friends'?" the other woman asked.

They both laughed heartily, spitting small specks of champagne into the air.

"No," William replied, his voice hard and stony.

Both women sobered.

A little.

"This is Arabella Sharp ... " He paused. I almost felt his cloudy brain spin for the right words to describe our relationship. Then, without looking me in the eyes, he stated, "She has worked with me at the hospital."

That was all he had to say about me. I stared at him, unbelieving. Hurt.

After walking across the room to shoo Toby, the parrot, away from his perch on the Polidori portrait's frame, William said, "And Abbie, these two lovely ladies are my cousins, Lettie and Lottie."

"Cousins?" I said, irritably.

"Yes. Are we second or third? Do either of you know?" he asked, eying them.

"Either way, Will, I think we're kissing cousins at least," Lottie exclaimed, laughing stupidly.

"William, might I see you in the hallway for a minute?" I shot him a fixed look as I said this.

William excused himself.

"*Will?*" I asked sarcastically as soon as we had shut Lottie and Lettie in the parlor. "Your cousins? Really, William." I tried to keep my voice down.

"As I said, second cousins." He took another drink of gin. "Or maybe third. Can't tell you, Abbie. My head is swimming a bit, to tell you the truth."

He shrugged. Perfectly handsome even when drunk.

"Oh well. Doesn't matter," he continued. "They're wealthy twins, both getting a bit up in years at twenty-eight and all, and their papa has it in his mind for one of them to marry me." William smirked. "I think the old man's getting a little desperate."

"I should think so." I frowned at the glass of gin. "I thought Christina didn't approve of alcohol in the house."

"She's gone—volunteering at New Hospital most of the night."

"How convenient. And her friends?"

"Currently we have a bit of a gap, as all of her friends now have sustainable wages and can live on their own."

The conversation was going nowhere, plunging into bitter talk and feelings—and with William drunk, I knew I should get to the point. But in that small foyer, I paused. In the glowing lamplight, I searched for the William I had known, or at least the William I thought I had known. That honest, terribly impolite, terribly self-assured William seemed gone. Taken away from me completely. I didn't know this person in his place; I searched the crevices of his still-handsome face to try to find ... him.

But who was he?

Then our eyes locked, and through his fog of alcohol, I saw William's transparent emotion—I saw desperate sadness.

I wanted to reach out, to embrace him, to take him

back. Tears stung in my eyes and I suppressed that desire. But I could not, not after what I knew of his past, and not after tonight—coming in upon him in this compromising situation. I loved him, but I could not plunge down that same path again … the end seemed far too uncertain.

So I cleared my throat and blinked back tears. "I received your note, William."

"Good." He drained his glass.

"So you believe me now?"

"I do." He set the empty glass down hard on a nearby side table. "Particularly after I read about the Brompton murders in the *Times* today. You saw something out of the ordinary that night. I actually believed you a little then, too. I was just angry."

William's eyes were shining. At least, even when he was drunk, he could be honest.

"Why did you take the trouble to send the note to my house today?" I asked. I had hoped that he'd left it to somehow right what had gone awry between us.

William shrugged, appearing uncomfortable.

"Did you want to see me?" I felt my heart in my throat as I spoke.

Then he looked angry. "It doesn't matter, does it? You've been seeing quite a bit of Dr. St. John, so I decided to have my own party."

So that was what this was about.

"Childish." I sighed, walking over to the dining room table and pouring a glass of wine for myself.

"If you'll excuse me, I have guests in the parlor," he said

coldly. "You should leave, and I would suggest taking a long detour away, from Swains Lane..."

"I thought, from your note, that you believed me." I heard my voice crack and damned myself for my vulnerability.

William raised his brow.

"Abbie—I believe that you might have seen the murderers, but how can you think that they are after you? Do you actually think that they have something to do with the Conclave?"

"William, I told you that I heard my name spoken, that evening in the graveyard. And why else would they take one of our hospital's children? It was as if they wanted to lure me there."

William sighed. "Come with me."

Both confused and excited, I followed him up the three flights of stairs to his apartment in Christina's attic. *Watch yourself Abbie*, I reminded myself, knowing how weak I could be when alone with him. Nonetheless, I followed him.

The dying fire lighted William's large attic bedroom only a little. Hugo lay in front of it, stretched out lazily. Lottie and Lettie probably feared the gentle beast.

My thoughts disappeared into shocked ecstasy when William shut the door and kissed me hard. His arms grasped around me about my waist in a near vise-grip. I could not move.

I did not want to move.

A thundering knocking from the front door far below interrupted us.

William pulled away. I still trembled. He looked into my eyes for a minute, his gaze unreadable. Detached.

"My apologies, Abbie. I'm drunk," he said, running his fingers through his hair. He looked at me again, his dark eyes momentarily fiery in the light of the dying fireplace embers.

My head reeled from the wine. And the kiss. "Why did you bring me up here?" I demanded. I felt tears sting my eyes.

William shrugged.

I stared at him, unbelieving, blinking back the tears. My head continued to spin. Hugo walked toward me and licked my hand.

The loud knock echoed again downstairs. I heard the parlor door open and Lettie and Lottie's voices ring out.

"Will!" one of them called.

"Will!"

"Excuse me." He left abruptly.

When I reached the bottom of the stairs, I stopped, shocked.

Simon stood in the foyer, surveying in bewilderment the scene before him: the two vacant-eyed blond twins, me still in my work dress. William, flushed-faced and reeking of alcohol. Both Lettie and Lottie were silent, cowed in the presence of Simon's formidability.

"St. John, you are out past your bedtime," William stated casually, pouring himself yet another drink. His tone was accusatory, even challenging. "Are you not?"

"I was just leaving, Simon," I said briskly as I buttoned my coat.

Simon stood absolutely still in the doorway—the front door still wide open behind him. I tried to pass him, but without a word he caught my arm at the elbow in a firm grip.

"Were you going to let her walk home alone, William?"

William shrugged, taking a deep swallow from his glass. "I'm not one to tell Arabella Sharp what to do."

There was an awful silence in the air. Simon seemed even taller than usual; William more explosive, angrier than usual. Their silence made the tense atmosphere worse.

I saw irritation in Lettie's and Lottie's expressions. Their little party with William was at an end.

Simon was the one to break the silence. "I've come from the hospital. We have some serious issues to talk of." He cast a brief gaze toward Lottie and Lettie. "Privately."

Before William could retort, Simon raised a long finger, silencing him. "Do not speak to me now. I am going to make certain Abbie reaches home safely, and then you and I will talk. I suggest that you secure a carriage for your friends, and that you...sober up a little."

Glaring, William drained the rest of his glass.

Simon ignored this. "Make some hot tea, anything, but I will be back shortly, and I expect to find you here, alone, and as rational as you are capable of being." He narrowed his eyes. "We must discuss some matters."

Still holding my arm, Simon led me away from the house.

"I just had a long discussion with Josephine," he said as we stood outside the house in the cool night air. "She was at the hospital on the night the child was taken, overseeing the rooms where the children slept. Although vigilant, Sister Josephine did not see the intruder and became quite distressed when William returned with the child—she had not yet noticed Christabel's absence. Fortunately, William had the sense to say nothing about your experience in Highgate. Josephine said that he told her he had found the child wandering in the streets, and that she had either walked out or that someone had taken her. The front door, as you know, is supposed to be locked, but William upon his arrival found it unlocked. There were no signs of forced entry—so it was probably due to carelessness from one of the workers. It has been left unlocked before."

Simon was correct about that; however, the unlocked front door usually presented no problem, as Whitechapel Hospital did not have much of anything to tempt an intruder.

"Anyway, the children were all asleep when Josephine left them alone downstairs to attend to something upstairs. That was around nine o'clock. It was during this time that Christabel would have been taken."

I thought of the two mutilated bodies in Highgate Cemetery and tried not to think of the awful possibilities if Christabel and I had not escaped. I shuddered.

Simon continued. "Apparently, William simply gave Josephine a firm lecture and said nothing more on the matter, when he should have alerted me. I did not discipline Josephine further, but security is imperative. I spoke to all the staff tonight about locking the front doors as well as all of the windows during night shifts. Also, we will have three nurses instead of one each night in the newborn and children's nurseries. I need to discuss all of these new policies with William, tonight. And also clear up our … communication problems."

Simon paused. I glanced up at him. The moon shone just brightly enough to illuminate the blond curls across his scalp and forehead. He began to speak again and then hesitated.

"Go on, please."

He hesitated for two seconds more, glancing down at me before continuing. "As I told you this morning, William has not been himself lately. He has become distracted in his duties to the hospital."

I said nothing. Nothing needed to be said in that moment. Simon knew the root of William's malaise. As did I. This break between us had hurt him, but his sudden plunge into irresponsibility only solidified my views that he was terrible for me.

A silence, awkward and heavy, settled between us. Simon spoke quietly. "I've heard that Scotland Yard did a thorough search of Highgate Cemetery, and of Brompton Cemetery today."

"And they found nothing?"

"Nothing. No hiding lunatics, and I did not see any indication in the newspaper's story that there had been evidence of a cult at work. This has been a suggested theory. But there were no signs of occult ritual. No candles. Nothing."

"Of course. But particularly in Highgate Cemetery, there are a thousand places to hide ritual objects." I said this more for my own reassurance; fears continued to rise within me.

Simon peered calmly down at me. I began to speak, but he hushed me with his eyes. Max was somewhere. Still alive. He had beckoned me. And he would draw me closer and closer until…

Moths fluttered around the lamplight in front of the Rossetti house.

Simon seemed like a lighthouse, a safe beacon in a storm at that moment.

"I am afraid," I whispered. The admission felt soothing, like a loosened belt.

Simon peered at me momentarily before his attention became focused on the moths.

"I fear, Abbie, that…" He paused. I could barely hear him.

"That everything is not over." I completed his sentence. My words had almost no volume, but they carried such weight for me.

Simon nodded and sighed, seeming unwilling to say more. "No more late-night walks, Abbie," he said lightly.

I laughed a little.

He became serious again. "Believe it or not, I am not only concerned about William's depression in terms of his work performance. I am concerned about how his problems might endanger himself and us. He is not thinking clearly—he had allowed himself to become overwhelmed by his feelings. If what we fear is correct, then this is not good. Who knows what William might say or do? We are all in danger, and William is blinded by his emotions."

My feelings piqued at this. I had not thought of this side of things. If we were all in danger, this would be a very bad time for William to lose his judgment or his mind.

Simon drew a deep breath and his marble-smooth forehead wrinkled slightly. "I am going to speak to him tonight, about securing the hospital and about being careful. I'll consider the best approach to this before I walk back inside."

We exchanged silent glances of amusement, as we both knew how resistant William could be to advice. I nodded to let him know that I would be careful.

Then, in a single feather-brush, Simon swept a lock of hair away from my forehead. I remembered when he had bandaged my hand; once again, I had forgotten how cool his touch could be. I felt a rush of warmth inside of me and silently cursed. Nothing. Nothing needed to become more complicated for me at the moment.

I stilled my feelings.

"Take my carriage home, Abbie."

"But…" Night had already fallen upon us. It had to be close to eight o'clock. I felt so agitated, suddenly nothing appealed to me more than a long brisk walk home.

Simon steadied his expression, and I knew that there would be no arguing with him, so I departed in his carriage. I settled back in the plush seat, shivering. These cool spring nights chilled me to my bones, and I longed for summer. The carriage jolted along the cobbled streets, and I hoped that I would indeed be home before Grandmother returned from Lady Violet's house. Grandmother's mood would be heightened by the wine and cordials, and her thoughts would revolve around the most current Kensington gossip. If I could rush to my bedroom before her arrival, I would not have to endure her reprimand, her prying questions. She would not even have to know that I had seen William Siddal.

The carriage had only gone a few blocks when the vision came. Everything became dark and shadowed. Then I saw the glow of gaslight in the night mist...I saw Londoners in dampened dark coats, the drawn collars of pedestrians out walking on a rainy evening. Then my vision became more focused and I saw Inspector Abberline leaving a pub.

My vision focused, blurred, rippled, and sharpened again. High Holborn. Abberline was leaving a tavern, somewhere on High Holborn. It was one of those rare moments when he was not at his office at Scotland Yard. *High Holborn.* My heart raced and I focused on the vision; he was less than a mile away from me.

In the vision, Abberline appeared older—paunchy and weary. He had always seemed so confident to me. But I saw that when alone with his own thoughts, he was almost...frail. Although I still did not like him, I felt pity for him. I realized that he was not a happy man. I had seen a photograph of a woman, presumably his wife, on his desk last year; that picture was all that I knew of his private life. I had an odd curiosity about his personal life. How consuming was his work? Then he turned off High Holborn, away from the moderately crowded street to the more shadowed, Bedwell. That street was smaller, much less crowded. Darker. Emptier.

My heart began pounding as the vision played out before me, and I suddenly sensed that Abberline was in danger. In the darkness, from the building alongside where he walked, a shadow crawled stealthily down the bricks. I watched in horror as the shadow moved closer and closer to Abberline, closing in on him like a spider descending upon a fly caught in his web.

Max.

"Stop! Stop!" I shouted at Simon's driver, leaping out before the vehicle even came to a complete stop. Simon's driver shouted to me, but I couldn't stop to listen. I ran fast toward Bedwell Street, feeling déjà vu as I kept thinking of that night of the double murder all over again—that terrible night when my visions led me to Liz and Cate, just in time to see them murdered.

No. No. My heart pounded as the shadow came closer. *Look up, Abberline. Look up.*

The memories propelled me to run faster and faster along High Holborn Road. I slammed into three pedestrians, but I refused to let this evening end as the night of the double murders had. I would not let Abberline die.

I turned a corner onto the smaller street—I could hardly breathe; my chest heaved from the sprint. I could barely regain my breath after the run in my tight corset. As my eyes adjusted in the dewy darkness, I saw Abberline's form ahead of me, walking in great strides, still unaware that he was being hunted, unaware of the killer closing in on him from the shadows.

Quickly, I scanned the tall, worn buildings and pulled the knife out of my boot. Part of me wanted to shout, but I feared that a shout might only spur Max on toward his deadly purpose.

Everything surrounding me was enshrouded in darkness, as Bedwell had no working lamps. I looked up at the building where, moments before in the vision, I had seen Max creeping downwards. But now I saw nothing.

Where was he?

I heard a thud, and saw Abberline pulled into the shadows of an alley with great force.

I heard him cry out.

Bloody hell! I hoped I was not too late.

I ran. Hard. My mind raced with terrible thoughts of Abberline being sliced apart, cut into pieces as the Whitechapel Hospital patients had been. Foolish Abberline! I desperately wished that he could forget about the Ripper case.

As I bolted toward the alley, I heard only my own breath, my blood pounding in my ears. Then I saw, in the dimness, the shadowy figure moving almost too fast for me to see. He had Abberline smashed against the brick wall of the urine-stenched place. I knew how fast Max could be and I had no time to hesitate, so I threw my knife hard, aiming at the figure.

Damn! I had missed. Max whipped away, my knife stuck into a bag of debris. Abberline collapsed upon the littered ground nearby; I saw the flash of Max's knife and my heart pounded. Then I could not see Max any longer, and I rapidly contemplated my next move.

Think, Abbie.

Think.

But in that split-second chaos, I could not decide what I should do next—whether to retrieve my knife or remain where I was, ready to fight. I whipped my head around, scanning the alley, trying to see everything at once.

I heard Abberline struggling to get up from where he had collapsed. He was still alive. Thank God! I moved to attend to him, but then Max was behind me. With great effort, I suppressed a shudder. In the darkness, I smelled the strong scent of an oriental cigar, and I felt his breath against the back of my neck.

"Max." I whispered his name into the shadows. My voice did not sound like my own. It exuded hate, revenge. I felt an alarming fire inside me, pulsing—the same fire I had that night before killing the other Conclave members; that was how much I wanted him dead.

"Excellent work, Arabella Sharp. I knew you would take the bait," he whispered from behind me. I smelled blood on his palm. He ran his finger along my left jawline; he continued to stand immediately behind me, whispering into my right ear. "Always so concerned for mortals."

One. Two. I gave a great kick backward, but my heel struck only air. I had forgotten how unbelievably fast Max moved; I had forgotten how strong he was. With the knife in his teeth, he whipped me toward him. It was a fast, hard spin—a grotesque ballroom twirl where he was the unchallenged partner. This could not be. I regained control, trying to summon my strength. Our fight was a sick one, a twisted dance where only one of us would survive. I had to make certain that it would be me.

Then he was gone.

For a few seconds I stood there stunned, gasping for breath and trying to ignore Abberline's labored breathing; I tried to focus on Max's scent, tried to see anything in the darkness now that my eyes had adjusted.

But he was gone. When I felt certain of it, I rushed toward Abberline. My chest tightened as I saw the black shine of blood on his hand and coat.

"Abberline," I said, quickly. "Did he…"

But without my assistance, Abberline managed to stand. He was physically built like an ox—not easy to bring down. Whatever wounds he had, I saw that he would survive.

Max could have killed him so easily, if he had been determined to do so.

"Miss Sharp," Abberline said in the darkness. A streak of light from a streetlamp showed me his face. Astonishment marked his features as his eyes focused on me. "What are you doing here?"

Without a word, I walked past him to retrieve my knife from where it remained stuck in the bag of debris.

"I just saved your life, Inspector." Although I felt fairly certain that Max had left by now, I remained alert. We needed to get out of this alley. I motioned for Abberline to follow me out, back to the street. Although uncrowded, unlit, and secluded, Bedwell Street seemed infinitely safer than this alley.

I glanced rapidly around me as I stepped out onto Bedwell, then turned to consider Abberline, who had followed me without a word. I didn't care a shred for him. But I felt terrible when I saw that the middle finger of his right hand had been completely severed—the white bone showed through the blood and skin. I felt a twist of surprise that he grimaced very little as he pulled a handkerchief from his pocket and began wiping the blood away, struggling to wrap his finger using the cloth as a tourniquet. As a long-time investigator in Scotland Yard, he knew what to do.

"Who is he?" Abberline asked, before I could say a word.

I said nothing. I just stared at him in the darkness.

He grunted in irritation and continued attending to the wound.

"Your finger, sir," I said, walking toward him. "Please allow me. It would be easier for me to secure the tourniquet."

But Abberline looked up at me sharply, his eyes gleaming in irritation as he pulled his hand away from me like an angry child. I could understand his reaction—perhaps it was wounded pride that a girl had just saved his life. Still, I thought that a shred of gratitude would be nice.

Abberline's eyes narrowed. "Who are you, Miss Sharp?" he growled.

I resisted the urge to turn on my heel, to leave him there alone.

"I'm Arabella Sharp, sir," I said, putting the knife back into my boot. Only then did I think about the problem of finding Simon's carriage again. I doubted the driver had waited for us on High Holborn Road. "I'm the granddaughter of Lady Charlotte Westfield. But you know all that."

He said nothing, merely stood there, irritated and perplexed as he held his wounded hand.

"Watch your back, Abberline," I said as I scanned the street and tried to decide whether to return to High Holborn Road or not. I didn't know what else to say to him. He needed the warning, but I needed to think. I began to walk away, rapidly.

Max was most certainly back. Everyone I loved would be in danger.

Something made me pause and turn toward Inspector Abberline. I knew he wouldn't stop—he would keep pursuing this until he was in too deep. At this point, I might, just might, be able to save his life. He still must not know enough yet, or Max would have already killed him. This would be his last chance.

I had to be direct. "Where did you see that symbol you asked me about, Inspector?"

He paused, as if sensing the foolishness of discussing classified evidence with a seventeen-year-old girl, a girl who had been merely a pawn for him when he'd tried to solve the Ripper murders. I saw the indecision in his eyes.

"Abberline," I said quickly. "I remember, last autumn, you warning me that I was caught up in a dangerous game. Now it is my turn to tell you that you are the one in grave danger. You had better tell me where you saw that symbol."

His response came out gruff and defensive. "You know, of course, that the symbol is on a small picture in the laboratory closet of Whitechapel Hospital."

Yes, of course. I remembered Simon's suggestion that Abberline might have seen the Conclave's symbol on that painting.

He continued. "I also saw the symbol on Dr. Bartlett's arm once, during the autopsy on Annie Chapman."

He paused, hoping that I would say more, but I said nothing. I was beginning to see that he truly did not understand the significance. This was a great relief to me.

Abberline sighed and lowered his voice. "The same symbol was found on a tomb in Highgate Cemetery, close to where the bodies of the resurrection men were discovered. Only myself and a few others know of this. We also found it on a tomb near the bodies at Brompton Cemetery. We are doing our best to keep it out of the *Times*; in fact, we will go to great effort over the next few weeks to keep this out of the newspapers, as much as possible. We don't want a massive panic."

My heart pounded with this information. The symbols in the cemeteries indicated, possibly proved, a connection between the recent graveyard murders and the Conclave. My mind swirled, this would also explain why Abberline knew about the symbol and was still alive. Max wanted him to know. For some reason, he was playing a game now with not only me, but also with Scotland Yard, just as he had done last October.

"Miss Sharp?" Abberline pressed.

"Yes, I know about the symbol, Abberline. In fact, I know a great deal." I looked at him sharply, and I saw from his expression that he had no idea how much danger he was in, even now, having lost a finger. "You have to trust me. You're involved in something much larger than you can imagine. If you choose to proceed in your investigation … watch yourself. I can't always be around to protect you."

"Miss Sharp … " He wanted to press me for more. He sounded angry, frustrated, and undoubtedly thought I was being cheeky.

"Be careful, Inspector," I said once again, walking away, knowing instinctively that he would not listen.

"Abbie!"

I heard the loud halt of carriage wheels on the cobbled street. Then I saw Simon's tall figure leap out of his carriage as he ran toward me. When he reached me, I told him quietly what had happened, and I saw his gaze move past my head toward Inspector Abberline, who was approaching us in the darkness with his wrapped hand.

"Miss Sharp refuses to give me any information regarding these graveyard murders." Inspector Abberline cocked his head under the dim streetlight. "Perhaps you can help me, Dr. St. John."

"Wait for me in the carriage, Abbie," Simon said quietly. I ignored him and stayed where I was.

"I will look at your wound, Inspector," Simon said quietly to Abberline; the Inspector appeared almost annoyed that everyone seemed to care so much about his severed finger. I couldn't help feeling a bit impressed by his continued disregard for it.

Gently, Simon took his hand and unwrapped the bandage. "The cut is clean, the flesh not torn too severely. It should heal well. Go to Whitechapel. Or to London Hospital. It must be cleaned to prevent infection and then sutured. I can take you there myself if you would like." Simon's voice, as usual, came out cool and reserved, but outstandingly polite.

Inspector Abberline said nothing, but he looked hard at me, then at Simon.

"Would you like us to take you to the hospital?" Simon repeated, his expression unphased by Abberline's agitation.

"No," Abberline growled. I knew he realized that I would not help him, and Simon would aide him only in the capacity of a physician. "I can get there myself. Good night."

On the ride back to Kensington, Simon said, "My driver

returned to tell me what happened. He knew the general direction where you had run. Abbie ... " His voice trailed off as he shook his head in disapproval. "I advised you to be extraordinarily careful."

In the darkness of the carriage, I turned away from his disapproving gaze. Then I felt his fingers lightly on my chin as he gently turned me back toward him, forcing me to face him.

"I couldn't ignore the vision," I said quietly.

Then I told Simon about what Abberline had told me—about the symbol appearing in the cemeteries. "We have proof now that the graveyard murders are likely connected to Max. And Max attacked Abberline. He was luring me into that alley, knowing that I would protect Abberline."

Simon remained silent, his face pale and handsome in the carriage darkness.

"Did you talk to William?" I asked.

"I did." Simon's look, as always, penetrated into me. I thought, in that moment as I had so many other times, how much he looked like the archangel Michael in an illustration in Grandmother's Bible. Beautiful, angelic, too ethereal to exist.

"William is far too indisposed to work safely at the hospital. I am requiring that he take some time off. What happened the other night—those murders—was awful, but it could have turned out much worse." His voice was stony, and I knew that he had very little respect for William. I suspected that he wasn't even surprised by William's current behavior.

William...what was happening to him? He had seemed like a different person when I saw him that night. And yet his behavior only fortified the wall I had built up around my heart, the wall protecting myself from him.

Fifteen

Seraphina burst into her house, feeling even more invig-orated than she had after consuming the French boy twenty years before. She took up her easel and began to paint. Her strokes were fast, furious. She felt her beast form melting away as she became human. Her skin became soft, pliable, again. Her fangs receded.

As with the other portraits, she knew she would not fin-ish this one, but it was more complete than many of her others. She was painting Julian Bartlett. She had not seen him in years, and yet he had been like a father figure to her. He and Robert Buck had been so kind—they were the only physicians who had ever helped her, at least before Robert's experiment had gone horribly wrong.

But she didn't think about that part. She felt strong enough now to face her other old memories. To recall Julian's face.

His trim beard.

His eyes.

Gradually, her pounding heart subsided. She thought again of her keeper's absence. If he was still angry about her outburst in November, perhaps his long absence was a lesson to her.

After her attack on the fishermen, she knew she would sleep well. There was a calmness in her blood, a bit of an ease from her restlessness. Immediately after the killings, she had swum about the island, then decided in the foggy twilight to fall asleep on her craggy perch. And her sleep had spun such peaceful dreams. No nightmares. Only the roar of waves.

She felt appeased, satisfied. Although she knew it was only momentary contentedness—her hunger was only held at bay.

"Per'aps we should turn around," one boy said to another.

"Nay, not at all," the other one replied. They had skipped out of school to fish. At thirteen years old, they wanted to do nothing else but fish on that day. And the day had indeed seemed so perfect for fishing. The sky burned white-bright upon their boat, and the calm sea emitted only a small, salt-tinged breeze.

"Don't tell me ye're scared, Timothy, after those mudders, those attacks the other night."

"Nay," the first boy said, shrugging. But Timothy was more timid than his companion, Rowan, and certainly the smarter of the two. This was the first time, in fact, that he had ever skipped out of school.

Rowan looked hard at Timothy, leveling his gaze. "The inspectors are saying it is a wild wolf. Perhaps a loosed bear. Nothin' more."

"Per'aps," Timothy said, willing himself to believe it. But now, as he looked toward the land, toward the shore of Bromwell—only a tiny, green, rock-strewn sliver on the horizon—and as he felt the flimsiness of their small dory on these waves, he felt uneasiness creep upon his flesh. He wished they had stayed on land. Or at least closer to land.

Then the boat jolted violently, as if a whale had hit the bottom.

"What was that?" Timothy asked, almost dropping his fishing pole in the waters.

"Dunno." Rowan said. His right eyebrow lifted a bit in mockery. "Scar'd?"

Something slammed even harder into the boat's underside. Water sloshed into the dory. Rowan looked frightened now—in fact, terrified. Both boys pulled their poles up.

"We should go back," Timothy said quickly, taking up the oars. He wasn't one to break the rules, and he had had a bad feeling about skipping school all day.

Something splashed in the water behind them.

"A whale perhaps," Rowan said, his voice only a small croak.

Timothy wished it were a whale. It was difficult to see as the noon sun glinted hard off the waves. But from the corner of his eyes, Timothy thought he saw the flash of a webbed hand—lizard-like, with talons. Horror overwhelmed the boy and his throat went dry, parched. Neither he nor Rowan could speak as an eerie calm set upon them and the waters.

They sat silently, breathing hard, staring at each other, frozen, their oars suspended just over the water, afraid to move.

Then the boat tipped, dumping both of them into the sea.

It had been three weeks since the night Inspector Abberline was attacked, and I had only been able to see Simon a few times. But my hours at New Hospital were long, and even now, on Sunday morning, my muscles ached. I spent each and every day at New Hospital, helping Dr. Carmichael and occasionally working alongside Dr. Anderson; then, in the evenings, rather than resting or sleeping, I often stayed up until midnight or even later, studying Dr. Anderson's anatomy books. Although I did not wish it, thoughts of William seeped into my mind. Sometimes, particularly when I felt weary and vulnerable after those late nights of studying, as I drifted into sleep, I would think of him, my weary mind finding the happily-ever-after ending that my more rational mind could not. In my dreams we would reconcile, forget the past. But I would always wake up, dawn breaking through my curtains, and my concerns about what he had done, and also about what he had become lately—inebriated, irresponsible—arose again. I would force myself to get up, dress, and become lost in the needs of the day.

Easter passed, and April and spring arrived in full force. But my memories of William lingered upon me. Unbidden, but beautiful and sharp all at the same time.

Then, one Sunday in church, as I found myself trying to stay awake while the priest droned on and on with the prayer liturgies, I felt someone slip into the pew and kneel beside me. I opened my right eye enough to see that it was Simon. Unlike me, he appeared to be lost in prayer, or at least in meditation. I would have given anything to read his thoughts, for I knew that he believed in humanity more than he believed in God. Also, I was surprised to see him beside me because he usually attended church in the deceased Reverend Perkins's old parish in Whitechapel. There must be a reason for his appearance now.

The liturgies faded in my ears as I studied his profile. Colored prisms of light from the stained glass windows shone on his face. His lashes remained light, almost as ash-blond as his hair. Particularly in this meditative pose, he looked, even more than usual, like a figure in a William Blake painting.

Saintly.

Inspiring.

I blushed and tried to turn my attention back to the liturgy.

Immediately after the service, Simon offered to escort me home. Grandmother lingered near Lady Catherine and

Lady Violet to chat with our new priest. "Young. Not yet twenty-eight," she had said about him at breakfast.

As we walked, Simon and I discussed Grandmother's behavior lightheartedly for a few blocks until we reached our neighborhood. The afternoon seemed almost normal—ladies walked small dogs, young children in their Sunday clothes walked primly beside their tight-lipped governesses.

Then Simon's face turned grave. We were very near his house, only a few blocks from my own.

"What is it, Simon?" I asked, alarmed.

"Can you step inside to talk with me in my study for a few moments?" he asked, looking not at me but ahead, at his front door.

"Certainly." I followed him inside. Although I heard his servants preparing Sunday dinner in the dining room, although I smell roasted pork and potatoes, I felt enveloped in Simon's intensity and I wanted, desperately, to hear what he had to say. As we ascended his family's ornate staircase, he told me that his mother had been home this past week but that she'd recently left, once again, for their seaside house, where she seemed to be spending most of her time.

Simon's upstairs study was exactly how I would have imagined it. The room was so unlike the rest of the house. It was simple. Functional. No gilded portraits. It was furnished with unadorned yet expensive sconces, all displaying beeswax candles. As I seated myself in a chair in front of his enormous oak desk, I surveyed Simon's many books. On the shelf nearest to me, a very small carved-ivory elephant, only the size of my hand, was the lone art piece.

I gingerly picked up the sculpture, feeling its cuts and angles with my fingertips; it was beautiful. Cool to the touch. Lovely.

"Where did you get this?" I asked as Simon shut the study door. "It's exquisite."

His eyes veiled, and I picked up on a brief pause before he spoke. "Africa."

"You were in Africa?"

As I stared up at him, it seemed as if his mind was soaring to another place.

"Were you there for travel or work?" I asked.

Simon was still far away from me. But after two seconds, he snapped out of his reverie and swiftly removed the small sculpture from my hands, returning it to its place upon the shelf.

"I was in the Congo, once. And to answer your question, I was there for work and study purposes."

"Extraordinary. You never told me about that."

"That is because"—Simon's voice was tinged acidic—"I do not wish to talk about it."

I felt startled. Although withdrawn and unreadable on many occasions, Simon had never spoken so sharply to me. I felt hurt. But then his gentle demeanor instantly resumed, and he sat at a chair behind his desk. He sighed, seemingly aware of the impatience he had just demonstrated.

"I think someone might be following me," he said quietly. "That is the reason I brought you here."

"Max?" I whispered.

"No. That is the odd part. My follower is blond, older.

Just beyond forty years old, perhaps. His face looks reddish, almost sunburned."

The man I saw in Highgate Cemetery, the morning after the murders!

I told him about the man I'd seen. Of course, it might not have been the same one, but there weren't many sunburned individuals in London.

Simon paused. "Your description certainly does sound like the same man."

"For how long have you seen him?" I asked, my heart pounding. Each day, everything seemed to become more confusing.

"I'm not precisely certain. I've only noticed him twice. Last week, when coming home from Whitechapel at a late hour, I heard footsteps behind me; I turned and saw him in the distance. But I was not certain that he was following me so I thought little of it. Then, last night, after working here at my desk until midnight, I turned to draw the curtains in the window." Simon gestured to the large window behind his desk. "And I saw him, standing in the shadows across the street. He tried to appear casual, as if just waiting for someone, but it seemed too much of a coincidence that I would see him twice in two different sections of London."

"It is odd," I said, perplexed.

"Have you seen him since that day in Highgate?"

"No, but I'm usually walking about during the day, when the streets are particularly crowded. I wouldn't know if anyone was following me. What about William? Has he been followed, too?"

Simon sighed loudly, and I saw exasperation in his face. He paused, looking hard at me, and I felt my heartbeat quicken. "I have not seen William since the night of the attack upon Abberline three weeks ago. William needed to know about Max, that the situation was serious, so I returned to his house immediately after taking you home to warn him and to require him to take some time off." Simon sighed. He hated William, but he knew that this was all difficult for me to hear. "He didn't seem to care when I warned him that Max has returned, when I told him of what Max had just done to Abberline. William seems to have entered a breakdown, a collapse of some sort. He hasn't even entered into the hospital since that night. As I said, that was three weeks ago."

I felt bewilderment. Grief. I hardly knew what else to say, particularly to my friend, to someone who had once rivaled William for my heart. So I said nothing.

I drummed my fingers on the chair beside me a bit, deep in thought—confused by these occurrences, saddened by all that had happened between William and myself.

A clock on one of the bookcases chimed. I knew Grandmother would be returning to our house soon.

I still heard the clank of silverware downstairs, and thought that, most likely, one of Simon's sisters was coming to visit. But, selfishly, I wanted him to myself that afternoon. Blinking back tears and controlling my voice, I said, "Take dinner with us. Please. Grandmother would like it."

There was no argument. "Of course."

Sixteen

As she surveyed the food supplies for the menagerie, Seraph-ina saw that her bags and frozen meats were running low. She suppressed feelings of panic, knowing that she could hunt for food for the animals; nevertheless, attaining grains and birdseed would be more difficult. Yet she had enough for now, and that was all she could think about. After feeding the animals, she ascended the cold wet steps of her home and dived off of a rock, slicing out into the waters to hunt for herself.

The sun, just breaking out, cast its light wild and pearl-ish through the seawater around her, and as she swam, alternating between higher and deeper depths, she felt her anxieties subside. In fact, once she had swum far out into the sea, she felt almost calm. The rest of the world might have forgotten her, but she still had her mind, her brains, her beastly nature, and her body, which made her a preda-tor of all. Even the rare large sharks passing through these waters never threatened her. Humans might eschew her, think her disgusting and monstrous, but they would inevitably become her prey.

The huge shadow of a sperm whale passed over her, far above. Its shadow lingered brilliant in the bright light of that day's sun. She considered who she was, in that moment in the depths of the water. Even the humans from her old life, before the experiment, had faded from her memories—her fiancé, her father. Her heart seized upon itself as she wondered if what she had experienced with either of them could be considered love. But her thoughts about this were scattered, foggy, caught in those recesses of her mind that belonged to another being entirely. Now a pang pierced her insides, and she knew she would give anything to be part of that world again, that human world. But as a cold current whipped at her body, she knew she would never think or be as she was before—anxious to marry, curious but uneducated and ignorant. Now, she knew that immortality existed; she wanted to latch on to the strengths and accomplishments of the Conclave. She wanted to contribute to the group—her best dream was to live and travel with them, to be their scholar.

But in the watery depths, as she considered her scales, her talons, she knew that unless Robert Buck finally found the cure, this could never happen. She considered her keeper. She remembered how he had nearly strangled her on his last visit, and once again wondered if his long absence was a means of disciplining her.

From her depths, she watched a jellyfish pulse by her, translucent and graceful. A sadness washed over her. Besides

Petey and her other animals, Max had always been her single constant. He had always been hers. But why had she expected their relationship to remain the same? He followed no rules except the Conclave's rules; he was their perfect assassin and enforcer because he had no moral boundaries, no limits. She shivered as she thought of this. But if he had not thought her worthwhile, he would never have convinced the Conclave to let her live. He had always tolerated her over the years, even become fond of her ... at least she had thought that he had been fond of her. Seraphina, with her beastly intemperate love, always hoped that one day—if she was ever cured—she might cut out into the world with Max.

But now, she believed in her heart that a cure was further away than ever. Once again she thought of how being part beast gave her an exclusive connection to Max, that they had been bonded as he could not be bonded to anyone else. She remembered the first time she saw him—she had been in such an awful state. She had done the unforgivable, and yet Max had not judged her.

Now he had someone else, someone who shared his psychic abilities—a bond with this girl, Caroline's daughter, Arabella. She would be the Conclave's immortal companion, and Seraphina would be forever banished to her island.

What would they do with her?

She swam upwards, her scaly arms slicing through the waters as she propelled herself toward the sunlight.

Would they destroy her?

No.

They couldn't afford to. The Conclave needed her to guard their treasury and their animals.

She spent the entire day in the waters, swimming, eating fish; she had not fed on human blood since attacking the two boys. If she killed too many humans, it would become risky for her. She had seen the search boats early that morning, near the shore. She had heard the baying of the hounds along the beach as they followed her scent. The search parties had been on land mostly, looking for wild wolves or bears. But since she had killed those boys on the waters, they now feared the presence of some sort of water beast, something exotic, perhaps a large crocodile—a beast not native to these parts, but nonetheless released or lost in the sea. She couldn't have them searching too close to her island home.

She swam to new depths, at a fast and furious pace. Her gills pulsating, she explored deep underwater caves, saw fish species that Robert Buck might only hope to see. She swam through long-forsaken wrecks of Viking ships, finding treasure that Orkney islanders would sell their souls for. She smiled, in the sparkly currents, as she poked a gold goblet with her talon—no human could reach or survive at these depths. These things were hers alone.

Sometime later, evening set in and she swam in the waters near the shore of Bromwell. The search parties were gone, and the moonlight was just beginning to show in the still-light sky. She liked the way it cut through the forest trees and rocky cliff places. As she broke the water's surface, she saw, surrounding her beneath the setting sun, the sea, inky as violet, shimmering, dimensioned and resplendent.

Calm and momentarily feeling more at peace, she let herself transform into her human form.

She floated nude in the cool waters of an isolated bay, in the shadows of a nearby cliff wall. She let her belly rise to the surface and felt her breasts—now soft, pale, and smooth, quivering in the waters. She floated like this for at least an hour. Then a boldness swept through her and she glided toward the sheltering cliff walls. Her urges, her appetite, made her monstrous again, and she began to climb. Her long hair hung heavy upon her head and back, swaying and dripping as she made the long ascension. When she finally reached the top, she was not even winded. She stood tall for a moment, feeling a high wind whip at her hair. When she saw a Pictish Stone, approximately four feet tall and illuminated by the moonlight, she stepped toward it, let her taloned finger scrape across the beautiful carvings upon the rock. The Picts, early medieval Scots, had made these symbolic stones as memorials—this one had a cross, with blossoms and ivy grooves about the base.

She smiled. This was made by Christianized Picts.

Funny... in that era, even the Christian people had believed in her. She was a selkie-lamia, the mythical Lilith, whatever monster dwelled among the damned and took humans fated to be hers. But of course it had been science that had brought her mythological life into existence. So here she was, an immortal lamia, a beautiful nightmare living on the margins of human society.

She moved on, the rocky surface of the clifftops gradually softened by scattered twigs and pine needles before giving way to a nearby scraggly forest. She walked through the forest until she reached its end, the edge of a green meadow. The meadow was pale-green in the moonlight. Then, as there was a hush in the rippling evening breeze, she heard voices.

She saw a young couple in the corner of the meadow. They spoke, leaning against a pine tree. Although she could not hear their voices, she knew they were lovers. As she watched them, her thoughts receded back to her life before the change, to her closest brush with love.

She hadn't known her fiancé well at all. To this day, she wondered if she might have loved him eventually. She also wondered if, at the age of eighteen, she had had any choice in the matter at all. She didn't know. All she knew was that she had felt the vague excitement of doing something new, and of moving away from her cold home.

Tristan had been her father's business partner. He was from London, and he was older than she was; she had not known his precise age, but she now assumed that he was somewhere in his thirties, about the same age as her keeper. Her governess, Maura, had seemed so excited for her, telling her over and over that she was so fortunate to be engaged to him. Tristan went on chaperoned walks with Maura and Seraphina, around the loch, whenever he was in Bromwell. And she still remembered walking into the parlor on the afternoon they had become engaged. She had worn her best dress, sleeves carefully covering her rash-covered arms. She remembered feeling warm and happy when he slipped the ring on her finger. Although she didn't know him, she had been excited, wondering if her own marriage might be better than her parents' marriage—although she did not even know, exactly, what that had been like. Her fiancé, like her father, was kind but distant. A complete enigma. And yet she remembered trying to be hopeful... she had looked forward to marriage, asking Maura what a wife did.

And then...

As her memories of her father and Tristan returned in a painful onslaught, she shut her eyes and felt her long talons dig into her palms until they bled.

She came out of the reverie and observed the two lovers. The couple was so enraptured in their own hushed words and kisses that they had no idea of her presence. The boy was a fisherman; even from across the meadow, Seraphina smelled the scent of saltwater and fish upon his clothes. The girl, plainly dressed, looked as if she might have worked at one of the Bromwell shops, a millinery, perhaps, or a bakery. As Seraphina studied them—both no more than seventeen—she thought of her own chance at love so many years ago, and the emotions of that engagement arose full force inside of her: the betrayal, the scorn from Tristan when he saw her transform.

These memories felt as painful as a re-opened wound. Her torn feelings swelled, and Seraphina feared that they would become too much, that she would split apart. That hunger, that old hunger that could never quite be dispelled or conquered, returned.

She had to feed.

She crouched in the high grasses, easing forward, her eyes glinting on the couple.

As she swam back to her island, the night sky deepened. She was late returning and the animals would be hungry. But her stomach felt full, her body invigorated. She rose and fell in the water, plunging against the rush of currents, against the splash of waves.

Finally she surfaced, sensing her island in the distance. A blanket of night mist parted like drapes, and her heart leaped when she saw Max's boat tethered to the rocky shore. She dove under and swam faster. Her keeper had returned to her.

I returned from work the next day, tired and exhausted beyond belief. However, Grandmother was angry at Lady Violet for some reason, and I knew that I would be expected to listen to her complaints during dinner.

"Violet knew better than to invite Lord Darton and his wife to dine the other night."

"What's wrong with them?" I asked wearily, only half-listening as I cut into my roast beef. I noticed that my meat was slightly bloody, a little undercooked. I liked it this way, but Grandmother would not be pleased.

She leaned forward, so close across the table that I saw the dust of her face powder upon her cheeks. "Why, I have no problem with Lord Darton, Arabella, only with his judgment in wives."

When she sliced into her meat, a bit of blood seeped out. I saw the immediate displeasure upon her face.

"Do not eat that, Arabella. Ellen!" she called shrilly.

I sighed. I would have to wait to hear about Lord Darton's wife while my meat cooked longer. I heard my stomach growl.

"Ellen!"

When the maid entered the dining room, Grandmother instructed her to take our meat immediately back to the kitchen to cook, and to bring us something else in the meantime. I argued this a bit, but then I saw Grandmother's nose wrinkle and her jaw stiffen, and I realized instantly that the argument was not worth having. Grandmother was already in a poor mood; Richard had left London on vacation, and Grandmother had had to endure Ellen's terrible hysterics.

She spread jam upon her roll. "Lord Darton's new young wife is divorced. She left her previous husband a few years ago, charging him with cruelty."

"It sounds as if she had good reason to leave him," I heard myself say, distractedly. My mind was so consumed with Max's return, with the news of Simon's follower, that I felt frightened even sitting in this lovely Kensington cage.

Grandmother's lips narrowed into a small slit. Before I could stop myself, I felt my eyes glance toward Mother's portrait on the wall near us. It was a painting done when she was my age, nearly eighteen, shortly before she eloped with

Jacque Sharp. I wondered how she had reacted to Grandmother's lengthy tales of gossip.

Fortunately, Grandmother seemed not to notice my inattention. "The young woman might very well have had reason to leave her first husband. Nonetheless, she is a divorced woman, and to marry so well, when she is so disgraced . . . it is unheard of." Grandmother clucked her tongue. She began muttering. "Violet would never have invited such a woman, but with her husband's . . . " She looked at me shrewdly; I think she knew I was aware of Lord Bertram's laudanum addictions and debt. "Indiscretions," she continued, "with his costly habits. They are in desperate need of money. They need this friendship with Lord Darton. Nonetheless, why would she invite *me* to a dinner party with a woman so eschewed by society that she cannot even attend Court? Violet might have at least warned me that notoriety herself would be at her dinner table. I would not have attended."

After a bit, Ellen returned with a more fully cooked platter of roast beef. Grandmother sanctimoniously unfolded her embroidered napkin. As we began eating, she said, "I don't receive such people in my house."

"Ma'am." Ellen stood in the doorway red-faced, flustered. "Miss Christina Rossetti is here. She most urgently would like to speak to Miss Arabella."

Grandmother groaned. "Now? At this time? What does the woman want?"

"Most certainly I will see her," I said, rising and wiping my lips with a napkin. I felt myself blush at Grandmother's rudeness. *Disgraced women. Bohemian families.* I despised the way Grandmother's world doled out kindness so discriminately.

Seventeen

I stepped into our parlor to find Christina Rossetti's frail figure pacing in front of the fireplace. She still wore her coat. When she looked up at me, her expression was absolutely panicked. Her face seemed paler than usual, her eyes almost the size of small saucers.

"What is the matter?" I asked, alarmed, shutting the parlor door behind me and advancing quickly toward her.

Christina gripped my upper arms tightly. "Oh Abbie," she said quickly. "I have not seen William in three weeks, and I haven't the slightest idea where he might be!"

"What?" I'd assumed, as Simon did, that William was at home with his aunt, hopefully resting.

Christina began pacing again as she talked quickly. "The first few days, I was not worried. I thought he might be so busy he was simply sleeping at the hospital. He has done that a few times. Then I became concerned. We have a place near Avignon, and he has been so distraught, I wondered if he had gone there. He took off there alone once after his exams in medical school. I wrote to one of our friends in the area, asking her to visit the house. She did, and replied promptly that it was unoccupied. And then..."

She lowered her voice and looked at me with pity. "You do know that he was engaged? It happened immediately before his disappearance."

"Oh, no..." I whispered, feeling my stomach. How could he do that? Move on like that so quickly. I had lost him. It must have happened a day or so after I last saw him, that evening of the attack on Abberline. My world spun a bit, and I sat down on the sofa.

Christina sat next to me and placed her hands on my shoulders. I felt shocked. Too shocked to even cry. But I could not speak.

"Abbie..." she whispered, soothingly. She removed her gloves and took my face in her hands, her palms cool and gentle upon my cheeks. "I helped my brother raise William; I know him very well, and I do know that his feelings for you are true. I didn't say anything earlier because I truly don't believe the engagement will last."

"One of the cousins?" I heard myself say, distantly. He could not love either of them. I couldn't believe it.

"Lottie," Christina said quietly. Then she bit her lip, "Or perhaps it was Lettie...I don't know. They're both ridiculously similar and remarkably stupid."

She paused.

I swallowed, folded my hands upon my lap, and stared into the fire. "Go on, please."

"I wondered if he might have eloped, but when I contacted the family, neither of the young women had heard from him. In fact, Lottie—or perhaps it was Lettie—blast, I wonder if William can even tell the difference—was furious with him for not contacting her in so long."

My head swarmed with so many thoughts at once. I became dizzied with jealousy, fear, rage, and worry. In spite of all of my conflicting and confusing feelings, I knew, beyond anything, that we had to locate William. I remembered his troubled face, how much he had been drinking.

"Do you think he might have hurt himself? Or that he might be hurt?" I asked. At Christina's expression, I saw that I had suggested one of her worst fears. I felt my chest tighten. "Max," I whispered in horror.

"Excuse me?" Christina asked, her eyes widening.

"Did William not tell you?" In that moment, I felt my anger at William rise. I'd simply assumed that he would tell his aunt all that Simon had told him—that he would warn her of Max's return.

Quickly, I told Christina about the attack on Abberline, about how my vision had led me to it.

"And William knew of this?" she asked.

"Simon drove back and told him. Simon told me that he had been apathetic, that he had not really cared ... " My voice drained off.

She had her hand on her stomach as if she was about to be sick. "He truly was not thinking clearly. And now I am even more terribly frightened."

Taking out a handkerchief, Christina wiped her eyes. I had never seen her cry before. "He was so distraught when I last saw him. But he would not talk to me. And his drinking ... he has never been like Gabriel in terms of addictions, but recently, he has been drinking too much. Far too much. He is hurt." The she looked hard at me. "He loves you, Abbie."

My emotions felt as if they would erupt inside of me. I suspected, *knew*, that he loved me. But did that make us compatible? Suitable? He had such a potential to wound me, and I wondered if the simple fact that we loved one another also meant that we would be good for one another. But I cut these thoughts short. In spite of William's state of mind, my future with him was of no concern now. He was missing, and we needed to find him.

I peered into Christina's distraught face, to her clenched hand where she held the crumpled handkerchief.

Trying not to allow my own feelings of panic to overwhelm me, I asked, "Have you contacted the police?"

"Yes, but ... they were not very helpful. They treated me as if I were an overbearing mother."

My mind raced. "Did you speak directly to Inspector Abberline?"

"No."

"Perhaps," I said bitterly, "he would be a bit more interested if he was reminded that William worked at Whitechapel Hospital. He's still quite obsessed with the Ripper case. A physician's disappearance from the place where all of the victims stayed or worked would seem suspicious." Quickly, I told Christina about how Abberline knew of the Conclave's symbol, about how he had sought me out after the Highgate Cemetery attacks for information.

Her face turned ghostly white. "We killed Max's friends.

Max will in turn torment us with fear, as he kills us one by one."

"We needn't despair," I said, taking her hand and squeezing it. But my words sounded so foolish as they came out. Of course we were in danger. William had been missing for weeks. In spite of my words, both Christina and I were despairing.

"And you are here, safe," I continued. "Simon and I are safe. We can't simply assume, just yet, that Max had anything to do with William's disappearance. Particularly if we consider William's mood and unruly behaviors lately."

Panic rose within me, but I didn't speak my other, more terrible thought: that perhaps now that William and I had parted ways, Max might have already murdered him—as he would no longer need William alive to control me. If Max still wanted me alive for some reason, he might have believed that he only needed Simon alive to make me submit to him.

Christina remained quiet. I felt a terrible helplessness. We had to find William, but I didn't know where to start.

I stood and walked to the fire, feeling the heat of the flames upon my skirt.

"He left me alive in that alley. Max is playing a game with us, Christina. But I can't make sense of it. I don't know what he's doing."

I drummed my fingers upon the mantelpiece, seeing the empty place where the china shepherdess, which I had flung at William, once stood. Richard had not been able to repair it.

"Tomorrow, I won't go to New Hospital," I said quickly, turning to face Christina. "We'll begin looking everywhere. Do everything that we can to find him. We should go first to Scotland Yard, speak directly to Abberline. Because of his ongoing interest in the Ripper case, and particularly after the attack on him, I am certain that he will find it odd that one of Whitechapel Hospital's physicians has disappeared."

Christina said nothing. She simply looked at me, her eyes searching and luminous.

"We will find him," I assured her.

I felt overwhelmed. I knew we both did at the moment. Christina soon left, promising me that she would try to sleep, although I knew that she would not.

By the time I left the parlor, I saw that Grandmother had retired to her bedroom on the first floor to read. I ascended the stairs wearily to my own bedroom. I didn't even turn on my lamp, needing the quiet dark to think, to cool my frenzied thoughts. I sat on my bed, hearing nothing but the ticking of the Grandfather clock on the staircase landing and the sharp click of Ellen's snuffers as she trimmed some wicks in the hallway, just outside of my bedroom.

I was too agitated to undress or to sleep, although I needed rest before Christina and I began our search the next day. And I felt bothered, chased by something. There was *something* that I wasn't comprehending—something I was missing. I walked to the closet to look at Mother's portrait again, and I stared at it in the darkness.

What are you trying to tell me? I thought once again as I stared at her. *What do I need to know?* I would have given anything to have her with me, to enlighten me. As I stood there, I wondered if she had loved Gabriel even in spite of his instabilities. Yet unlike Gabriel, William had seemed to be faithful to me when we were together. Christina herself believed that his feelings for me were sincere. My heart felt painfully torn.

And then, the vision slammed over me, but this one felt frustratingly short. I saw her—the hazelnut-haired creature from my first vision. She was swimming, her movements wild, heedless, her webbed fingers and long claws stretched out far before her in the dark greenish waters. I saw the glint of a thick gold bracelet on her serpent wrist, tight against the scales. Then I gasped as the shroud of bubbles surrounding her cleared and I saw, across her back, the Conclave symbol. It was not small as theirs had been—the creature's tattoo was larger, covering her entire back.

Then everything darkened.

No. No. I struggled to retain the vision. I opened my eyes and saw my mother's portrait.

Who is this creature?

Who is she?

What is Mother trying to tell me?

Then I was back, in the vision, and I saw him. William. He was dead, his bloodied corpse on a floor somewhere.

I panicked, felt dizzied. No, he wasn't dead! I saw his chest heave very slightly with raspy breaths. My mind strained to see him—this vision was less clear than the others. My heart pounded. *No. No.* I tried to still my panic, the waves of help-lessness that I felt. *Focus, Abbie.* William's body lay on a marble floor somewhere, and the place was only dimly lit, resembling a grotto; I saw marble columns, torches, candlelight. I heard a great roar from somewhere. A hiss.

My mind reached, arched, to focus upon William—his face was bleeding. He had a gash, a terrible wound in his chest. His clothes were torn, ripped all over. And he had a chain tied around his neck, bolted into a marble column or wall behind him.

Where was he? I had never seen this strange place before.

William! It sounded like a scream in my head. Then the vision was snatched from me. Taken away too soon, before I could get a good picture of his whereabouts. All I knew was that he was being held. And he was hurt badly.

Also, the lamia. Was she real? She had that tattoo on her back. Was she somehow a member of the Conclave? Max had lied to me about my mother—he never told me that he'd poisoned her, or that he'd saved my life so that I might someday replace her as their female member. What else did I not know of the Conclave? What other monstrosities had they committed? What other secrets had they harbored?

Max. What *did* Max have to do with all of this? I paced in my room. At this point, everyone in the house was asleep. I heard the grandfather clock chime eleven o'clock.

I needed more information—to re-enter the dream. If Max had sent me the vision, he wasn't finished, and my mind was too distraught to summon it again myself. I tried, perspiring at the effort. I stared at the lamia portrait again and tried to lose myself in my thoughts, but my heart kept pounding. I was too worried for the psychic part of my mind to work.

What could I do? I couldn't get that image of William out of my mind—wounded, seemingly close to death. I felt stricken. I needed to open my mind again.

Simon. An idea materialized in my mind, and I peeked

out my bedroom door. The hall was dark and quiet. Richard was gone until morning; Ellen was probably asleep in the servant quarters, and she was so much less attentive than our butler.

Eighteen

When I reached Simon's house, I saw that most of the lights were out. Suspecting the Simon would be up late, studying or reading, I tossed rocks at the panes of his study window until I saw the drawn curtain ripple. When he opened the door, I saw even in the darkness that his eyes were bloodshot. And disapproving. But he was also still fully dressed, so I knew I had not woken him.

"Abbie, are you aware of how extraordinarily dangerous it is for you to be walking about at night? Particularly given our present circumstances."

Indeed, I was very aware of the danger, and also of the impropriety of this—showing up at the St. John house so late at night. However, the idea that had come to me in my room ... I couldn't let it go.

Nonetheless, I must have looked stricken, because Simon's disapproval melted as he ushered me through the door.

"What has happened, Abbie?" he asked quietly as we stood in the dark foyer and he took my coat and gloves.

"I'll tell you momentarily. Your family is all away?" I whispered.

"Yes, and the servants are all asleep or gone for the night."

In what seemed like one breath, I told him about Christina's visit, about how she hadn't seen William in three weeks.

Simon's ice-blue eyes flickered, and he sighed. "I know you think highly of William, Abbie, but he's probably—"

"He's hurt. I just saw him."

Simon looked bewildered.

"That's why I came here to talk to you tonight, Simon. We need to get to him. Would you please help me?"

"Abbie..." Simon began.

"Might we go to your study?" I asked quickly, already ahead of him on the stairs. Even with his family out of town, I felt more comfortable having this conversation in the privacy of his study.

When we entered, I sat down on a plain, wine-colored settee near his desk. After shutting the door, Simon seated himself beside me; he was patient, but unreadable as always. The light in the room, from a single reading lamp on his desk, shone dim and seemed to accentuate his handsome paleness. Remembering his bloodshot eyes, I thought about how many hours he must be working at the hospital daily, now, during William's absence. I noticed several books on his desk, and pages and pages of notes. Simon must work or study every second of his life.

I told him about the vision—about how I had to get to

William but I didn't know where he was. And how, when I had focused and concentrated, I could not re-enter the vision. Then, summoning my strength, I looked Simon in the eyes and said, "Hypnotize me."

"No." His reply came out firm, without hesitation. This was what I had feared.

"But you must. It is the only way…"

"I cannot do that to you, Abbie."

"Simon, you know much about the mind, do you not? You never questioned my sanity when I began having the visions last year, when I felt uneasy discussing them with anyone other than you." I lowered my voice, looked away. "Even with William."

As he glanced down at the carpet, uneasy, I leveled my gaze at him. "You have hypnotized before," I continued. "I have seen you do it in the hospital. You would not endanger any of our patients. I know that about you. Therefore, there cannot be a risk."

"There could be." Simon stood and began pacing, then walked behind his desk and looked at me in the glow of the lamplight. "That is why I refuse to perform the procedure upon you."

I wasn't about to give up. "But I sat in my bedroom only moments ago, perspiring, trying to force another vision. All my efforts were futile. I think I was too agitated. Hypnosis might be a way to open up my mind."

Simon stopped pacing, but said nothing.

"Please, Simon." I cringed as I heard my desperate whisper.

He leaned forward across his desk, his knuckles white upon the oak surface. "As you know, I use hypnosis as therapy. I have studied it. It puts the patient into a somnambulant state—essentially, the mind functions as if one is sleepwalking. Once there, the mental senses are heightened and the nervous system is suppressed. The mind is highly suggestible. Usually, physicians employing the method make suggestions to the patient—to stop drinking, or in a mental illness case such as monomania, to quit obsessing about an object or issue. I have used hypnosis to treat alcoholism, monomania, and even nymphomania. But most of the patients I treat are hysterical—not in control of their capacities, anyway. There is no risk of peeling away their conscious faculties because they're so weakened anyway. You, on the other hand—"

"But I want this, Simon. Doesn't my will matter at all?"

"It does help in the matter—a patient who believes in the process and submits to it is usually more successful, but I have worries."

"What?" I asked. I was alarmed, hearing the clock tick away and knowing that every moment we debated this was another moment preventing me from finding William's whereabouts.

"I have never used it, or heard of using hypnosis, on a psychic patient; I have never used it to enhance psychic abilities. I am concerned about how it might affect you."

"What do you mean?"

"There are two issues to consider. One, that Max might be sending you false visions."

"I have already considered this," I said quickly, cutting

him off. "But the stakes are too high for me not to believe him. William might die. Furthermore, all of my visions last autumn were true."

"Secondly," Simon continued as if he had not heard me. He came around from the desk and sat beside me. In an oddly intimate gesture, he pushed a lock of hair away from my face. "Memories, thoughts that you might not like, could surface. Become real to you."

"What are you saying?"

"Abbie... after learning the truth that night at the Conclave's house, that Max killed your mother, you have had to re-remember her sudden illness as not simply illness, but as murder. You have undoubtedly had to 'rewrite' those last days in your mind. Max was there in Dublin during those last days, probably watching you."

"I have thought some about those days..." I heard my voice trail off. I swallowed hard, trying to keep my facial muscles composed. Roddy, his death, my rescuer—who I now knew was Max—carrying me home after I'd nearly drowned... Max was the person I'd heard arguing with my mother while I struggled to regain consciousness. He had saved me even as the poison ravaged my mother's body. And I had lost my friend, my dear friend, Roddy. I had hardly allowed myself to think of that day since coming to London. It had been a chapter closed, sealed away in my mind. Now, fear seized me as I thought that I might somehow revisit it— be brought to that nightmare's threshold. But nonetheless, William needed me, and although I couldn't imagine a future with him, I knew that I wanted him to be safe.

Simon paused, then pressed on, gently. "What I am saying

is that hypnosis does not come without its risks. Very real risks, Abbie." He cleared his throat a bit. "I do not want to harm you."

William. Saving William was paramount. I could not focus upon my own hurts and traumas.

Simon was quiet. I knew he thought William was a sloth, unstable. And I saw, in the layers of Simon's expression even in the study's shadows, how Simon still felt about me.

I felt my heart flutter a little.

"But, Simon, if I'm strong enough to handle even those memories, then it is a possibility that hypnosis might heighten my psychic abilities."

He paused. Shrugged. Then Simon's expression became agitated, and I saw his eyes rest for a moment upon the ivory elephant on the bookcase. "I'm simply warning you that it could have unanticipated results. I have seen ... inexplicable things in the past. There is much we still do not understand about hypnosis, and I feel it is best to be cautious."

My heart thumped. What was he talking about? What had he seen?

I felt myself, against my will, wring my hands in frustration. "Simon, as my friend, will you please help me? I don't beg of you often, but now I am begging. If you do not hypnotize me tonight, I'll find someone else to do it tomorrow. I must try to conjure that vision again, and I am too distressed at the moment to focus and bring it up." I set my jaw. "You must. This is my decision now, whatever the outcome might be."

Simon said nothing, but by his expression, I sensed that I had won.

"All right Abbie." His voice leveled. "But you must do as I say."

Without a word, Simon drew the drapes tighter around the window behind his desk. Then, after taking a wide candle from his desk and lighting it, he put out the lamp, leaving us in darkness except for the flicker of the candlelight.

In that moment, I suddenly felt inexplicably fearful, on the verge of this new experience. Previously, I had thought that at worst the process would not work or that I would see other visions, unhelpful visions that wouldn't give me the information I needed to find William. But now, something instinctual, an energy that I didn't fully understand, recoiled within me. I ignored this surge, telling myself not to be fearful. I told myself that Simon was overly cautious, that hypnosis was regularly used at Whitechapel Hospital without any "unanticipated" results.

"Look at the flame. Focus upon it. Keep your breaths regular and think of nothing other than the candle flame," he said.

I tried, focused, watching the light flicker in the darkness. But I also felt my heart pounding, racing at the thought that if this worked, I would see William in that terrible position again. Every time I started to feel my breathing, even my system, calm down, at the very moment when I thought I could surrender, my heartbeat would leap and pound, and I was back in the room with Simon and the candle.

"It's not working…" I said, frustrated.

I saw relief wash across Simon's face, and I knew that he would give up soon.

"Is there nothing else we can do?" I asked.

He sighed. "There is one other way."

Blowing out the candle, he placed it back upon the desk. Then he knelt before me in the dark. I saw him only because of the tiny stream of moonlight seeping through the slit in the drawn curtains. "Look only into my eyes. Think of nothing else but my eye color."

I stared, noticing in this closeness the icy depths of his eyes. They were glassy blue, with flickers of deeper whitish and turquoise hues. Simon, who always kept his eyes so veiled, was showing them to me, unabashed. I thought of the ocean—not the ocean in summer, shimmering, sunkissed, but the ocean in winter—lovely, flicked with icy darkness, and yet gray and unyielding. I felt an almost painful hook in my heart, and soon my interest in his expression turned from curiosity to arrest as I plunged into those winter waters, surrendering myself to whatever awaited me there.

I faded away from myself, from my body, from Simon's study, until I found myself on a speck of land, a treacherous rocky island with sharp peaks and cliffs. I felt, smelled, salty seawater. I moved, drifted phantom-like, into a crevice in one of the rocky places until I found myself in a warmer place, an unusual place—a small, dim, marble hall. The place was too dark to see well in—there were columns, the dull glint of many, many portrait frames on the walls. But the unlit torches lining the marbled walls made discerning my whereabouts difficult.

William. Where's William? I channeled my focus, letting myself spiral deeper into the vision.

William, I'm here.

William, where are you?

Then my mind faded and sharpened again, leaving the hall for some sort of elegant bedroom illuminated only by a fireplace. In the firelight, I saw more columns, identical to the ones in the hall, more marbled walls, a large bed—the headboard made of seashells. Pale green curtains, with twists of threaded gold, draped from the high ceiling to hang long and sheer around the bed, while the bed itself remained unmade, its tossed sheets and coverlets the color of sea foam. In spite of the beauty of the place, I sensed an unpleasant dampness in the air, tinged with mildew along with other vague, foul odors—of acid, of rotting meat. Of blood.

Then I saw William. The enormous bed had blocked me from viewing him. As in my previous vision, he lay on the floor, the large shackle around his neck chaining him to a column near the bed as if he were an animal, a pet mastiff. My own terror and fear threatened to overwhelm me, and I had to remind myself that this was a vision—I was not there in flesh and blood and could do nothing to help him in that moment. I worked hard to suppress my emotions, fearing that if they became too strong, the vision might leave me as it had before. I saw him clearer then. His face was bruised, one eye swollen shut, his lips cracked, bleeding. His dark trousers had been ripped in places and were coated almost entirely in dried black blood. His white shirt was nearly shredded, but the remaining fabric pieces were dried with both rust-brown and fresh-red blood. In horror, I saw what seemed like bite marks, deep wounds all over his chest, his neck. Some looked older, scabbed with oozing pus where infection had set in. And William, although breathing, lay quite still.

Dear God.

The vision wavered a bit, like rippling water, and then I steadied my mind.

Who did this to him?

I knew Max was somehow behind it, but those wounds, those bite marks, were deeper than a human could inflict. I thought of the lamia in my visions—because of her tattoo, I knew that she was somehow connected to the Conclave...

With great effort I calmed myself, hoping that the vision wouldn't leave. I needed to know where this place was. Rocky islands. Cold winds. I searched my mind—this could be anywhere in the British isles. Or elsewhere.

I felt overwhelmed with frustration. Desperate. I refocused on the vision, streamlining it, trying to pull it toward me. I remembered how I had seen street names when I chased the Ripper in my attempt to save Liz and Cate, how I had recognized High Holborn the night I had saved Abberline.

Focus.

I pulled my mind away from the underground bedroom, pulled myself through the marble walls, through the rocky walls again to outside.

Then everything faded and I found myself standing on a thin strip of land surrounded by water, a great expanse of sea to my right and to my left. The land strip stretched ahead of me and behind me for what seemed like miles, disappearing in both directions into a mist of fog. The fog, in fact, moved aggressively around me and out across the water as if alive. I walked ahead a bit, my heart pounding. I did not know this place.

Where was I?

I heard a splash near me, breaking through the eerie silence like a gunshot, and I jumped. I looked down into the water surrounding me. Hundreds, indeed probably thousands, of goldfish swam in the waters. I paused. Something seemed odd—I had expected to see only greenish sea depths, but these masses of domesticated goldfish were exactly like the ones I had seen last summer in the ponds around the London zoological gardens, when I had gone there with Grandmother after arriving in London.

The hairs on my neck prickled and I felt a small, breeze, warm and breathlike, upon my neck. It was only then that I noticed that when the shroud of fog thinned a bit, something was unusual about the color of the sky. Instead of regular grayish clouds, lavender puffs billowed out, rippling and rich; cream-colored, lacelike shapes trimmed the edges. In spite of my unease, the sky felt lovely, dreamlike ... it reminded me of something.

Mother's dress! The dress I'd worn to the dinner party at the Conclave's house when I first started work at Whitechapel Hospital. The sky was like the lavender folds of her dress, and the cream-colored edges like the white lace that trimmed the cuffs and throat. Why would I be seeing it here?

Then the thick fog ahead of me parted. I saw, at the end of the strip of land, the cottage I'd shared with Mother on the Edgeworths' property. But this cottage was entirely displaced—I was not on the Edgeworths' land. I was on this narrow strip, surrounded by a sea of goldfish. Nothing fit. Everything seemed out of place. Wrong.

I approached the house, inexplicable fear mounting within me. I felt my body pulse, my ears roar with trepidation. I feared, foolishly, that the cottage would consume me. Once again, I remembered that last terrible day vividly, right after Roddy died, when Mother had died. I had never forgotten it. But I had closed it off, pushed it aside like an undesirable book. But now, I felt intensely all those memories of that day flood over me as if I experienced them again—Roddy's dead corpse floating above me as I drowned in that pond, Mother wasting away dying; I remembered vividly being pulled from the pond and carried away by Max, I felt viscerally all that information that I had been forced to rewrite in my head after my experience with the Conclave, since knowing that they had given Max her execution order.

Now I had the cottage before me.

I felt my body quake violently and stumbled to the hard ground, unable to open that door. I realized, then, that I was not so much in the vision as somewhere in my own consciousness, somewhere where my own memories mingled. I was meeting up against the place I most feared—that day. Memories of my mother permeated everything, not just the sky color but the wind itself; I smelled the faint scent of her hyacinth perfume. And I felt my own feelings of failure. Of loss.

Then everything around me stilled—the clouds, the mist. The waters became flat as mirrors and I heard a noise; I stared in horror behind me, down the strip of land, as a taloned, webbed hand came up out of the waters, a gold bracelet hanging heavily upon a scaly wrist.

I did not want to open the cottage door, afraid that I would find Mother dead or near death. I felt tears burn my eyes. I could not face it. But the terror of being trapped in my own psyche, unable to move backward or forward, strained upon me.

And now, the lamia. That serpent woman from my nightmares. I was seeing her coming for me.

I felt panicked, and yet I still couldn't go inside the cottage; I couldn't move to open the door. I felt suffocated, and realized that I couldn't breathe. It was as if a hand had been clamped over my mouth.

No.

No.

I felt as if I were dying, and as I fell, sank, to the ground, I prayed that I would wake up. But it didn't happen. My lungs felt as if they were going to burst, just like they had when I nearly drowned in that pond under Roddy's body. And I saw, in the distance, the serpent woman, far down the strip, crawling at an agonizing slow pace out of the water. I knew, instinctively, that she was coming for me.

Then I heard my name called, distantly. From somewhere far away.

Abbie.

Abbie.

I felt my body quake, and pain seared through my lungs as if I were dying. What was happening? Full panic set in as I felt myself spiraling somewhere. I could no longer see or breathe. For all I knew that serpent woman could be nearly upon me, ready to strike.

Abbie!

The voice sounded louder now, desperate, and somewhere, distantly, as I seized blindly in the dream, I felt my knees hit a hard floor. The pain, the burning, the suffocating inside my body was too much, I thought I would die. Then the pain eased a bit, and I felt myself floating somewhere, somewhere away from myself. Soon all would be oblivion.

Then I felt lips upon my mouth, and I gradually became aware of my own body, feeling the hot throbbing pain on my kneecaps, each of my hands clenched in a fist with my fingernails digging hard into my palms. I became aware of my own legs. I felt my arms gripped tightly. Although I had not fully surfaced yet from my psyche, I began to feel other, more physical sensations. Desperately, I pulled myself deeper into the kiss. This drew me upwards. Outward. Away from the nightmare.

Confusion slowly faded, and I found that I was on my knees on the floor of Simon's study. I must have fallen from the settee during the hypnosis. Simon was in front of me, on his knees, clutching my arms tightly as he kissed me. But this kiss wasn't as controlled as the one we'd shared in Sir Bertram's library. Rather, Simon crushed me to him, and I sensed something raw and reckless in his feelings, an urgency that I had never felt before. I felt my stomach lurch when I opened my eyes and pulled myself away a bit, to focus. The veil over his eyes had loosened and I saw deep worry.

Dear God. I felt myself tremble at the realization. *He loves me.*

Simon fought to regain his old composure.

I couldn't bear that. I couldn't bear the anxiety I saw in his eyes.

And yet, shocking myself, I pulled him back to me and kissed him again. This time, I felt fully in my body again; I felt flushed, breathless, and bit his lower lip a bit to make him feel more. I thought of a time in Dublin when I had tried to ride Sir Edgeworth's most obstinate horse. The horse had taken off across a meadow, running at full speed. I'd felt initial terror as I held the reins, and then, once I realized I had no control, I felt a strange elation in surrender. The feeling had been delicious, and I had embraced it. I wanted Simon, like this, as he was now. And I wanted to be as I was now. Authentic.

William.

With great effort, I pulled away. My thoughts and feelings were still reeling from the vision and from my near-drowning in my own memories.

Simon and I remained kneeling on the floor, staring hard at each other, unsure what to say or do. His lower lip bled a bit, but he didn't seem aware of it. The trickle of blood looked oddly unnerving on his white-marble chin.

"Abbie." He put his long fingers in my loose hair at my temples. "I was afraid."

He placed his palms, cool now, gently upon my cheeks. It felt soothing, good. And I felt how sweaty and damp my cheeks were, burning as if I had a fever.

"What did you see?" he asked. "When you fell onto the floor, seizing."

I quickly related what I had seen of William, telling him also that I thought this lamia creature was behind it.

He interrupted. "No. What were you thinking of after that? When you lost control of your body?"

I told him of being at that place in front of the cottage.

"Damn it," I heard Simon growl as he pulled me to him in a crushing embrace. I had never before heard him curse. "The hypnosis brought you to your memories, as I'd feared. You imagined the lamia—whether she exists or not, you see her—possibly also because your mother assumed her disguise for the portrait. Your mother, your memories of her, your inability to understand her, and your need to avenge her, are, as you feel, your greatest threats. The conscious mind delving too deeply into the unconscious can be dangerous."

I had a thousand questions on my tongue, but I said nothing. I still felt my body trembling at all that had just happened. Simon continued to hold me, and I felt his breath warm upon my hair.

"I worked one summer in a mental asylum near Brussels," he said. "I saw a few patients, who had been sane all of their lives, brought in with sudden hysteria, dementia, an absolute separation from reality. None of it followed the patterns of what we are learning regarding traditional mental illness. They had died within their own psyche—withered and become lost to themselves. Many died soon after arriving."

"So I might have 'died' to myself in that vision? I might have lost my mind, become permanently imprisoned in my nightmare?"

"It's possible," Simon said softly.

I focused. "Is that why you kissed me?"

He paused. "Partially. I was trying to wrench you, physically, from the place where you were as quickly as possible, and it seemed kinder than a slap."

I remembered my sudden insight that he loved me. What had happened between us? I paused, and yet could say nothing in my confusion. This was too much to sort through at the moment.

"We need to save William," I said instead, as Simon helped me to my feet. "He is imprisoned somewhere."

"But the place you saw could be anywhere, Abbie. We need more information." I could tell, based on his expression, that Simon still had doubts that William was really imprisoned.

"You don't believe me."

"No, I believe you. But how do you know he isn't in some sordid brothel?" Simon's expression was perfectly serious as he said this. "Or that he didn't anger someone in a drunken gambling match?"

I frowned. "Do I have your help or not, Simon?"

"I will assist you. But not for William. This is no excuse for William's poor choices. Whatever muddle he is in now is probably of his own—"

"I know, I know," I muttered, smoothing my hair back, putting on my coat, and regaining my composure.

Simon sighed. We were both exhausted.

"I said I would help you, for you. I'm taking you home now. Let's both rest and think rationally. Perhaps, if you get some sleep, something, somewhere, in the vision will give you a clue to the location of the place." He caught my eye. "And yes, I will help you."

The lurch occurred in my heart again, and I felt that old bewilderment of not knowing myself, not trusting my own feelings.

The hues of early morning began to penetrate the room, and I knew that I would have to return so that I could slip into the house before Ellen arose. Still, as I stared at Simon, I felt my chest heave in a small riot from freezing anxiety ... and from something else, warming and sweet. I blushed.

Simon walked me home, making me promise to sleep a few hours before he returned so that we might begin our search.

Part III

---

*"We fear, indeed, you spent a stormy time
With our strange girl; and yet they say that still
You love her."*

—*The Princess*

Nineteen

After quietly slipping in the front door, I forced myself to try to sleep for a few hours. But it was a restless sleep, not restorative or deep. Through those early hours of the morning, my mind continued to churn and spin, trying to figure out where the place was that William was being held. I felt spent, exhausted, knowing little more than I did before the hypnosis session. The vision during the hypnosis had been clearer, but I still had not learned the location. Furthermore, my mind now felt agitated and jittery over what had happened with Simon. I knew he still loved me, and I felt something deep within me respond.

But did I love him?

I truly did not know how to read my heart.

After my dreamless but frenzied sleep, I awoke, hearing the grandfather clock strike nine o'clock. I bolted upright. I needed to talk to Christina, to tell her about what had happened last night. And Simon and I needed to begin our search. I blushed as I recalled our kiss again. I remembered the elephant sculpture, the wintry expression in Simon's eyes.

What draws me to Simon?

I knew I was drawn to him, needed him—even if I was not certain that I loved him. I finished securing the last button on the gray walking-suit dress.

Distractedly, my mind spun, thinking of all the places we should look for William. If William was being held by this creature, perhaps we should research various newspapers to see if there had been any animal attacks around the British Isles. I bit my lip. There were the cannibal attacks ... but I knew William was somewhere along a coast; it didn't seem possible that this creature had something to do with the cemetery murders. Furthermore, I had seen people—the walking dead—in the cemetery that night. That part of the puzzle I did not understand.

I was so deep in thought that it was only as I secured my hair in pearl combs that I noticed voices downstairs. Grandmother had a visitor.

It was rather early in the morning for someone to call. I wondered if it might be Christina, but I heard Grandmother laugh loudly and I knew that she would not be so warm to a Rossetti.

Quickly, I hurried down the stairs, intending to eat breakfast quickly and leave. But I froze when I reached the bottom of the stairs and could see the guest in the parlor. Horror and rage rose within me.

I saw Max, dressed formally in a dark waistcoat, seated in a mahogany chair and conversing with Grandmother.

I saw Jupe unashamedly sniffing his top hat and gloves, which lay on a nearby bench. Max looked terrifyingly handsome. His dark hair curled wild about his face, and his eyes gleamed brilliant green in the pale gold light of the morning. His tone toward Grandmother was cheerful, indeed charming.

I walked into the parlor, determined to get him out of her house as quickly as possible.

"Arabella," Grandmother exclaimed when she saw me at the door. Her cheeks flushed, and I could tell she was enjoying the visit. I remembered her reaction to the young priest at church and I knew how susceptible she could be to charm and flattery. "This visitor is a most marvelous surprise. Have you met Dr. Bartlett's nephew, Mr. Max Bartlett?"

The Ripper. My mother's murderer. If Grandmother only knew. I felt my stomach lurch and feared that I might become ill. I had wanted to protect Grandmother, keep her safe in this lovely world of hers. But I couldn't keep him away from her, and the perversity of Max's presence in her parlor infuriated me. I had to keep Grandmother safe.

Nevertheless, I felt overwhelmed.

Focus, Abbie.

Simply find a way to get him out of the house.

There was an awkward silence, as I stood silent and unsmiling in the doorway, too angry, too distraught to speak. With great effort, I stilled my pounding heart.

When Max turned to greet me, his eyes sparkled. He stood up and bowed a bit, in keeping with his act as a gracious young gentleman. "I am afraid that I'm here at a shockingly early hour, but, as I have already explained to Lady Westfield, I am in London only until this early afternoon. You see, I have been in Austria, where business has kept me ever since the tragic accident that took my uncle's life."

He shook his head regretfully, although when he caught my eye again, I saw the glimmer of a wink. He loved this charade.

What is he trying to do here?

This was the first time, other than during his attack on Abberline, that I had seen Max since murdering the rest of the Conclave. He had told me, that night, that if I refused the Conclave's offer or did anything outrageous and he had to intervene, it "would not be pretty." Was this what he had been holding out for? To murder Grandmother and myself on an ordinary morning, in our own parlor? No. Instinct kept telling me that something else entirely was going on. I felt sure Max was behind the cemetery attacks, and I suspected he somehow knew of William's whereabouts. He still needed me for something else . . . I felt my eyes narrow.

"Currently," he continued, "I am on my way to Oxford for business. My train will leave at one o'clock this afternoon."

I wished I could get my knife—but that was impossible. I wasn't about to leave Grandmother alone in the parlor with Max for even a second.

I saw confusion cross Grandmother's face. She paled, undoubtedly wondering why I was acting so rudely toward our guest. I willed myself to be calm. Grandmother had

had such great respect for Julian Bartlett, and in her mind a visit from his handsome young nephew from the Continent was an honor. This cordial, dapper Max Bartlett was the illusion that she had; it was all that she knew.

But I can play his game, too.

Straightening up, I flashed my most brilliant smile. "Of course. Forgive me—I had difficulty placing you, since I have only met you once, one evening at Dr. Bartlett's house."

He bowed again, as if my worry was a mere trifle.

Bloody bastard.

I saw Grandmother relax a bit; Jupe, finished with his exploration of Max's hat and gloves, leapt up onto Grandmother's lap. She began scratching his back with her thin, heavily veined fingers.

"I understand that you worked closely alongside my uncle during his last few months in the hospital? Is that correct?" Max asked.

"Of course. He had such care, such affection for our patients." I leveled my gaze at him and felt my face flush even darker.

Max smiled, his perfectly white teeth gleaming.

"I know it is early, but"—he turned to Grandmother—"I was wondering if I could take Miss Sharp on a brief walk, just around the neighborhood, of course. I was unable to attend the memorial service for my uncle at St. Paul's Cathedral, and it would give me great pleasure to hear of Miss Sharp's memories of my uncle. He was like a father to me."

"Of course," Grandmother said warmly, gazing up at him in admiration. I felt nauseated.

Stepping forward, I said quickly, "I would be delighted to share some of my memories. If it would comfort you."

He bowed gratefully.

Twenty

Once Max and I had walked several blocks away from Grandmother's house, he took my arm in his in an intimate gesture, as if I were his wife. But I knew it was a way to control me, to keep me from turning upon him or from running away. The streets were rather busy this morning, so I couldn't possibly attack him without making a scene. Carriages sped loudly along the street beside us, but their noise seemed like nothing compared to the thuds of my own heart. Although I wanted to kill him, I couldn't possibly in this setting, among these people. Furthermore, I needed to figure out how he was behind William's disappearance.

But my urge to hurt him, to kill him, was too strong, now that I knew he had murdered my mother; now that I knew he had been the one to take her from me.

"Keep your bloody self away from my Grandmother," I growled softly as we neared Kensington Gardens.

"Ah, Abbie," he said, patting my arm lightly. "But we have so many other important matters to discuss."

"Where is William? And who is this creature I keep seeing in my visions?"

Max smiled widely, brilliantly. I saw, in the shadows under his hat brim, the small crescent-shaped scar on his chin from where I had bitten him that night he attacked me in Christina's house. I felt much satisfaction upon seeing the scar, and I wanted to hurt him again. The rage rose within me to the point of being unbearable. But there were too many people—I couldn't do it. I needed to deal my cards out carefully if I wanted to save William.

Still, I couldn't hold my tongue from one matter: "You killed my mother, you smarmy cock."

"I saved you, remember. I saved you from drowning." His stare was enigmatic in that moment. "I couldn't let you, my best project, drown. Frankly, I would have expected a bit more gratitude, love."

"How did you kill her?" I snapped, a bit louder. "What poison did you use? How did you do it?" I felt myself trembling a bit.

Max looked down at me through his eyelids, clearly bored. We were passing a Catholic Church on Kensington High Street. Max stopped, keeping my arm locked in his own. He stared above us at a small crowd of pigeons perched upon the blackened stone carvings. "I don't know about you, but I've lapsed a bit in my church attendance, and I'm feeling the need to make confession."

He grabbed my wrist painfully hard and, almost before I could breathe, pulled me swiftly into the cathedral. Although the morning was bright and busy, we were enshrouded in darkness, silence, and solitude the moment the doors closed behind us. I had never been inside a Catholic church, and in these shadows, statues of saints with rose-painted lips and pale faces glowed eerily in the candlelight. The sanctuary seemed empty, and just as I wondered why no one attended a morning mass, I saw blankets and enormous canvasses covering the pews and half-empty paint buckets set upon the floors. The smell of fresh paint and splintered wood pierced the air sharply. It seemed as if the interior was being renovated, which explained the sanctuary's emptiness.

Max pushed me behind a curtained doorway, into the interior of a tiny confessional.

In the dark, stifled air, before I could move or speak a word, he had his gloved hand at the base of my throat, and I felt his fingers tighten a bit through the lace of my high collar. "Your mother is a forbidden subject. Her death is a matter that I would advise you not to bring up with me. Ever again."

I saw something dark flicker in his eyes, the lingering of something that I didn't understand. I trembled in fear and confusion, but anger also pulsed within me. Max had no feeling toward his victims; he was sadistic. Part of me thought he would almost relish describing how he had poisoned my mother. I had not expected this reaction.

William. You must save William.

Only after I stilled myself, stopped struggling, did he loosen his grip upon my throat.

Then I stated quietly, trying to blink back tears, "You know where William is."

"I do." Max smiled. He stepped back from me a bit in the shadows as he lit a cigar. The confessional was terribly closed off, and I fought the urge to cough as the sweet smoke merged with the already persistent odor of wine and old wafers. "William is, actually, what we need to talk about— why I arranged this little rendezvous with you. You did a fine job last autumn."

A fine job.

I felt shocked. Baffled.

"When I initially discovered what you had done, killing off Bartlett, Buck, Perkins, and Brown, I was, of course, enraged," Max continued. "It had seemed impossible. I therefore planned to kill you, your friends, Lady Westfield and her nasty pug for that matter. You see, I will not surrender my immortality. Fortunately for you, I located something of interest in the interim, and I think matters will work out for the best. In fact, matters are working out quite well. I have a bit of a project going on, an experiment of my own..."

The cannibal murders? Simon's follower? What is Max doing? Who else is involved?

"What do you mean?" I leveled my gaze at him.

He sighed and blew smoke through one of the creased places in the confessional's curtain. "That is another matter, which we will deal with at a later time. I think there is some more pressing information that you want from me..."

"William," I whispered, coldly. "Tell me where he is."

"You must know, Abbie, that we have had another immortal in our group for years. This one is our very own Lady of Shalott." He smiled, pleased and languid.

"Your what?"

"Our princess in a tower. Or on an island." He tapped ash into a nearby communion-wafer dish.

The serpent woman. The lamia.

Max's eyes glittered. "You seem to have already seen her. I've sent you some images of her, and no doubt, now that she has your paramour, your psychic powers have extended a bit on their own."

"Go on," I hissed. "Who is she?"

Max smiled. "About eighty years ago, not too very long after I had joined the Conclave, we lived in northern Scotland, in the Orkney Islands near the small seaside town of Bromwell."

Orkney! Of course! The rocky, windswept seacoast. I wondered why I hadn't thought of that place before.

"Long before Gregor Mendel, Robert Buck was extracting material from humans and animals to determine their structural essence. He was particularly interested in how animal essences could prove beneficial to humans, particularly in curing human diseases, or in strengthening human mental and physical abilities. There was a young woman in Bromwell, Seraphina Umphrey, daughter of the opulent merchant Joseph Umphrey. Julian Bartlett had been treating her for rashes, for painful and severe eczema, and Robert suggested injecting extractions from various serpent material—Komodo dragon genes, as well as a few other species of lizards and snakes. These breeds had particularly adaptable skin, and Robert hoped that the best part of their essences would merge with the young woman's to heal her body, her skin. Robert had not yet tried merging these genetic structures, and he was anxious to see if it would benefit Seraphina. And of course"—Max paused—"he was insatiably curious about the outcome."

"She was an experiment, then," I said.

Max finished the cigar and tossed it into an old silver wine flask. He chuckled. "Of course she was. And the experiment might have helped her."

"But it did not." I felt a coldness creep over my skin.

Max moved closer to me in the shadows. I heard the cathedral bell chime the ten o'clock hour. But its sounds seemed dull compared to the roaring in my ears—I was anxious and furious. During my struggle with him, one of the combs in my hair had come undone. Max secured it back in its place now, his movements thoughtful.

"The possibilities inherent in animal structures are extraordinary," he whispered. "Although the experiment had unexpected results, the results were nonetheless ... interesting. We'd created a new species. Before, she had been a beautiful but dull woman. After Robert Buck's injections, we found that we had created our own mythological beast."

"A lamia," I muttered. My warring emotions continued inside of me—pity for this girl, and yet fury. In the vision, William was hurt. How much humanity could be left in her after all of these years?

"Of sorts." He smiled proudly. "Robert's injections permanently affected her human essences. After the first round of treatment, her skin improved dramatically, but then she transformed almost immediately. What was remarkable was that the transformation could come and go—sometimes at will, sometimes as a result of extreme emotion. These transformations made her highly adaptable. Not only could she hunt on land, but she had gills and webbed feet and hands for hunting in water—it was as if the best survival mechanisms rose to the top of her own structures."

Max was speaking of her as a specimen. As a pet.

"How did she feel about her change?" I asked bitterly, knowing where this was going—that my worst fear, that she held William, was true. My insides tightened.

"Why, she hated her new self, of course. She escaped from the cell in Robert's home where he'd been keeping her while we decided what to do with her. Robert didn't want to kill her—she was such an interesting study. But when she escaped, she killed a few Bromwell natives. Once I'd caught her and brought her back to them, Robert and the rest of the Conclave had already decided to destroy her. She was too much of a liability."

Before continuing, he paused in the confessional's darkness. "But, as I have always had too much of a fondness for lovely women, I saw how we might use her."

I recoiled, pulling away from him and pressing my back even further into the thin wooden wall of the makeshift confessional. It was a futile effort to distance myself from him. He continued. "I thought that she might perhaps benefit us as a guard for our accumulated wealth. We have always, as you know, moved among our residences. What to do with the animals, where to keep them, what to do with our wealth, was always rather a complicated issue. So it was my idea to have an underground home constructed, on a tiny island just off the coast, where we could keep everything. I imported the architects from the Continent—they took great care in the construction of the place, and adhered to the secrecy of the project as I required them. Then, once they were finished, they were her… housewarming gifts, of sorts."

I felt nauseated. "She eats humans."

Max smiled. "Well, she's not supposed to. We forbid it, requiring that she keep her existence secret and restrict herself to the island. But every so often, her appetite overwhelms her a bit."

I glared at Max. "So you already have your female member of the group. Why did you want me?"

I knew the real reason, of course—because of my psychic powers and because of Dr. Bartlett's romantic feelings for my mother, which he later displaced onto me. Still, I needed to know as much as I could about the lamia woman.

"Yes. Our situation with you has always posed a bit of a complication for our dear Seraphina, or Effie, as I call her."

Effie. A pretty pet name. I didn't want to consider the ways in which she had been used by Max throughout the years.

"The cruel irony of everything is that Effie indeed wanted to be part of the Conclave. She gladly takes the elixir I bring for her and the animals every year. She has always believed in what we do without bothering to ask questions about our means—the petty details."

"Does she know how you gutted patients in Julian's own charity hospital?" I asked.

"She knows that we have to employ special means at times, if that is what you're saying, to do what we have to do." Max sighed, tired of my ethical considerations. "Nonetheless, she had no 'special abilities' that would make her a worthy member of the Conclave. Simply put, she is a lovely and useful pet. Truth be told, I am quite fond of her. But the fact remains that there is nothing extraordinary about her. Nothing that would be an asset. The Conclave has kept her throughout the years, promising a cure. But she has become more demanding in recent years, particularly when she learned that we were offering the elixir to your mother and then to you. Our Lady of Shalott is becoming increasingly restless. She has killed several of the locals this year."

"And William. He is my concern. What does this have to do with William?"

"Oh, that is quite the fun part." Max smiled widely in the darkness. "I thought it would be more amusing if, rather than destroying her myself, Arabella Sharp destroyed her for me. You can slay the beast, so to speak. William is merely the bait to lure you to that place, and to put you in your best fighting form. William..." He clucked his tongue. "Truly, Abbie, your taste in men is deplorable. It was quite easy to capture him—incapacitated with alcohol as he has been lately. A blow to the head and then some chloroform was all it took."

Poor William. Poor stupid William.

The bell chimed again. Once. It was ten thirty.

"I had best send you back on your way to Lady Westfield, lest she think that I am not such a respectable gentleman."

I glared. "Will she leave William unharmed until I arrive?"

"I told her not to hurt him, but I must say, the young lady has a temper. I would encourage you to make haste in your journey."

I felt my own rage rise to unspeakable heights, but I knew losing my temper now would do no good. This was not the time for revenge. That would come later. But it would certainly occur.

Max carefully took an envelope from his inside jacket pocket. "You will find directions to the island in here."

I took the envelope from him and tucked it carefully into my handbag. "You must leave all those I love alone, including Christina and Grandmother. You must not harm them," I said fiercely.

He gave a little bow.

Then he stepped forward, his expression no longer languid. Rather, there was something greedy in his eyes—something wildly undecipherable. He took my chin in his hand and I trembled with fury. He was only one man, yet I could not conquer him. I slammed my arm into his chest to fight him, to push him back, but he caught both my wrists, vise-like. He smiled; he had wanted me to strike out against him, to remind me that he was always one step ahead of me, anticipating my movements perfectly. I gritted my teeth and, in a futile attempt, tried to push him away from me. But his grip was too strong.

Then, hungrily, he kissed me. Hard. Again, I tried to push away but I could not; he merely smashed my arms and my wrists against my skirts, immobilizing me. His kiss deepened, as if he were trying to pluck something from me, and our touch brought forth a vision of the lamia.

The vision was strong and my head ached. I saw her clearer than I had before. She was beautiful, even as a lamia, with green eyes and hazelnut hair; I saw her perched upon a high rock on her island, the Conclave's symbol tattooed across her back and illuminated clearly under the morning sun. I tried to fight against Max, but he only crushed me harder to him. I saw the lamia's eyes—although serpent-like and slitted, they were the most tragic, the most dangerously tragic eyes I had ever seen.

I surfaced from the vision, still unable to push Max away, and I hated him—hated him for the deep shame he inflicted upon me, the shame of kissing my mother's murderer inside a confessional and feeling the fire of that terrible vision, feeling the psychic bond we shared. There couldn't be a hell—because if there was one, I would be burning in it already.

At my first window of opportunity, I pulled away from him, trying to kick him hard away from me. But he spun me around, still holding me in a vise-grip so that my back was pressed against his chest. I was in a position where I could not even kick backward. And biting him was now impossible.

I thought he was going to hurt me, but instead, he kissed me lightly on the back of my neck, just above my high lace collar. "We're alike, Abbie Sharp. Survivors. Assassins."

"No!" I yelled, hot tears in my eyes.

But he slammed a hand over my mouth while maintaining his grip on my arms against my chest with his other hand. A plate of stale wafers rested on a small makeshift shelf only inches from my eyes. A tarnished crucifix gleamed dully on the wall beside the wafers.

"Shhh … shhh … Abbie Sharp," he whispered lightly, as one would to a child. "We are destined to be together, my love. You are mine. Do not squander your boundless possibilities for baubles, for the sake of the brief human life you cling to and for those you love around you. They will be gone, gone in a breath. But me, I offer you eternal life."

Eternal life? I'd assumed that the elixir must be gone, lost in the fire, but he'd said that he'd "found" something … had he located the Polidori papers? The elixir notes? Did they not burn? I remembered seeing the woman I'd thought was Mariah, that awful night in Highgate Cemetery, and I then I remembered Simon's follower.

I fought feelings of weakness. The mystery seemed more confusing and deeply layered by the second. Despair now rose. I had done so much already, I worried that I might not be strong enough for this, for whatever was to come. I knew that I might have to kill Seraphina—that tragic girl-beast. I hated to kill, but I would kill again; in fact, I would make a bargain with the devil to save William's life. But what would come after that? Would I spend my whole life fighting the remnants of the Conclave?

"What are you doing, Max?" I whispered tearfully in the darkness.

He spun me around so that my face was inches from his.

"Terrible, terrible, wonderful things. I am offering you something extraordinary, but I will let you die—I will kill you, Arabella—before I will let you live forsaking the gifts I offer. Do not make me do that."

The look in his eyes frightened me.

He kissed my tear-streaked cheek, moving his lips up my jawline to my ear. "We have a jolly fun time ahead," he whispered. I shuddered. "A bloody jolly fun time."

I felt another great tear slide down my cheek and my emotions threatened to overwhelm me. A phantom memory of my mother's good-sense governess advice rose within me: *One task at a time, Abbie. Simply focus on the immediate task.*

That was all I could do.

I closed my eyes. "As I've said, leave Grandmother and everyone I love alone. Don't go into Grandmother's house again."

"Of course." He bowed a bit. I knew Christina and Grandmother were another means for him to control me.

When I surrendered completely, when I stopped struggling, he let me go, took out his pocket watch.

"Confession time is over. Shall we rejoin the land of the living?"

As quickly as he had pulled me into the Cathedral and confessional, he pulled me out into the blinding light of the street.

"Goodbye, love." And by the time my eyes had adjusted to the blinding light of morning, he was gone.

My heart pounded and the envelope he had given me weighed heavy in my coat pocket. Quickly, I tore it open, finding a map with specific directions to the Orkney town of Bromwell, as well as directions through an archipelago of rocky, uninhabited islands to the place where Seraphina lived.

Dizziness swept over me, and I leaned into the cool shadows of the cathedral to keep from fainting. My time with Max had been overwhelming, and I couldn't trust him. I knew that he wanted me, but I also wondered why he seemed so certain that I would slay this creature. Was this a further test? Another way for him to determine my competence as his immortal partner? And what was he planning? I thought of the graveyard murders. Who was Simon's follower? Had Max recruited others into his schemes?

I began to walk wearily down Kensington High Street, attempting to narrow and focus all of these thoughts. But above all, I knew that I had to get to the Orkney Islands.

Twenty-one

I was halfway down High Kensington Street, my mind racing with how to secure tickets to Bromwell and what to pack. I had no idea how to fight the creature, and, beyond what the visions had shown me, I had no certain knowledge of how she would act.

Fight.

Kill.

I hated those words. I thought of all the memories, all the nightmares I had had this year about killing the Conclave. If I had the opportunity, I knew that I would kill Max in a minute for what he'd done to my mother, and to assure that he could kill no more. And yet, if Max's story about Seraphina was true, she was as much a victim of the Conclave as anyone else. Her mystery puzzled me entirely.

A hand grabbed my shoulder. Hard.

Startled, I turned to find Simon, his carriage stopped in the street immediately behind me.

"Dear God, Abbie, are you quite all right? I arrived at

Lady Westfield's just now and she said that you had left with Dr. Bartlett's nephew. I have sent my driver all over the place in the past hour, looking for you—"

"I know William's whereabouts." I pulled out the envelope. "That place I saw, according to Max, was in the Orkney Islands. It looks from the map to be near the south islands, just over the waters from the mainland, from Caithness."

Simon gave instructions to the driver to take us back to our neighborhood and pulled me quickly into the carriage. "Max—where is he?" he asked as I took my place on the carriage seat.

"Gone. But we need to leave London as soon as possible." As the carriage lurched forward, I told him everything about what Max had said of the lamia's origins.

Simon's eyes veiled a bit. "How can you trust him in all this? How do you know this isn't some sort of trap?"

It was at this point that I burst full force into tears. Simon was correct—I couldn't trust Max at all. "I don't know, Simon. I don't know. And it all does seem like madness. But I think it's likely that it's true. My visions have never been misleading in the past." Then, before I could stop myself, the true root of my anguish came out. "William was terrible, awful in fact." I wiped my nose on a handkerchief Simon silently handed to me. "And yet my life feels shattered without him. Absolutely shattered."

Simon remained silent, but when I looked up in the curtained darkness of the carriage, I clearly saw Simon's own anguish. I saw jealousy in his expression; I thought of our time together the night before. In spite of his reserve, he cared about me, loved me. Now that I felt certain of Simon's love, it was as if my heart had come to be balanced precariously on a thin bough, seriously in danger of falling. His compassion and goodness extended enough that I knew he would follow me on this mad journey, helping me to rescue my prodigal love. Last autumn, that terrible autumn, I had questioned Simon's capacity to feel, to love; but now I knew he could feel. And he could love—that realization had come to me sudden and unbidden. Like an icy blast.

As if Simon could read my thoughts, he embraced me, pulled me to him, and I felt the strength of our bond even more painfully. Whether or not Simon was my love, he was a brother—my friend in a way that William never could be. While Simon didn't care if William fell off the face of the earth, I knew that he would go to the ends of the earth to make me happy.

"I will go with you, on this journey, even if it is one of madness," he whispered against my hair. His words, as always, came out soft as down.

Although Max had not forbidden me to bring Simon on the journey, I felt vaguely guilty for looping him into it. Yet Simon was already part of this. I knew, beyond a doubt, that my chance of surviving and saving William would be much stronger with a partner.

In whispered breaths, we discussed our plans. Simon would immediately go about securing tickets. I needed to pack my bags. Simon would arrive at Grandmother's house later with an excuse to take me from her for a few days. I knew of Grandmother's fondness for Simon, and I knew that he could persuade her of anything.

I also needed to warn Christina. She might have arrived

at Grandmother's house to begin our search for William, and I worried that, like Simon, she would panic upon hearing that I'd left the house with "Dr. Bartlett's nephew."

The moment Simon's carriage reached Grandmother's house, I stepped out, holding his gloved hand in my own.

"Thank you, Simon," I said, squeezing his hand.

He said nothing, and a bit of his old shadowed expression returned.

His heart rests upon a bough, too.

Twenty-two

Grandmother's house was quiet when I went inside. Ellen was running errands, and Grandmother was on a shopping excursion with Lady Violet. Richard had just returned home from his trip, but I would never have known it—he looked perfectly composed, as if he had been occupied by his household duties all morning. When he let me into the house, he told me that I had a visitor waiting for me in the parlor. For a moment I panicked, worried that my visitor might be Max yet again, but I felt instant relief when I saw that it was Christina. I was surprised to see Hugo as well, seated tall by her skirts. Grandmother must have taken Jupe with her, for the pug would have never allowed another dog in our house.

"It's so pitiful, Abbie," Christina said. "He howls nonstop every time I leave home. He has done this ever since William disappeared. So, for the last two days, I have simply brought him with me."

I knelt down. When I was on my knees, the dog towered above me. He leaned over, licking my face while I petted him.

"I apologize for not arriving earlier," Christina said quickly. "I have taken in two more friends just this morning…"

But I cut her off, telling her all that had occurred. That I knew where William was, and that Simon and I were going to bring him home.

As disbelief and shock registered in her luminous eyes, she fell into a coughing fit. It was only then I noticed that her normally pale face was flushed and her eyes seemed even larger than usual. I remembered William mentioning once that Christina had had a health condition since childhood, which sometimes flared. And in spite of her paleness, when I touched her cheek she seemed to burn with fever.

I called for Richard to bring her some tea.

"Oh dear," she said after recovering from the spell. "The lamia… the portrait. This seems impossible. Are you certain it is not a trap?"

"No, I cannot be sure. But Simon and I are going nonetheless. For whatever might meet us there."

"What can I do? How can I help?"

I bit my lip, thinking of her long history with my family. I needed to gather as much information as possible. I needed to know all that she knew of the portrait.

Richard brought Christina some steaming tea and after seating herself and taking a few sips, she regained her breath and composure.

"Do you feel well enough to come upstairs with me to see the portrait?" I asked as she finished the tea.

"Please tell me all that you know about it," I said as we stood in my closet, staring at the lamia portrait. Christina had not seen it since it came into my possession; in fact, she had not seen it in all the years that had passed since it was in Gabriel's studio. She crouched down, put on her spectacles, and brought the lamp even closer to the painting. I saw marvel and amazement on her face, as if she were deciphering the most exquisite hieroglyphics.

"I don't know very much about it at all," she finally said. She stood up, still staring at the portrait but removing her spectacles and furrowing her brows a bit. "I can tell you that your mother chose the portrait subject—the lamia—and she directed much in the portrait's style and arrangement. But I think you already knew that. It is so much more daring and poignant than my brother's other portraits. It has been so long since I have seen it, and I forgot its intensities. The hues, your mother's expression. Extraordinary."

Once again this raised questions in my mind. Did my mother know of the existence of the real lamia? Had she actually seen the creature, or did she have visions of it, like my own? I once again looked to the painting as some sort of message. As always, my mother's cryptic nature presented itself before me.

"I know nothing about Caroline's reasons for choosing the lamia as a subject. But Abbie..." Christina looked at me through the dimness. "If this is true, if this creature is real as

Max has described her, I tremble to think of what you are up against. It might be very much like slaying a dragon."

I had already thought of that.

"Then if I am to slay a dragon," I replied, "I shall need a sword, as well as my knife." If this creature had William and refused to surrender him—or even if she had already killed him—destroying her would be paramount. Simon and I should be able to secure weaponry somehow on our route; he was resourceful, and he had unlimited funds.

"If she was indeed a woman at one point, you shall have one advantage." Christina smiled darkly. "You might think like her a bit."

I shuddered, wondering how much of a beast I would be by the end of this ordeal. And I hardly knew what to say; I might be going into battle with an opponent that I couldn't possibly understand.

Christina continued. "But then again, if Max's story is true, Seraphina has no problem taking the elixir. She probably doesn't have the same moral considerations that you have. Also, we can't be certain what Max has told her about you, but if she does know that you have been invited to join the Conclave, she will already have a vendetta against you. You have everything she has must long for."

I hardly knew how to respond.

One year ago, I would have thought my current situation unbelievable. But since that time I had had to face an immortal brotherhood, and now it seemed I was going on a wild journey where, like St. George, I must slay a dragon. This was not the life I had chosen, the path I had sought out. I wanted to be like Dr. Anderson, a physician in a hospital like Whitechapel or New Hospital. I thought of how the Conclave's existence had brought so many more fathoms of trouble to England than, surely, Queen Elizabeth had ever intended when she sanctioned the group. Now it fell upon my shoulders, and Simon's, to weed through the mess they had left behind. To sort it out and restore order.

"Abbie." Christina's voice interrupted my thoughts. She put both of her palms upon my cheeks. "You are Gabriel Rossetti's daughter. As such, you are my niece, and as dear to me as William is. If something happens to both of you...it will be as if I had lost my own children. I cannot bear that."

"I know," I said soberly, not speaking my thought of that moment: that if I died, she would also be dead. As would so many others. Max would no longer need to keep her alive to control me.

She wiped a tear from her face, saying crisply, "At least take Hugo. He might offer a little protection."

Before Christina left, I asked her to speak to Dr. Anderson, to let her know that I would return at a later point but that there were family responsibilities I must attend to. This was the truth. I did not want Dr. Anderson to think that I had abandoned my work at New Hospital.

After Christina kissed my cheek and descended the stairs, I began throwing everything into my small luggage bag. Hugo lay on my floor, sad and mournful. I packed an extra change of clothes, and then carefully placed the bowie knife in my bag. But I felt immensely troubled leaving Grandmother. Christina, at least, realized that she was in danger. Seeing Max in Grandmother's parlor had alarmed me; Grandmother had no idea that he was a killer. Because of this, I feared greatly for her.

Simon's perplexing statement about Grandmother's butler Richard returned to my mind. On the night when I'd been forced to confront the Conclave, I had feared for Grandmother's safety. Simon, the next morning, had slipped Richard some money, which Richard had refused.

"You obviously don't know your butler well…" Simon had said to me.

Grandmother always discouraged me from going into the kitchen—something about well-bred ladies not lingering among servants. Another nonsensical Kensington rule. But she was still out with Violet, and her rules didn't matter, especially now that I was trying to save her life from the psychopathic killer she had let into the parlor.

When I reached the kitchen on the first floor where Richard was preparing dinner, I realized how long it had been since I had been in the room. Paint peeled in many places, and I saw that some remnants of ancient wallpaper near the back door had become so faded, the floral designs were barely discernible. Grease markings spotted the high ceiling. Nevertheless, in spite of the woeful lack of updates, Richard kept the kitchen clean—the floor swept and the counters impeccably wiped. Something in a large pot on the stove smelled wonderful, and the pork, roasting on a spit over the roaring fireplace, smelled excellent. I almost wished that I had an appetite, but I had too much before me, too much on my mind to think of eating.

Richard was wearing an apron, his sleeves rolled nearly past his elbows as he sliced carrots and potatoes on a chopping board. He had several dried herbs, including thyme and rosemary, sitting on the counter ready for use.

He raised his eyebrows, surprised at the sight of me. "Miss Sharp, are you in need of something?"

I smiled. "No, I'm not hungry." I took a seat upon a chair near the counter while he meticulously chopped leeks and onions. It felt a bit awkward. I played with a ring on one of my fingers and made a hideous attempt to appear casual.

"I feel as if I know so very little about you, Richard."

Richard remained quiet as he began slicing the carrots in perfect orange circles. But I saw something tense in his jaw.

"Truthfully, I am not very interesting, Miss Sharp."

"Oh, I'm not sure about that," I said quickly.

He caught my eye and I saw a knowing glint. "What would you like to know?" he asked cheerfully, dumping the carrot and potato pieces into the boiling pot on the stove. He returned to the leeks and onions.

I had a feeling that I would have to tread carefully as I went about this. Richard needed to know that he could trust me.

"Do you have family, Richard?"

He paused, then began dicing the dried rosemary and thyme. "I have one niece. The only daughter of my only brother. My brother and his wife are both deceased now. The young lady is married and has a child, and they live in Chatham. Her husband works in the dockyards there, and she embroiders dresses for ladies. So, when I am not here, I am usually with them, taking their infant Thomas on long walks. He is almost one year old now, so there is much adventure to be found on our excursions."

I liked this image of Richard, of his life apart from working as Grandmother's butler. I liked seeing him in a grandfather's role. I asked him several more questions about his niece and great-nephew.

But as we talked, I felt myself becoming impatient. I had not yet heard from Simon, and it was now one o'clock. At any moment he might come to the door, and we would have to leave immediately.

I cleared my throat and decided to simply plunge forward. "I'll speak candidly, Richard. I'm in a bit of a muddle at the moment."

Richard glanced up from his vegetables at me, but he said nothing. I waited. I would have to be more specific.

"My friends—Dr. Siddal and Dr. St. John and I—were involved last autumn in something, a situation that I do not want to bring you into, but one that could be dangerous for you and for Grandmother."

I leveled my gaze, praying he would not think me mad if I had reason to believe he'd understand something of the nature of my "muddle."

"Particularly," I continued, "I fear for Grandmother, as she has no idea of the danger she is in." I paused, not knowing what Simon had already said to him. I didn't want to involve Richard in something that he couldn't get out of. But I felt desperately worried for Grandmother, and certain that there was more to Richard than a mundane life as Lady Westfield's butler.

He seemed as if he was about to speak, but Jupe came running in at that moment. *Blast that dog.* This meant that Grandmother was home, and I would have to hurry the conversation. I thought of Hugo, shut away in my room upstairs, and I prayed that he wouldn't bark, and that Ellen wouldn't walk in upon him and scream. I watched as Richard gave Jupe a small piece of sausage.

The little dog swallowed the piece quickly and looked back at Richard expectantly.

"No, young man. There will be no more. Madame has been worried that you are getting fat."

I gazed at the bit of bulge, under the bare place on Jupe's back where I had accidently shot him with the arrow.

"Richard . . . " I said, feeling tears in my eyes as he turned to the stove to stir the pot and remove a boiling kettle. Why was this so hard? "I will be away for a few days, and I simply want Grandmother to remain safe."

"Lady Westfield will be quite safe," he said firmly, although he kept his eyes on the contents in the pot.

Then, as he bent over the stove, he brushed against the hot pan of stew and jerked his arm away suddenly, rolling his shirtsleeve further past his elbow to examine the burnt spot. I moved quickly to help him, and then gasped when I saw it. Just above the burn was a tattoo. It was some sort of seal—a coat of arms with the Queen's markings upon it: the lion and the unicorn. I had seen the Queen's coat of arms many times, but this was a different version. The colors were deeper, and these markings had gleaming swords protruding from the arms.

Our eyes met.

"What is it?" I asked quietly.

As he placed a cold cloth on the burn, Richard replied casually, "Oh, just a minor indiscretion from my youth."

He met my eyes again, and I knew that that was not all there was behind the markings. I also had an almost certain feeling that Richard had intended for me to see it.

"Never fear, Miss Sharp, your grandmother will be quite safe," he assured me again. "Quite."

I caught my breath at the tone in his voice, and a weight lifted from my chest. I felt instant relief.

"Thank you, Richard."

Before leaving the kitchen, I took several old copies of the *Times* up to my bedroom to read. I had given Simon the map, to have while he organized our journey, and not being able to study it made me feel agitated and restless.

As I sat on the floor, Hugo's horse-sized head on my lap, I scanned the headlines and editorials from recent weeks. I needed to do something, and I thought that in the newspapers I might find more information about the cemetery murders. I remembered how Abberline had said they were trying to avoid a mass panic, but I had seen journalists present at Highgate Cemetery that morning. And the story about the Brompton Cemetery murders had been on the front page of the *Times*.

So I was a bit surprised at how, in spite of the fact that two gruesome murders of resurrection men had occurred in two different graveyards, there was actually very little about the murders in the papers. There were a few articles theorizing about them: that the murders had been perpetrated by a Satanic cult, or, as someone from the Royal SPCA suggested, they were the work of a loose wolf. But none of the articles mentioned the symbol that Abberline had found on the tombs near the bodies. Furthermore, all the direct statements from Scotland Yard seemed to downplay the sensationalism of the cases. There was no mention of cannibalism in any of the recent articles, and Inspector Abberline was quoted as supporting the loose wolf theory, stating that the Zoological Society of London had just imported five gray wolves from the Continent and two had been missing upon arriving in London. He assured Londoners that all of the attacks had been upon common criminals—resurrection men in locked cemeteries at night—and thus law-abiding Londoners had nothing to fear.

Another short article quoted a local sexton as stating that he had seen strange figures around the graveyard, specifically a woman in white, beautiful and barefoot. But this was the lone article mentioning any graveyard sightings similar to what I had seen.

Then, as I scanned the paper again, ignoring the multitude of advertisements and announcements, I found a small article about some odd deaths of fishermen and townspeople around the Orkney Isles. It mentioned that decomposing body parts had washed up on the shores of Caithness. That article was short, no more than ten lines on the third page. Typically, Irish and Scottish news rarely made the *Times*, especially news from the Scottish Highlands.

Grandmother had arrived home an hour earlier, and I was sure that she would now be taking tea in her parlor. It was three o'clock, and I began pacing my room. Finally, there was a knock at the front door, and then voices. Simon! I heard his lovely hushed voice speaking to Grandmother.

As Grandmother still did not know that she had a Great Dane in her house, I shut Hugo in my room and descended the stairs, trying to appear casual.

"Of course, Simon. Of course," Grandmother said to him quietly, just as I reached the bottom of the stairs. She walked toward me, Jupe in her arms.

"Arabella dear, Simon has just told me that his sister Rosamund is in Bath, and a friend that she had been expecting has fallen ill and cannot join her. She is quite unwell in spirits and would like a companion. You must go to see her"—Grandmother's eyes narrowed, as she knew my usual excuse for staying in town—"even if it means forsaking your duties at the hospital."

Simon was a smooth liar. His expression seemed so earnest as he said, "I do apologize for the short notice, but our train leaves in one hour. Of course, our servant will be accompanying Abbie and myself as a companion on the way to Bath."

In that moment, Jupe began snarling in Grandmother's arms. Somehow Hugo had escaped my room and was padding down the staircase even as I began running up the stairs to retrieve my bag. Jupe tried to leap from Grandmother's arms as she shrieked, "Arabella, what is that beast?"

"William Siddal's dog," I called, and I could almost hear the hundreds of questions brewing in her head.

I grabbed my bag and was out the door, with Hugo, before she could speak.

Twenty-three

The moment Simon, Hugo, and I left Grandmother's home, I said, "What a wonderful lie, Simon. I'm worried however, that a single conversation between Grandmother and your mother, when she returns from the coast, might unravel it."

Simon smiled. The late afternoon sky had begun to change to dull plum. "I've sent a note to Rosamund, who has indeed recently arrived at Bath. She will of course uphold the story."

He held my bag as I stepped into his carriage.

I knew that Simon was closer to Rosamund than to his other sister, and that Rosamund would do anything for him.

"Of course."

In the carriage on the way to the train station, Simon explained our travel plans. We were taking a train to Edinburgh, and then a carriage through the northern regions, the Highlands, until we reached Caithness. At that point we would take a ferry over to Bromwell.

On the way to Victoria Station, I told Simon about what I had discovered in the papers—about the murdered fishermen in the area. Simon responded quietly, "I have never been to the Orkney Islands, but I have read much about the area. The waters are fierce and the currents unpredictable in many places. Many shipwrecks have occurred there since the time of the Vikings. The people, well ... it is Scotland. We are Londoners, therefore not particularly endeared to them. We will have to be careful when we get there, but still find a way to get information, to discuss the details of these murders—that will be our best means of determining the nature of the beast and her attacks. Also, we will need to secure a reliable guide to help us reach the creature's island. If the map is correct, it's a bit away from the mainland. Navigating those waters will be as difficult as cutting our way through a jungle. The Conclave's selection of an island was brilliant—it's almost unreachable, and terribly treacherous to ships and boats."

We arrived at the station. Our own train would leave shortly, and Simon had told me that it was the last one of the day to Edinburgh. As he secured our luggage, I waited outside the coach, Hugo beside me, watching the crowds of people and railway guards upon the platform. The hot steam from the engines swirled about me, and I saw rain trickle down the bricks of an outside wall of the station.

I'm coming, William.

He was in danger, and there were so many miles between us. I would be with him soon, in two days at most—it was seven hours to Edinburgh, more hours by carriage to the coast, and then the time spent on the ferry to Bromwell and securing our transport to the creature's island. I prayed we would not be too late.

I felt Hugo stiffen and growl beside me just as someone tapped sharply at my shoulder. I turned to find Ellen standing before me, a long narrow case in her arms. My first thought was that I had forgotten something superfluous, like my best pair of gloves or a hat, and that Grandmother had sent Ellen to the station to bring them to me. But the moment I met Ellen's eyes, I stifled a scream; I recognized that glazed, glassy sharp look well.

"You might be needing this, dollygirl."

Ellen's voice came out raspy, and I knew that it was Max speaking through her. I saw Mariah's possession again in my mind. Ellen's expression was shocking, disgusting.

She handed the case to me. "A little something to give you a bit of an edge when you get there." She smiled quietly.

I looked hard into Ellen's eyes, angry, unable to speak.

"A sword, love. You will need it. Best of luck to you." Then she turned and disappeared into the steam and the crowds of people.

"You look pale..." Simon said when he returned to me to help me into the coach.

"It was Max speaking through Ellen. He gave us this."

"What?"

"A sword."

Simon had secured us first-class seats so that we would have a comfortable journey. With only four other passengers in our roomy, cushioned coach, we had neither the background noise nor the privacy to discuss Seraphina. Still, we freely talked about other aspects of our trip.

"So, you said you have never been to Orkney?" I asked.

"Never. The place is mostly populated by fishermen— although there are some wealthy families on nearby estates around Bromwell."

I thought of Seraphina's father, the merchant. I wondered if she had lived in some lovely mansion just outside of town.

Simon smiled. "And you do remember that it was on the Orkney Islands that Victor Frankenstein created and then destroyed his monster's mate."

"And then the monster murdered his best friend, Henry," I said.

"Ah, you do recall the book details, then."

I bent to scratch Hugo's ears. I felt miserable, terrible for bringing Simon along on this trip when all of us might die. And yet I knew that I needed him.

"You should sleep, Abbie," he said gently. "We have several more hours of this journey, and I doubt you will sleep well on the carriage ride this evening."

Seeing the half-circles under his eyes, I almost suggested that he sleep, too. Sometimes I wondered if Simon ever slept. Nonetheless, the rational part of my brain knew that sleeping was the best thing I could do at the moment. I closed my eyes, not expecting to drift off, but I soon fell into a deep slumber.

It was then that the nightmare began.

Grandmother and I were walking Jupe near Highgate Cemetery. It was sometime in winter, as Grandmother and I were both bundled in wool hoods and muffs; light spits of snow fell on our faces. The sky was thick—a dullish gray. In reality, Grandmother and I never walked outside in such weather.

No constable stood in front of the cemetery. The atmosphere felt calm, and the gates to West Highgate Cemetery stood wide open.

Suddenly, Jupe, seeing something, broke away from his leash and ran through the gates into the cemetery. Grandmother shrieked. Dread overtook me, but I ran to catch the pug. After I entered the gates, the calm feeling evaporated. Like in so many dreams, my limbs felt as if I were moving through water. Jupe was always just beyond my reach. I would almost grab him, touching his tail even, and then he would dart ahead, slipping away behind another tombstone. I chased him deeper into the cemetery and the snow increased. When we reached Egyptian Avenue, I chased him into the shadowy entrance. My hood slipped away from my head as I ran faster, hoping that I might finally corner him.

As I entered a darkened corridor, I heard the scuffling of Jupe's nails around some crypts to my right. I darted that way and then all became silent. I could neither see nor hear Jupe and the air grew colder, freezing even, although I could no longer feel the gusts of wind from outside. Terror overtook me, and I knew that I was not alone.

"Abbie."

I heard my name spoken, immediately behind me. A whisper.

I whipped around.

Mariah.

I had not even heard her approach and now she stood inches from my face, her hair loose, sweeping thick and dark across her shoulders. In spite of the weather, she wore no shoes; in fact, she wore nothing except a long white gown, not even undergarments. In the dim light I saw her nipples, the rise and fall of her breasts beneath her gown.

Even amid my terror, I gasped at her loveliness. Sorrow and guilt spread through my chest.

"Abbie," she said again, moving even closer. I felt her breath on my cheek, saw my own breath puff before me.

Entranced, overwhelmed, I wanted to touch her.

"You're dead," I said sharply, trying to break the spell.

She smiled. It was a classic Mariah smile. Glorious and wicked.

She leaned toward my ear, as she used to when telling me a secret. I felt her lips brush against my skin, and I could not move as I smelled something sweetly rancid. Dizzied, I closed my eyes; my world spun.

"No," she whispered. "You are."

I opened my eyes again, and found myself in a coffin. Mariah was lying still, dead, a corpse beside me. I pounded the casket lid, screaming, suffocating, and frenzied.

I must have gasped in my sleep, because Simon was gripping my shoulder, and I saw an elderly female passenger glancing in my direction, clearly annoyed at my outburst.

"What is the matter, Abbie?" Simon asked.

I tried to suppress the terror that I felt. Then I saw more unfriendly gazes from the other few passengers as I struggled to regain my composure. "Just a nightmare."

The semicircular windows of the coach showed that night had come. Everything in the coach interior was dark, shadowed.

"We're almost to Edinburgh," Simon whispered quietly.

***

As Simon arranged for a carriage ride from Edinburgh to Caithness—paying extra, I was certain, for us to travel alone and to leave immediately—I scanned the busy train platform, waiting for his return. The platform was unusually busy for this time of night. It was difficult to see, amid all the harsh gaslight and foggy night air, but as I watched for Simon's tall form, I saw a flash of straight, ash-blond hair. It looked like the distinctive hair of the man I had seen in Highgate Cemetery that morning, near Mariah's grave. But when I looked again at that spot in the crowd, I saw nothing.

"We have to hurry, Abbie," Simon said, appearing quickly and taking my arm.

I cleared my throat and said nothing. After the nightmare, and with all the stress of the journey, I felt certain that my strained eyes were playing tricks upon me.

Once we were settled in the carriage and the journey began, I knew exactly why Simon had recommended that I sleep on the train. Although we were the only passengers, the ride was fast and jolty, and Hugo took up so much of the floor space, that it was impossible to sleep. Simon had mentioned that the trip would take at least four hours with no stops.

Perhaps it was the late hour, but I no longer felt like respecting Simon's many secrets. There was a reason behind his melancholy, his wintry eyes, and I felt determined to discover it. I thought of his refusal to tell me about his time in Africa.

"Simon. What happened in Africa?"

My voice sounded like a gunshot in the darkness, jolting and a little cruel.

He turned to look at me. A bit of moonlight shone through the drawn carriage drapes and I saw his face tighten a bit. "Abbie..."

"I know something happened, Simon. Something, I would guess, that you've never even told Rosamund about."

His lips tightened. I was correct.

"Please, Simon. We might all die anyway before this journey ends. Tell me."

He sighed. The carriage had suddenly become stuffy, cramped, so he opened the window. Cool, very cool air swept through the interior for a moment; I had forgotten how very far away from London we were. Both Simon and I remained silent as the carriage cooled for a few minutes. Then he shut the window and drew a breath.

His voice was low. Even. Barely audible. He pulled aside the curtains to look out the window, and I saw the sharp shadows of branches across his face.

"I have always been sober, distrustful, even disdainful of the life I lead in Kensington with my mother. Six years ago, before I attended medical school, I made a decision to also attend seminary. My mother, of course, was not terrible happy about that. Her brother-in-law, my Uncle Fitzwilliam, had become a priest as a young man, and after becoming a missionary, descended into the Congo and never returned. We knew where he was posted, near Port Francqui in the Belgian Congo. His mission was to convert and attend to the needs of the natives there, and he had every hope of being well-received, as I heard from my mother that he was of an intelligent and generous nature."

Simon turned back to look at me. "He wrote to us often. I listened eagerly to my mother read us his letters. This uncle, to my young mind, seemed to be living life the right way, not living in ease like myself and our other relatives. Rather, he was living a life abroad, a life of simplicity, serving others. Then suddenly his letters stopped. We assumed he was still at his missionary post, but my mother fretted occasionally. Then suddenly, a year later, when I was seventeen, we received a brief note telling us that everything at the post had gone well. He said that he was living in perfect community with the Congolese."

He looked at me hard. "I was young. The idea of that life seemed so inspiring. I had felt certain of my belief in God then—that God had purposes for men. I requested, from my mother, the funds to travel to Africa to meet with my uncle. She reluctantly agreed. Europe was just beginning to colonize in Africa, and the journey was very dangerous. But I was determined."

He paused, swallowed as if his throat were parched. I saw him look down at his long, pale, slender fingers in the dim coach light. "The journey was difficult and arduous. I became sick with ague for one week during it, but recovered quickly. Once I reached Port Francqui, I inquired about my uncle, asking many if they knew the whereabouts of Father Fitzwilliam St. John. What I learned from the local merchants in the area was that they had not seen him in three years. Apparently he'd gone off into the jungle and never returned.

"I found this odd, particularly since he had only recently written to us. I won't tire you with the details, but I remained at the Port Francqui post for a month. I realized that I wasn't going to get anywhere with the Europeans, even if I did speak Dutch moderately well. I studied and learned enough of the local Bantu to communicate with the native Congolese."

Hugo raised his head and growled as a dog barked somewhere in the distance. When he relaxed, Simon began speaking again. "We talk about imperialism like it is a noble concept, as if we are helping other nations. But we are not. I saw such terrible atrocities in the name of imperialism, and, I have heard that it has only become worse now that the area is completely controlled by King Leopold. Imperialism is an excuse for exploitation. It was only through communicating with the natives that I learned that there was talk of another post, somewhere deep in the interior of the jungle. I had difficulty getting information because few Congolese would talk of the place. Eventually, with extra money, I secured two guides to take me to this secluded post. It was a three-week journey, and I became covered in mosquito bites from head to foot. My leg was infected by a snake bite. Nonetheless, we eventually reached the post."

He stopped talking and stared at me as the carriage

lurched violently. We were ascending a hill, and the road seemed to be extremely rocky. Still, Simon's face remained immobile, statuesque, and I felt as if he were far from me.

"And then?" I whispered. A dread set in upon my heart. "When you reached it..."

I saw the weighted, anxious look in his eyes, the same look I had seen when my hypnosis session had gone terribly wrong and he'd kissed me, saving me from becoming lost in my psyche.

"We smelled the place before we saw it. It reeked of rotting flesh. My guides and I had had to put cloths around our faces to keep from fainting. And then we saw the spikes, on the walls surrounding the post. The spikes had heads: Men's heads. Women's heads." Simon paused. "Children's heads. Even the heads of infants. Many of the heads were no more than skulls. But some heads appeared to have been from recent deaths."

I put my hand over my mouth. Unable to speak, I thought I might vomit. I had never heard of anything so awful. I did not want him to continue, and yet I knew that he had to. I knew the weight of memories, and I knew that for his own sake, Simon could not carry his own in solitude forever.

"As we passed through the broken front gates, I saw that this 'missionary post' was merely a small village. It seemed empty. Isolated. The only thing greeting us was that smell of rotting flesh. The flies in that area were intolerable. I saw a few, very few, half-starved people—they had a distracted, fearful look in their eyes. Many were missing fingers, arms. I saw a five-year-old boy missing a leg. It was easy to locate my uncle, as he was in a large mud hut in the center of the village. When I entered the hut, I saw that he was nothing like the handsome, youngish man I had seen in Mother's photographs. He was thin, dreadfully thin. He wore a turban over his head and had markings upon his face. Crucifixes covered every inch of the wall behind his bed. Silver, golden, carved wood crucifixes. I saw a platter of raw meat in the corner of the hut.

"My uncle said nothing, but rather stared at me through deep hollow eyes, eyes that resembled so many of the skulls upon the village walls—expressionless, empty. He said nothing for so very long that I wondered if perhaps he had forgotten how to speak English. I hardly knew what to say, except to tell him who I was.

"But Uncle Fitzwilliam had not forgotten about our family. He suddenly spoke of how marvelous his post was, of how happy he was that I had decided to join him. He said he would send a servant with me to my quarters to make certain that I was comfortable after my long journey.

"I remember feeling speechless. It was as if he was ignorant of all the grotesquery surrounding us, of the almost empty village with its hollow-eyed, mutilated inhabitants.

"A native woman escorted us from the hut. She had all of her limbs and I suspected that she was my uncle's mistress. Something terrible was quickly becoming clear to me. The story behind this place was becoming clearer. As I walked beside her, with my guides at my side, I asked her in Bantu who God was. She pointed into the hut and explained that my uncle was God. As one of my guides questioned her further, I realized that my uncle had told them he was God—

that he was the true God. I learned that my uncle had taught them heresies, twisted the notions of communion and sacrifice to create a cannibalistic ritual system. The villagers I saw were the few natives who had stayed, who believed that my uncle was who he said he was, and they gladly gave up their limbs, their children even, for his cannibalistic appetites. He had told them that this was the only way to heaven. The eyes of that small boy haunted me. As I began to understand the situation, I found myself shaking, trembling violently. I was only eighteen then; I had grown up so sheltered—this sort of cruelty was catastrophic to me."

Simon paused again for several minutes before going on. This time I did not urge him on; I felt a tear slide down my cheek in the darkness. I had considered sharing the trauma of Mother's death, of losing Roddy, but I knew that my story paled in comparison to this. Another tear slid down my cheek. How could he keep this to himself for all of these years?

"I went into his hut again, and he was eating the meat from the platter. He ate it raw, and I still remember shuddering, knowing and believing that it was human flesh he consumed. But I had to be certain.

"'Who are you?' I asked him. 'God,' he replied, barely pausing as he chewed. I wondered how he could stay so thin if he ate human flesh so frequently. I knew that what I feared was true. He was delusional.

"'And who are these people to you?' I asked him. 'They are my followers. Gladly giving up their flesh for me.'

"I don't know what I was thinking, but I was terribly shocked, beyond belief, to hear him say it. I pulled out my revolver." Simon turned his gaze away from me. "And I shot him in the head.

"The mistress ran into the hut, wailing. She dropped to her knees. I took my guides around the village; we took account of all the huts and found that there were even fewer people there than I'd thought. Only twenty. I thought they might kill me for murdering their god, but they seemed too weary, too starved. The boy was the only living child. I took him with me when I left with my guides. I left a murderer."

I couldn't speak, yet I knew that I had to say something. I knew the anguish he felt, and I knew the powerlessness of words to comfort in such a situation. I had so little to offer him.

"You had no choice, Simon. He was killing, torturing people. That boy would have lost more limbs. Died."

Simon's face darkened. "I couldn't even save him. An infection had started in his leg. He died before we even reached Port Francqui."

Dawn was just breaking over the cliffs outside the window. I remembered that odd conversation we'd had on my first visit to the Conclave's home, as we stared at those cases of weaponry, of human hair. Simon had enigmatically mentioned his "search for God"—an odd comment for a theologian, I'd thought, but now I wondered if Simon believed in God at all.

"As you suspected, I have never told anyone what I just told you. Not even Rosamund. Upon returning, I simply told my mother that her brother-in-law had died from a fever—that he'd died before I arrived. She has no idea that

I killed him. It has haunted me over the years. He did terrible things..."

"He was a madman," I said.

"But he might have been institutionalized, perhaps." Simon rubbed his temples as if he had a headache.

I knew Simon was back in that terrible place, that he saw the faces of the dead, that he remembered vividly as in a photograph what he had done to his uncle. I remembered losing Roddy; I hadn't been able to save him, and, like Simon, I knew what it was to have killed. Our shared feelings of guilt, vinelike and strong, bound us together, and I felt them swell between us like a terrible energy as we prepared to face whatever was before us now. Tears fell down my cheeks, and I leaned forward across Hugo's enormous body to take Simon's hand.

"Simon."

I waited until he focused upon me, surfaced from his haunting memories. "Simon, I too share this albatross."

He said nothing, but I knew he heard my words, for I saw a ripple in his expression. As we finished the ride in silence, I felt a powerful connection with this man who had previously been so enigmatic. Simon knew the terrible weight of having to kill someone—even a heinous, murderous person. And now I understood more of his nature. He was haunted by his past, by what he had seen and by what he had done. And while William, Simon, and Christina shared my horrific experience of the Conclave and knew what I had done, Simon, thus far, had shouldered his burden alone.

Early morning light broke through cracks in the clouds outside the windows. I peered out, staring at the craggy beauty of the Highlands. I had never been north of Edinburgh before. Light fog stretched along the green pastures and rocky plains like an unyielding blanket. As the landscapes came into my view, their rose and periwinkle hues were resplendent in the morning mist.

I felt Simon's eyes on me, and I turned my head to meet his gaze. His expression no longer seemed veiled, but kind and open, which gave him an even more startling resemblance to a character in a Blake painting. I felt arrested and could not look away.

"Thank you, Abbie."

Twenty-four

When we stepped off the coach in Caithness, in the north-ernmost town of the county, we discovered that we would have to wait for several hours for our ferry. I groaned at this; William was just over the waters, and we were so close. Apparently a northern storm had blown in, and the ferry had been delayed for several hours as the waters were unusually choppy.

Simon and I took lunch at a local tavern. I had no appetite—I felt an unbearable anxiety to reach William. But Simon reminded me that eating, like sleeping, was necessary to keep my strength up.

"We're husband and wife," Simon said.

"What?" I said, almost choking on my overcooked mutton.

"The towns in this region are quite small. We cannot be seen traveling about unmarried. As I've already mentioned, we'll be outsiders. If we are to gather information, we must appear as benign, as ordinary as possible."

I couldn't believe that I had not considered this. I remembered all the times Mother and I had moved, how we sometimes had difficulty fitting into communities even larger than these.

"So, then, what am I to be called? Abbie St. John? Or are you to be Simon Sharp?" I asked wryly. I found that I was stabbing at my meat particularly hard. I couldn't wait for the storm clouds to roll away so that we could continue our journey. I hated this stall.

Simon smiled and took a sip of water. As he did, his eyes glinted and he stared out the window behind me. Then he froze.

"Abbie." He spoke quietly, but I heard him even above the noise of the loud tavern crowd. "We are being followed."

"Is it the same blond man who was following us in London?" I asked quickly. "I thought I saw him in Edinburgh, at the train platform. But I wasn't certain. I thought my mind was playing tricks on me, after that experience with Ellen at the London station."

Simon's eyes now turned to me. "He was walking down the street in front of this tavern, and he glanced through the window at us as he passed by. Of that I am certain. If you look quickly, I think you can still see him."

I turned and saw, just disappearing at the end of the street, the same straight ash-blond hair I'd seen before.

"I think that's him," I said.

"He must have followed us from London," Simon said thoughtfully, his eyes still on the street. He took a long sip of water.

"What could he want?"

"I don't know. We need to go about our business, but we must be watchful."

"I agree," I said in what I hoped was a confident tone, but I felt as if I stood at the base of a mountain—a mountain far too large to climb.

She hadn't meant to nearly kill him. She didn't want him dead. But she had forgotten how weak humans could be, and, well … he was barely breathing now. His face was pale, far too pale. It had been flushed with fever the past few days as the wounds oozed pus. The pus still seeped a bit, but the wounds were mostly dried and scabby. His body was wearying; he would not be able to fight the infection much longer. Seraphina surveyed all the dried blood on the mat surrounding him.

She sighed.

He had lost too much blood.

"You must keep him alive," Max had told her. "I need him."

That evening, almost three weeks ago, when she'd returned from devouring the young couple in the meadow near Bromwell, she'd felt her spirits rise at the sight of Max's boat, at seeing that he had returned to her.

"She turned us down," he had said, simply, informatively, as he dumped the unconscious body of the young man onto the floor of the great hall. Seraphina had knelt over the body. She'd only just transformed back to her human form, and she felt water still sliding from her wet hair down her naked body. The boy her keeper had brought her was young and strikingly handsome, with dark wet curls on his head and flushed, vibrant skin. His breathing was even but shallow. Undoubtedly Max had drugged him.

"You've wanted more responsibility in our Conclave, so we are offering you the task of killing her," Max had said. "This is our bait, our lure." He stared at the young man in the puddle of water on the floor and then shook his head vigorously, flinging the rain out of his curls. "Arabella Sharp deserves a cruel death." Max's eyes lingered upon Seraphina. "And I think that my lovely Effie will be up to the task."

Seraphina had felt herself blush at the compliment.

"Who is he to her?" she asked. "Her brother?"

"Unfortunately, her paramour," Max said quietly, his lip crinkled upwards in a cruel grin. He looked down at the body, disdain in his voice. "He's a hot-headed prig, daft and foolish, still … try not to kill him."

Seraphina felt a cruel pain. It was a stab of empathy for the young man, as he was the most handsome man she had ever seen. Furthermore, although he was more attractive than her fiancé had been, his face shared some physical similarities with her own paramour.

"I brought feed for the animals, and then I have to leave."

"Tonight?" Seraphina asked, her hopes dashed. She'd wished that Max would stay longer, particularly since he had been away for so long.

"Yes, I have important business in London. Miss Sharp will soon be on her way here. Once everyone is certain that William here has not eloped and that he is not traveling abroad, they will suspect I have taken him. When Miss Sharp arrives here, kill her." His eyes glinted and became distant. "And kill anyone who might come with her. She might have a friend, a pale-faced young man. He should be an easy kill—but be careful, my Effie. He's smart. Very intelligent."

"And this one—William—I mean, what happens to him after I've finished with her?" Seraphina looked down at the young man's body. She tasted the venom in her mouth and felt her stomach growl for human flesh. Odd. She was in her human form, and that had never happened before. The transformation seemed to haunt even her human form now.

"No." Max looked at her seriously, his eyes bright in the darkness. "As I said, keep William alive, and I'll return later for him. He needs to know what I can do—he needs to see you kill Miss Sharp, to know what lovely monsters I have to do my bidding. I need him. I have a bit of a large project I am working on back in London, and it turns out that this young man, Dr. William Siddal, is rather important to me."

William had stirred a bit, the drugs wearing off. "And whatever you do, don't let him escape. We shall secure him now."

After moving William to a mat on the floor of her bedroom, they locked shackles around his wrists and one around his neck. He was then secured to a column between her bed and the fireplace. Seraphina had wondered, then, what it was that Max needed from this young man, other than to serve as a lure for Arabella Sharp. She remembered the Conclave's many experiments, their many projects, and bit her lip thinking of how she had been the unintended result of one of those projects. But she had learned not to ask too many questions;

Max already shared so much with her, probably more than the Conclave ever intended. She always hoped that at some point her distracted lover would come around, would see how valuable she could be to him. That night, she'd hoped his disappointment with Arabella's decision would prompt him to realize her own worth.

Seraphina had thought of the young woman who was coming to save William. *Arabella.* She'd spoken the girl's name quietly to herself, in the shadows of her bedroom, as Max left to ready his boat for the journey back to the mainland. He had to leave quickly, as a storm was blowing in. *Arabella.* Foolish girl—she could have the world at her fingertips. She could have everything that Seraphina had longed for, and yet this Arabella Sharp had turned down all of that.

On that night, Seraphina had walked outside with Max to watch him leave. She'd felt an emptiness, a loss of their old intimacy, and tried to push away darker thoughts—suspicions that her bond with him had never truly existed. Shivering, she'd clutched her arms about her body in the cold wind. She'd donned a robe, her favorite gauzy lavender robe that Max had brought to her from Venice a few years back. He'd also brought her the pearl-colored slippers she wore. But these were no protection against the elements, and she shivered again, violently. Although the rain at this point was light, featherlike, the wind swept in from the ocean in great blasts.

"I hear you have been straying from your typical meals," Max had said before stepping into his small boat.

Seraphina had blushed, remembering how angry he'd

been when she had tried to attack him back in November. She had not wanted to make him angry. She felt her lip tremble.

"I am sorry," she said. "I had not heard from you in so long. I did not know if you would return, and ... I was hungry."

He held her to his shoulder, patted her head. "There, there ... do not cry." He tightened his embrace, kissed her temple.

And then a strong blast blew up—scattering some papers, what looked like letters, from the front of the boat.

Quickly, she pulled away from him and helped collect the letters before they fell into the waters or were damaged in the rain.

He thanked her, kissed her again, and promised to return to her sometime after she had slayed the girl. *But be prepared*, he had told her. Arabella Sharp would be there in a few weeks.

As Max rowed his boat away and she turned to walk back inside her house, she saw that she had missed one of the papers. The wind and rain were whipping even harder, and she fought to stay upright as she walked toward the paper and picked it up. It had been glued to a rock by the pounding rain, and when she opened it, only one line was readable. She frowned, not knowing what it meant, but saved it nonetheless.

When she returned downstairs that evening, she had hope that William might regain conscious. But he remained unconscious for the rest of the night and for half of the next day. It was only on the following evening that he awoke. She was sitting in front of the fireplace, near the place where he lay, painting, in large brush-strokes, another portrait of her keeper.

This time, she painted his eyes dark, darker than they actually were. She painted them such a dark green that they were nearly black—for they seemed black to her then, a library of secrets.

"She'll kill you."

Seraphina had turned sharply, seeing the beautiful young man still lying on the ground, the shackles about his neck. She'd expected him to fight against the restraints once he awoke, for she'd seen the bruises, the marks upon his body and knew that he had probably fought against Max. But now he was weary, and wisely knew a fight would be futile.

Seraphina had smiled. She had ignored him. But as she painted, she kept feeling William's eyes upon her, his gaze fiery and unnerving.

"I know your plan," he said. "I heard what you're planning to do to Abbie Sharp. It will never work."

Although she said nothing, she felt her hand shake a bit. William had a scratch on his arm, and she smelled blood even from it. Her stomach growled.

William laughed. It was a mocking laugh. "What has Max told you? It sounded like he has not told you what happened to the rest of the Conclave."

She looked sideways at him. Glared. Then returned to her painting. "They are in London still, last I've heard."

William threw back his head and laughed. He roared with a hearty, frenzied laugh that echoed throughout the bedroom and the great hall. After several moments, he straightened his head and considered her seriously. She felt her hand tremble; the paint under the brush had dribbled,

bled black upon the canvas. She felt fear rise within her. Then the fear gave way to rage.

"You're a pretty but foolish one," William had said contemptuously. "What are you? One of his whores?" The rage continued to rise within her as his voice trailed off. "I'm weary of foolish women. Poppets. Pretty, stupid things." He paused. "Like you."

She'd felt the venom flow a bit, in her mouth. Her hand trembled even more. Violently this time. How dare he? She tried to control her breathing, but she could not. She snapped her paintbrush handle. She tasted the venom again; this time it pooled on her tongue and she wiped a trickle of the fluid away from the corner of her mouth.

William's voice had sharpened. "They're all dead except for Max, you know. She killed them all." He gave that terrible laugh again. "She nearly beheaded Reverend Perkins."

Seraphina stood up from her painting stool, looking down upon him. "You lie."

He laughed, crossed his arms over his chest, the chains making a terrible rattling noise. "Never. I never lie. Max lies, though—all the time. Abbie Sharp killed the Conclave last November, immediately after refusing their offer. If you think you have a bustle-clad, well-behaved London miss coming here who can barely lift a teacup, you couldn't be more wrong. She killed them all. She'll kill you easily."

Seraphina couldn't repress it anymore. "Do you know what I am?" she roared, feeling her insides shake as if they were on fire.

But he didn't look a bit afraid. She smelled his blood once again. The smell was overwhelming, and her stomach continued to growl. She remembered how her breathing had quickened in that moment. Max *wouldn't* lie to her. The Conclave couldn't be gone. What would happen to her if they were? They were the only ones who knew how to make the elixir. And who was this pert young man?

He was her prisoner. She could kill him in one bite.

She stood immediately in front of him, trying to control her rage. Again, she asked: "Do you know who I am?"

She was wearing one of her favorite gowns, one her keeper had brought back to her two years before from Paris. She wasn't about to rip it because of this stupid young man before her. But she couldn't help herself. Since returning to her diet of human flesh, she'd found it harder and harder to control her transformations. And then it happened. In one instant, her painting bib burst and her lamia body exploded out of the dress, tearing it to pieces.

At the sight of her, the confident, darkened expression had melted away from the young man's face. But he'd seemed not so much fearful as bewildered. As bewildered as all of her victims were, not trusting their own eyes. It was always the same expression. William, like all of those she killed, thought he was in a beautiful, terrible dream.

"It cannot be," he had said, amazement upon his face.

It was then that she'd taken her first bite. Lurching forward, she ripped his shirt apart with her claws and bit him hard in the chest, avoiding his jugular, the place where she usually dealt her fatal blow. He screamed out in pain, and Seraphina tasted the faint traces of chloroform and alcohol in his blood. The distaste of this might have saved his life, as it prevented a feeding frenzy. She pulled back and steadied herself hard, to control her breathing.

Do not kill him.

Do not kill him.

Do not kill him.

William was screaming and writhing in pain, and she saw the bite wound on his chest oozing blood. She saw that her talons had punctured his shoulders and chest as well, from when she had grabbed him. She watched him yell for a few minutes and realized that he could not merely be screaming over the wounds, which were deep but certainly not fatal. Rather, he screamed as her venom swept through the veins like fire.

She steadied herself again, but she could not will her human form to come. She'd thought he would be fearful of her, that he would be quiet after this attack. If he did remain quiet, and if she could stand the sight of him—his fresh flesh and the smell of his blood—she might even help attend to his wounds. After all, she wasn't supposed to kill him.

To her surprise, William recovered his composure after only a few minutes. Although she saw that his expression was still contorted in pain, his face had turned scarlet in anger and he'd strained hard, jerking both arms hard against the restraining shackles.

"Bitch! Freak!" he screamed. "What are you? One of Robert Buck's specimens? Something he found in the Amazon? In the wild somewhere? Let me out of these, and I'll tear your throat out. She'll still kill you. And if you hurt her—if you hurt her at all, I'll tear you to pieces myself. I will not let you hurt her!"

She couldn't help it. She lunged at him again, this time biting his thigh, hard. She tried to keep the bite from going too deep, but she wanted to make it hurt. She wanted so badly to hurt him, to eat his heart.

The venom and blood dripped from her face.

Leave. Leave. She knew that if she didn't leave immediately, she would kill him.

Still quaking, she felt confused and baffled—both by him and by what he had said. She could kill him quickly, swiftly, and yet he had yelled at her that way, called her a freak. Her mind flashed back to when she had transformed in front of her fiancé, his reaction ...

Who does William think he is?

"One of Robert Buck's specimens." Those had been his most infuriating words. She tried to forget the words, knowing that in a way, she was indeed one of Robert Buck's experiments. She ran through the doors of her bedroom into the empty hall, surrounding herself with all the half-finished portraits. Most were of the members of the Conclave. She felt their eyes then upon her, staring at her. Robert. Julian. Marcus. John. Were they indeed dead? Could that even be possible? Had Abbie Sharp killed them?

Seraphina's bewildered emotions coursed through her. She had thought that they would help her someday, that Robert would find a cure, that they would make her one of them. Although she hadn't seen the Conclave in almost a century, they had become protective fathers to her in her mind. However, like her own father, who had never quite accepted her, the Conclave seemed troubled by her very existence. And in that moment, as she'd stood in the great hall, she'd been forced to face the truth: that they cared as little for her as Joseph Umphrey had.

These thoughts were too much, too heavy. And how could she make sense of the Conclave, of her life, when her only link to reality had always been Max? He had loved her. She thought of all those nights they'd spent together. He must love her.

She had run up the stairs, gotten herself outside, before she could change her mind and finish her attack. She dove into the water, swimming deeper and deeper into the icy depths, her gills pulsating under the currents. She needed to hunt fish. But she also wanted flesh, human flesh, and she knew the temptation would be too much if she headed toward the shore near Bromwell. She'd seen the boat parties during the day, and at night, their lanterns scanning the waters around the shore.

Except to pour water and broth down his throat, Seraphina had tried to avoid contact with William since her attack upon him that first evening. The smell of his blood was too tempting for her. It had been almost three weeks now since Max had brought her William, and thus the Sharp girl should be arriving soon. Seraphina hungered for her more and more, each time she restrained herself from biting William again. But her willpower was weakening, weakening to the point where she did not trust herself even to clean his wounds.

She wondered exactly when Abbie Sharp would arrive.

In the firelight of her bedroom, she watched William as he lay upon his blood-soaked mattress. In the days following her attack upon him, he had faded in and out of consciousness and his words had been nonsensical, delirious. Now he had not moved in four days; the venom, infection, and loss of blood had taken its toll. He would be dead soon.

Seraphina sighed. This was not what she had wanted, and for the first time in a century, she regretted her rotten temper.

Twenty-five

When Simon and I finally stepped off of the ferry onto the muddy shores of Bromwell, Hugo by our side, I saw that this town was even smaller than the last. Houses lined the streets tightly, uneven but clustered together as if for protection against the strong Arctic winds. We held on to our luggage and scanned the place. I smelled the strong odor of sea, the odor of fish, everywhere we walked. The storm had diminished and the sun now shone brightly, glaring white as it reflected off the roofs of the houses.

After Simon inquired about the location of an inn, we began walking through the town. As we walked, I saw sketches of the lamia posted on many of the shop doors. Many sketches advertised rewards for the creature's body. If she hadn't been real in my mind, it would have seemed so peculiar as to be almost humorous.

As we stood in front of some sketches, I said quietly to Simon, "At least we know for sure that she exists, and that she's been attacking people here. We know that that part of what Max has said is true."

"Yes, our lady has created quite a stir," Simon replied.

My nerves felt more heightened. We were so close to William, and he was in the clutches of this creature. My anxiety increased by the second.

"We don't need rooms," I muttered grumpily as we walked across town toward the inn.

"Abbie," Simon said, nearly cutting me off. "Now that we're here, we need to study the map carefully. As I've explained, we must do this patiently if we are going to be successful. We might even need to study the shoreline. Remember, even the people here do not know of this island. We need to formalize a plan, and to do this, we need rooms."

I knew that what he was saying made sense, but I felt my blood rush through me. Hard. I couldn't imagine sleeping or studying at that moment. The sword case felt heavy in my hands, and I wanted to act.

After securing a room for ourselves as husband and wife, we spent the evening studying the map. I felt more practical about our planning. I pulled out the bowie knife and two of my old tournament knives from Dublin. They were a bit rusted, but still gleamed sharp in the dingy room's light.

I took the sword out of its case. It was a thin blade—Parisian. The hilt was ivory, solid to the touch. I saw, almost with revulsion, the Conclave's symbol engraved upon the hilt.

A Posse Ad Esse.

"This was their sword," I said, almost to myself. "I'm not used to swords."

"Take it." Simon said, not even looking up from the map, which he had spread out at the desk in front of him. He had brought several books along for the journey, too: one about the Orkney Islands and another about mythical creatures. He had also brought Charles Darwin's *On the Origin of Species*. He had all of the books open before him on the desk. "We don't know what we're up against. We should take everything—the knives, the sword. I brought a revolver."

I walked behind Simon, stepping over Hugo as I peered at the open books. Simon's usually smooth-as-marble forehead wrinkled as he studied. I saw that he had written notes in nearly all of the margins of his books.

"Abbie. How large was the lamia in your visions?"

"I think about eight or ten feet. Significantly larger than a tall woman."

He sighed and ran his fingers through his hair as I returned to inspecting the weapons. "We can't be certain of her traits at all, at this point," he said. "We keep calling her a lamia, but we cannot assume that she is like the literary or mythological lamia at all. If she has a mix of species in her structures, which she might, considering Robert Buck's extensive travels and studies, she likely has some undiscovered species, possibly even extinct species, within her."

"You mean, like dragons or dinosaurs?" I asked as I began sharpening my bowie knife.

"I do." Simon closed the book and stood. "Most mythological creatures have been based on real, actual creatures.

Many share similarities to fossils. I am not aware of any current ten-foot lizards that can swim or stand on two legs, but as I have stated, it is possible that Robert Buck used the essences of extinct creatures. I simply don't know. I'm only theorizing. And frankly, I'm infuriated by our lack of information. In light of this, we must consider all possibilities."

"I feel as if we might be walking into an ambush. We are up against an enemy that we do not fully understand," I said wearily.

"We are," Simon replied. "We're going to have to be sharp, figure her out quickly as we go—second by second. Is she venomous? How far can she leap? Can she see better in light or dark? What are her weaknesses? We must continuously figure out these sorts of questions once we see her."

"What we need to do is to find somebody not just to take us out to the island, but someone who knows something about the nature of these attacks," I said quietly.

Simon rubbed his eyes. I knew my heart was more into this than his, that Simon probably blamed William for getting himself into this mess in the first place. In his inebriated state, William must have been an easy capture for Max.

"I wonder . . . " Simon's voice trailed off wearily. Evening had begun to set in and the room had darkened. He stood up from the desk and paced a little, near the window. "I wonder why, although she's been in service to them for almost a century, she would feel the need to go on a killing spree now. What spurred her to do this?"

"It could be anything," I replied. Through a nearby window, I scanned the horizon, out over the roofs of the village homes that blocked our view of the sea. I recalled the rage I had felt when William told me about his past, about his dalliance with Jane Morris. I felt almost ashamed of it now, even though my feelings of anger at the way he had treated me persisted. I then remembered my conversation with Christina as we stood in my closet. "Of all the mysteries about this creature, we can be sure of one thing…"

Simon lifted his head to look at me. His hair became a halo, caught in the bronze light of the setting sun.

"She is part woman," I said. "Of that we can be certain."

Simon suddenly stepped toward me, caught my hand, and lightly kissed my fingers—the shock of his gesture felt lovely to me. He had never done that before, and I realized that I had still not sorted out my feelings for him. I felt my heart upon the bough again.

He looked quickly away, his pale face reddened slightly; I couldn't take my eyes off of him in that moment—he was so beautiful in the sunlight. "You are correct about that, Abbie. But her woman-ness will make her all the more unpredictable."

We walked to Bromwell's only tavern to take dinner that evening, hoping to learn something, if anything, about the attacks and to secure a reliable guide. Then we could go across the waters to meet Seraphina. I had insisted that we leave for her island tonight.

As we approached the pub, I saw a large man seated near

the doors, his hat pulled over his face. I noticed longish gray tufts of hair hanging out from under his hat. I signaled for Hugo to sit, and he lay down near the entrance.

If it hadn't been for our long journey, Simon and I would have looked very out of place. But my hair had fallen from its prim knot and felt ratted and tangled; my dress, which I had worn since yesterday, was untidy and wrinkled now, with mud splatters from when Simon and I had stepped off the ferry. Simon was not dressed in black, as usual; he wore only a white shirtsleeve and muddied brown trousers. Even so, he maintained the angelic aura about him.

"We should fit in," I said, quietly. "We look as if we've been fishing all day."

Simon glanced down at me, amused. "We don't fit in at all," he said, holding the door open for me. I saw immediately that we were Londoners. My dress, even with the wrinkles and mud stains, seemed overly prim and formal, and sported far too many buttons.

The place was small and crowded. As we stepped inside, the smell of ale, grease, and dirt assaulted my nose, and I felt at least fifty pairs of eyes upon us—probably half the population of the town.

Simon and I seated ourselves, and I felt my face turn scarlet.

"Whit will ye be havin' tae eat?" the tavern keeper asked when she came over to greet us. Even though I had worked in a charity hospital for prostitutes, I had never seen a dress so low. While I gawked, Simon calmly told her what we would be eating.

When our food arrived, I found that I had no appetite. I knew we were supposed to behave naturally, but my heart pounded. My ears rang and my stomach twisted upon itself. I couldn't do this. I couldn't conduct a normal conversation knowing that William was near death somewhere not very far from us.

The tavern keeper eyed Simon and me carefully when she brought out our ales. I watched, amazed, as Simon charmed her, bringing the conversation around to the curious sketches of the monster displayed on the buildings of the town.

I saw the woman's lips tighten at this, and I wondered if the people of Bromwell were touchy about their local monster. Her gaze became unfriendly and she stopped speaking to Simon immediately. We noticed, after our meals came, that the gazes from other Bromwell natives became steelier. Although Simon masked his emotions well, my nervousness continued to mount and I felt as if going to this pub had been a futile and disastrous endeavor.

We are wasting time.

I think Simon felt the same, because very soon, we left, calling Hugo to come with us; we walked away as quickly as we could. The cool night air had set in, and I could see our breaths puff out in the shadows.

I was about to ask Simon about their strange reaction, but I heard footsteps behind us—steps in the dirt. Just as Hugo began to growl, I turned around, immediately on my guard and thinking that it might be the ash-haired stranger. But I saw then that our follower was the gray-haired man who had been seated near the door of the pub.

Hugo continued to growl, but Simon calmly silenced him with a wave of his hand.

"Whit is yer interest in th' monster?" he asked. At first, I thought it was a threat, but his tone did not seem threatening. It seemed merely inquisitive.

Unsure of how to answer him, we said nothing.

"Coz ah saw ye Londoners git off th' ferry today. We don't git many visitors like ye."

"Our reasons for being here are personal." Simon said quietly. Then I saw Simon pause and gaze thoughtfully at the man, assessing him. I knew that he was trying to read the man's character. *Please Simon,* I thought. *Think of a way to get him to help us.*

"One of our friends, from London, stayed here recently, on vacation," Simon began. "He disappeared, and we're trying to find him."

The man said nothing, and I believed now that he was trying to discern our character.

Simon continued, knowing that we would need to provide more information. "More specifically, from what we have learned, our friend went out into the waters in a boat. He never came back."

"Yer friend is dead," the man said quickly.

I started to retort, but Simon laid his hand on my back and asked the man quietly, "Why are you here?"

The man's nervousness increased. "We don't loch talkin' abit it. We hav' enough jokes abit us believin' in monsters in our lochs and aw 'at."

I saw, in the moonlight, that he was not as old as I had

first thought. No older than perhaps his late fifties. He seemed hardscrabble, as if he had been out in the sun every day of his life, but there was also a vulnerable nervousness about his demeanor in this moment.

He looked sideways, back in the direction of the tavern. "Ah wuz watchin' ye baith through th' window, and ah think ye know mair than yoo're sayin'."

Simon's expression must have brought affirmation to the older man, because he continued talking.

"That thing out thaur in th' waters killed mah granddaughter. She was aroond yer age," he said, pointing one thick finger in my direction. "If yer friend was here, and he disappeared in those waters, it's likely she got 'im."

Perhaps it was impetuous, but I said quickly, "We think we know where the creature is."

The man's eyes widened. "That so?"

The three of us stood in awkward silence for a full minute. The man was the first to speak.

"Neil MacDiarmand," he said quietly. After Simon and I introduced ourselves, as husband and wife of course, Neil glanced around to make sure no one was nearby. "Come wi' me, and we'll talk."

His house, nearby, looked like so many of the other houses in town—small, cottage-like. His wife, like the man, had a sunburned face. Her grayish red hair reminded me quite a bit of Ellen's, but the resemblance stopped there. She seemed so melancholy, so bleak. As she stood in the kitchen, wiping her hands on a rag, her eyes appeared so dark and void that she seemed almost dead. I thought of the grief she must have experienced, losing her granddaughter.

Still, she greeted us politely and brought us steaming cups of tea; she even took a bowl of water outside for Hugo.

At the table, Simon pulled the folded map from his pocket. "We believe she's here," I said, pointing to the specific island Max had marked.

Neil took a long sip of tea and studied the map. "Whaur did ye' fin' this?"

I glanced at Simon, feeling slightly nervous, not knowing how we could explain it. Simon, however, seemed unalarmed and spoke confidently. "We have researched the area, the geography. Based on the locations of the murders, we estimate that her lair would be in this place."

"We want to go there, to this place, to see if she's there," I said firmly. My impatience had mounted to the point of being unbearable. "We want to go there to find her and possibly find our friend, but we don't know these waters, so we need someone who does know them to take us there."

I felt almost like a madwoman, speaking so bluntly, and I knew Simon would have eased more smoothly into asking Neil for his help. Neil eyed me sharply, his eyes a lovely glassy gray, bright against his tawny skin. We were all quiet, around the table. The room was lit only by the nearby fireplace and a few tallow candles. I heard Hugo bark from the front porch.

Finally, after a few moments, Neil spoke. "Ah'll go wit ye, but this might be a fool's errain. Why, there's nae inhabited islands in that place. Only rocks. Rocks we'll smash against if we go at the wrong point of day, fer certain."

"We have reason to believe she is there. We must at the very least find and explore the area," I said urgently. Simon shot me a split-second gaze, and I realized that I hadn't taken a single sip from my teacup. Although my stomach churned, I immediately took a sip in order to appear sociable.

Neil finished his tea and sighed. "Best time to go out will be early mornin'. Three o'clock. I don't want people around here knowin' I've befriended ye."

I took another sip of the hot tea. "*Why* are you befriending us?" I asked. Other people in Bromwell had lost loved ones; I didn't understand why Neil had sought us out, why he was troubling himself for us.

He was quiet for a moment, then finished his tea and sighed. "Ah'll show ye. Go up that stair."

We followed his wife, who had just come in from outdoors, up a creaky set of stairs until we were at a room at the top of the house. She opened the door to a small bedroom. It was simple, like the rest of the house, but had been brightly painted. Whitewashed. In a small bed with a lace coverlet lay a little girl, no more than seven or eight years old. She had long stringy dark hair and her eyes were black and hollow. She lay on her side, unmoving, not speaking, as if she was unaware that we were there. The woman sat by her bed and stroked the girl's hair gently. The child clutched a one-eyed, threadbare doll in her hands.

I had seen this look on a few of the children in the hospital—most of them had been beaten. We'd had one terrible situation soon after I began working at Whitechapel, where a young girl had been raped by her drunken uncle. She came to us with her wounds, along with the same hollow, terrible look. Trauma.

I sat at the end of the bed, near the child's feet.

The girl did not look down at me, even as the bed moved with my weight. She did not speak.

"How long has she been like this?" I asked the woman.

"Three weeks," she said. "Ever since … "

She didn't continue, but I intuitively knew what she could not speak of, the root of her speechlessness.

The attack.

There was no point in talking about it in the room. The woman stayed with the child, and as soon as we closed the door and were in the narrow hallway outside the room, Simon whispered, "The child witnessed the attack?"

Neil nodded. I could see, under the wrinkles in his face, that he was still highly affected by the state of the child. "She did. Her older sister, Margaret, was to git married next month. She and her fiancé were in a meadow, on the northern part of the shore. My Laura had arrived there to meet her and saw the attack upon 'er sister. She saw 'er sister devoured before 'er eyes. And she saw the beast."

"The lamia," I said, stunned, feeling coldness creep through my veins. William was still with that creature.

"The child is a strong one," Neil said quietly. "She'll be fine. But ah don't feel safe til the beast is gone—she's smart—been livin' in these waters for years. Mostly left us alun. But not lately. Disturb'd, she is. Ah can't let mah Laura out of the house wit' this she-wolf still alive. Ah wan mae grandchild to be saf' agin. Their father, mah son, is dead. Their mother gone. Ah've raised them. This beast, this creature, has taken everything from me. Ah've ridden my boat out at nights, in the places the search parties have not been. She's out there, she is. Ah've seen the gleam of her back in the distance."

We spent the next hour discussing where and when we would meet him.

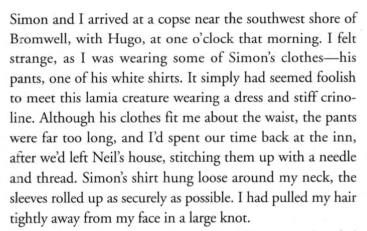

Simon and I arrived at a copse near the southwest shore of Bromwell, with Hugo, at one o'clock that morning. I felt strange, as I was wearing some of Simon's clothes—his pants, one of his white shirts. It simply had seemed foolish to meet this lamia creature wearing a dress and stiff crinoline. Although his clothes fit me about the waist, the pants were far too long, and I'd spent our time back at the inn, after we'd left Neil's house, stitching them up with a needle and thread. Simon's shirt hung loose around my neck, the sleeves rolled up as securely as possible. I had pulled my hair tightly away from my face in a large knot.

My heart pounded as we waited. I felt as I used to feel when anticipating a knife tournament in Dublin, but this endeavor was so much costlier, so much more frightening.

William was so much on my mind.

Simon and I sat, leaning against a rotten tree trunk in the reflecting light of the water. Hugo lay beside me, looking out over the waves. Occasionally, he perked his head up, laid his eyes back, and growled or whined, and I wondered what he sensed out in the depths. I knew that we all might die, and so much remained unspoken between Simon and myself.

"Abbie," Simon said suddenly, quietly. "You are under no obligation to love me."

I laughed a little as a tear slid down my face. I had always felt amazed at Simon's level of perception, at his ability to know how to read me, how to read my heart.

I looked at him, feeling as if I might split in two. The sea roared ahead of us and a breeze pushed through his curls. This situation was so different from the one last fall, when I had rejected Simon's proposal of marriage. I had not known him well then. The break from William had, painfully, allowed me to see Simon's heart—to know that he did not merely *seem* good, true, constant. He *was* good and true and constant. And we were so similar. The story he had told me of Africa ... for someone to live through what he had and to still believe in humanity at all ... it was nothing short of miraculous. I felt another tear slide down my cheek and I choked awkwardly.

Simon leaned forward, wiped the tear away.

"I'm sorry, Simon. You are so bloody perfect for me—in every way. Grandmother would even approve. I do love you, but ... " How did I explain that the love I felt for Simon was too temperate? My thoughts didn't make sense even to me, and yet I knew the choice had already been made. In spite of good reason and judgment, I knew, suddenly, that I had and always would love William.

Simon leaned forward and kissed my lips lightly, in what I knew would be our last kiss. This journey to the Orkney Islands marked the end of so much. I tried clumsily to speak, but Simon placed his finger upon my lips, urging me not to speak another word.

A streak of green light flashed across his pale face, and I turned out to the water to see where it came from. In what was probably the most beautiful sight I had ever seen, I saw what looked like enormous green yarns, green serpents, glowing beautifully, weaving themselves across the dark skies as if alive. Flashes of fires. I had never seen anything like it, but scenes from "The Rime of the Ancient Mariner" came to my mind—"a hundred fire-flags sheen."

I murmured the line under my breath.

"Northern lights," Simon said, gazing out, and I knew that he had heard me. I looked out at the display with him, and then I felt his eyes upon me.

"It's beautiful," I whispered. The beauty only made my heart more sorrowful.

"Odd," Simon responded, his light blue eyes focused over the waters again. "They appear more often in winter. But this is lovely."

The lights played around his hair in slithering auras. His beauty, as it had back at the inn earlier this evening, almost overwhelmed me. Yet, I knew he was not my own. I also knew in that moment, tragically, that I was the only person he would ever love. This realization came instinctually. There would be no one else for Simon St. John.

"I'm sorry, Simon," I said again. It sounded weak. Pathetic.

He turned in the darkness to face me just as an intense streak of light fell upon us, illuminating our forms, blinding me for one second before I could refocus on Simon's face in the darkness.

"Inexplicable," he whispered. "Wild. Unruly. And yet the lights still stir the heart."

More tears now. I knew his point, deftly identifying the nature of my love for William.

He reached for my hand, and somehow this felt more intimate than the kiss had. "It's all right, Abbie." He paused, looked away. His voice cracked. I saw a tear in his eye. "There are some matters, some paths of the heart, that even the will cannot conquer."

A little before three o'clock, even amidst the night winds, we heard Neil's boat approaching us, softly coursing near the shore.

"Our ride," Simon said gently, helping me rise and leading me down the rocky mounds to the water.

Part IV

"O fair and strong and terrible! Lioness
That with your long locks play the Lion's mane!"

—*The Princess*

Twenty-six

A storm rolled in as we neared the island. Indeed, the island seemed to be all rocks—a small sharp bundle of cliffs and crevices jutting out in all directions, a craggy, pointed starfish. I would not have noticed the place if we had not been looking for it—the island seemed to rise up from the waves only when we were almost upon it. Even Neil said that he had been in the area but had never seen it. "Th' currents veer away," he said. "E'en on sunny days, a blankit ah mist settles in the area an' it's guid as covered."

We had been forced to steer the dory hard against the current, and then, just as we almost reached the shore, fighting to near it, the current altered course and began sucking the boat violently toward the rocks.

"Paddle 'arder!" Neil shouted over the winds, just as we were almost dashed against a towering cliff wall. Hugo lost his balance and fell hard against the side of the boat, nearly tipping us. It was only when we steadied and escaped the sucking current that I felt myself breathe again. But the moment we steadied, Neil shouted at us to veer sharply again, and we washed up on—or rather, crashed upon—a narrow, almost hidden strip of sand. The boat slid so violently onto it that both Hugo and I were thrown out of the dory, landing hard onto the packed wet sand.

As Neil secured the boat and Simon checked his medical bag to make certain that the supplies he brought for attending to William hadn't been damaged on the rain-soaked journey, I surveyed our surroundings and checked our weapons. I had my own knives strapped tightly to me, and I'd taken the sword out of its case. Neil had brought gunpowder, but that, like Simon's revolvers, had been soaked during the journey.

"Useless." I cursed and tossed them back into the boat.

"It doesn't matter," Simon said quietly, placing the useless revolver in his medical bag. "You're more comfortable with the knives, at any rate."

Hugo uttered a low growl, and the hair on his neck stood on end. I felt goose bumps rise all over my skin; we were all highly alert.

Taking out my bowie knife, I stared above us at the cliffs. Seraphina could be anywhere—in the surrounding waters, somewhere in her underground home waiting for us. She could even be in the rocks looming above us, crouched in a crevice, ready to pounce like a terrible mountain lion.

The sheets of rain had ceased a bit, but thunder roared in the distance and the wind had picked up, even more so than when we were crossing the water. The storm was far from over.

"We're too exposed," Simon whispered as we eased away from the boat.

"We must get underground," I whispered. I turned to Neil. "You have been so kind to bring us here. You should stay here with the boat." It was me that she wanted; at least Neil might have a slim chance of escaping if Simon and I were murdered inside the lair. I remembered that little girl, and I wanted her grandfather to arrive home to her, safe.

"Nae. I'm stayin' with ye." His answer carried a stubborn tone with which I could not argue. And although I wished he would stay on the shore, his bravery bolstered me a bit. I tried to ignore how violently my hand shook as I held the bowie knife.

Simon insisted on going first, and, trying to watch everything at once, I followed him and Hugo away from the sandy strip, toward the peak of rocks. Neil followed me. Simon carried the sword, and I gave Neil one of my two short-bladed throwing knives.

Simon led us to a narrow crevice in the rock wall.

The crevice was so narrow that it looked almost as if Simon had stepped into the rock. I tried to push away images in my mind of Seraphina habitually slipping, silently, serpent-like, into that place.

Following Simon, I glanced behind me. Neil was behind me, close and alert.

A narrow stone staircase descended downward.

Dull light seeped up the staircase from far below us, and I recalled the eerie glow of the jellyfish tank in the Conclave's home. Images of my terrifying experience there pulsed through my mind, and I shuddered as I feared what was ahead of me now.

My fear increased when I saw that Seraphina had been along these stairs recently—I noticed as we descended that the steps were puddled, slippery. I gripped the rocky walls to keep from falling.

I gasped as we stepped out of the narrow rocky stairwell into the underground house. My visions had been accurate. This place was lovely and elaborate; Grecian in style, almost grotto-like. Graceful and terrifying all at once.

We were in a short but wide corridor lined with columns and doors; it was some sort of great hall. The surrounding walls were high and smooth, composed of white marble. The floor was marble. Max had spared no expense here. He had clearly hired the best architects and builders. A dome cathedral ceiling loomed above us, displaying a breathtaking mosaic of a kraken attacking a ship, the tentacles spiraling in and out of doomed vessel's wooden beams. Eight large glowing lamps had been bolted into the walls along the corridor. Two unlit torches rested in sconces. Quickly I pulled them from the wall and Simon lit them for us.

"Where ur we?" Neil whispered.

"Her humble home," Simon muttered as he handed Neil his torch.

I swung mine around to get a better look at the hall.

Lining the marbled walls, from the floor to the bottom of the ceiling mosaic, were painted canvases of half-finished portraits. The faces were painted mainly as black oil-brushed outlines, but many of the portraits had been marred, with slashes across the faces and smears in the dried paint. My insides grew cold as I recognized several of the portrait faces as Conclave members. But there were other portraits, faces I did not recognize. Family and loved ones from her previous life? Victims, perhaps? I shuddered.

"An artist." Simon whispered softly into my ear. "She must have been a painter. Although..." He stepped closer to the portraits and my torchlight. "The nature of the portraits indicates a very disturbed mind."

"It is as if she could never complete a work. Not a single one," I said.

I saw Julian's noble face—an oil paint drop had dried like a black tear across his cheek. A slash cut clear through the face of Robert Buck, the slit so wide and deep that I could see the marble wall upon which the portrait hung. Three almost-finished portraits of Max hung on the wall to my right. My heart leapt at his expression—laughing, ruthless.

The storm must have moved directly above us, because although we were far underground, I could hear the thunder. The gilded portrait frames rattled a bit against the walls. My mind ticked away as I tried to recall from my visions the rooms in the place: a bedroom...she fed the animals here, so there must be a menagerie somewhere...and a treasury for the Conclave's wealth as well.

"William will be in the bedroom," I whispered in the darkness.

And Seraphina. She could be anywhere, behind any of these doors.

Then I saw Hugo, whining and pawing as the base of some wide double doors to our left.

William. "He's in there," I whispered. Simon said nothing, but asked me to hold his medical bag as he stepped ahead of Neil and me, the sword in his hands. He advanced silently toward the doors. He paused, then gingerly opened one of the doors.

Cautiously, we entered an enormous bedroom. This room was completely enshrouded in darkness. No glowing lamps. I saw, in the darkness, the enormous curtained bed, exactly as it had appeared in my vision, and I saw, on the far side of the room, an unlit fireplace.

A tiger suddenly roared from the darkness, and I waved the torch in front of me. Hearing a clink of chains, I froze. A large Siberian tiger rose from the floor near the bed and growled. I stepped forward, the bowie knife poised. But even as the tiger stood, I saw that he had a great steel collar around his neck that had been chained and bolted to a column.

But Hugo, ignoring the tiger, ran past it to the other side of the bed, the place closest to the fireplace. I felt Simon leave my side in the darkness, following Hugo.

"He's over here, Abbie," he said as he crossed the room.

"Guard the door," I said to Neil. "Do you still have the knife?" As soon as he nodded, I ran past the bed to the corner of the room, where William lay on a dirty mat.

A bolt identical to the one around the tiger's neck had been clamped tightly around William's neck and attached to a nearby column. He wore nothing except his pants and a torn shirt. Blood soaked through the shirt, which had been ripped apart, revealing his chest. Pus had dried, crusted around his wounds.

"William!" I hissed under my breath, kneeling on the floor over him.

His skin felt cold, clammy cold. When I touched his shoulders, he did not respond. In relief, I noticed that he was still breathing, and I felt a very weak pulse.

"William, I am here."

I held his limp hand and still there was no response. Hugo whined, licked William's face.

Simon had already opened his medical bag, and now began tearing off the rest of William's shirt. "Shock. He's in shock," he said as he worked. "That collar." He nodded toward it. "It has to come off."

In the glow of the torchlight, I saw the dried blood and bruises under and around the collar. "Where are the bloody keys?" I whispered desperately.

At that point, Simon had completely removed William's shirt.

"Dear God," I whispered.

Bite and claw marks nearly completely covered his throat and chest. Although none appeared fatal, some wounds were swollen, purple. There were bruises and smaller claw marks covering his arms, and a large seeping wound on his thigh.

"Loss of blood," Simon said. "Infection has set in on some of the wounds. I believe our lady is venomous, as there is unusual swelling about the wounds. His entire system is inflamed. I don't, of course, have an antidote."

"Oh, dear God." I felt panicked, so overwhelmed that William might die, I forgot about the lamia. "We have to do something."

Simon considered William for a moment, his eyes unreadable, ice-blue in the darkness.

Then he began acting at lightning speed.

"There's nothing to do about the infection now, but he's going to die if he does not get more blood. In fact, he *is* dying from loss of blood. It's imperative that he get more blood." Simon began rolling up his own sleeve.

"Blood transfusion. He needs a blood transfusion," I said quickly. I would give him my own blood, but I did not know how to conduct the transfusion. "You have done them before?" I asked Simon quickly.

"Once," he said.

"And?" I asked.

He looked at me as he pulled the equipment from his bag. "The patient died. The transfusion often does not work. But I did see it work once while I was in medical school."

I began helping Simon organize the necessary syringes, needles. With a cloth from the bag, I began dabbing carbolic acid across some of the larger wounds as an antiseptic.

Simon disinfected William's and then his own arm.

I heard a thud in the great hall.

I looked at Neil, on the other side of the bedroom, near the door. My heart seized upon itself when I saw the transfixed expression on his face as he stared out into the great hall. Fear marked his weathered features, and then something else: rage. Fury. In horror, I saw what he planned to do.

No. No. No.

"Don't, Neil!" I hissed, standing up. But Neil had already run out into the hall. I almost could not make myself leave

William, but Neil was old—he couldn't face that creature on his own.

From the hallway, I heard a low growl, a smash. And then silence.

"I'm going out there," I said, making sure I had the short-bladed knife and bowie knife in my belt.

But Simon grabbed my arm. "No, Abbie!" he hissed in darkness.

I jerked myself away. "Just save his life! Please. Neil went out there by himself. She's out there. I need to go after him!"

A wave of indecision passed over Simon's face, but he knew there would be no arguing; William was in a desperate condition. Simon plunged the needle into his own arm, securing it before injecting the connecting syringe into William's arm. Immediately, Simon's blood began flowing into the connective tubing.

Before he could pull the needle out and argue with me any more, I ran toward the doors.

The moment I stepped into the great hall, my foot kicked Neil's extinguished torch. In horror I saw that all of the lamps in the hall had been extinguished. Everything was dark.

Motionless, I held my bowie knife poised.

Neil. I didn't hear him anywhere. A sick feeling washed over me. As my eyes adjusted to the darkness, I saw an enormous puddle of water. A gust of wind blew down the staircase far ahead of me and I smelled a salty, fish odor, mingled with the odor of blood.

I trembled violently but stepped forward—I had to keep Seraphina away from the bedroom. Simon would be too weak to defend himself as he lost blood, and, of course, I didn't want her near William.

I heard a noise somewhere at the end of the hall, in the unlit shadows behind me.

She is here.

Somewhere. Lurking. Hunting me. The portraits rattled again as the storm continued to rage far above us. A flash of white from the lightning above spilt down the stairwell entrance, illuminating the hall. And I saw, in that second, Neil's body on the floor at the base of the stairs.

I worked hard to suppress a scream, and I almost dropped my bowie knife. Neil's corpse had been eviscerated; the intestines spilt out around the body.

She was here. She had killed him—silently, swiftly—before he even had time to cry out. And I knew I was her next prey. Still, a strange curiosity about Seraphina broke through my terror. She had been waiting all of this time for a cure, to become fully human again.

"Arabella Sharp."

Her words came out in a thick Scottish accent, a ripple in her voice when she hit the "r" in my name. There was something melodic, antiquated, about her voice. It was an older dialect, an Anglo-tinged dialect. She spoke like the Scottish heroine in a novel.

When I saw her, my heart dropped in my chest.

She leaped down from her perch on the crown molding near the ceiling mosaic. She had obviously just returned from the sea. Even in the shadows, I felt stunned by her size, shape, and beauty. Long hazelnut hair dripped loosely around her face and back. She was the woman from my nightmares, from my visions. In her lamia-form, she stood at least eight feet tall, her legs dragonlike, with talons for tearing flesh. Scales covered most of her body, but I took note of her exposed breasts and the skin around her face and neck—that was probably the best place to attack. Although she wore no clothes, she had jewelry—thick rings upon some of her fingers, a bracelet, rusted and bronzed, wrapped tightly around her wrist. Apart from the talons, I saw that long claws extended from her webbed hands.

I will have to watch those.

Simon had said that we would have to figure her out as we went along. My mind raced rapidly as I tried to take notice of how she moved; I searched for her weaknesses.

From where she stood, fifteen feet away from me at the bottom of the stairs, I smelled her scent. Pungent and deadly. That tangy scent of sea salt and blood become stronger. And I saw, in the gleam of the corridor, the dripping blood around her mouth. Neil's blood.

But there was something else—an acidic odor.

She opened her mouth, hissed, and began walking slowly toward me. I saw the fangs extended, glistening.

Venom? I remembered William's inflammation. Simon was correct—she had to be venomous. I would have to avoid her fangs, too.

Hugo suddenly sprang out of the bedroom, snarling, running straight toward her. She turned, hissed, and with one hand picked him up and hurled him against the far wall. He didn't even have time to yelp. I saw a deep puncture wound in his side from her talons, as he lay very still on the floor.

She hissed again, so loudly it seemed more like a roar.

Some of the canvas portraits quivered. Seraphina looked from me to the bedroom door and then back to me again. Her eyes dilated, and then diminished into serpent slits as she considered me.

"You've finally arrived," she said.

My chest pounded heavily. I fought panic and gripped the knife handle tightly even as my hands slipped upon it, my palms cold, clammy. I had never fought a monster before. I had never believed that anything like her existed, and now she stood before me, and I knew I would have to kill her.

Keep your distance, I told myself, hoping that my general rules for fighting humans would work here. *Don't let her pin you. You can't match her for strength, so keep your distance.*

I saw how gracefully, how quickly, she moved, reminding me of so many predators at once. She had the smoothness of a snake, the swiftness of a lizard; her enormous haunches, her legs reminded me of a crouching lioness hidden among the grasses, moving strongly and stealthily toward her prey.

"Seraphina." I swallowed, almost feeling ridiculous talking to a beast like this. But the breasts, the hair—she was still a woman. I cleared my throat to keep my voice from cracking. "I don't want to kill you." In spite of everything, even what she had done to William, I knew that Max was the true devil in this game. He had kept her here, in this lovely palace-prison, fueling the predator in her with dashed hopes for a cure. The half-finished portraits surrounding us—they might as well have been her half-finished dreams. They were manifestations of her rage, her misery—testaments to the half-finished life that had come to be frozen in this purgatory for almost a century.

"Seraphina, these killings need to stop. And I need my William."

I felt my heart flutter. Something about hearing me claim him as my own emboldened me.

She hissed, and I saw out of the corner of my eye that her long dragon-tail was too close to me, whipping back and forth a bit. We moved slowly in a circle.

She hissed again and moved forward a bit, in a threatening lunge. That tail. I had to keep watching it. She could trip me, and then, if she pinned me, if she leaped on top of me, there would be nothing I could do. I tensed, perspiration dripping down my forehead, and I clutched the knife even tighter in my hand, thinking quickly.

"You are the red-headed girl," she hissed. "Caroline's daughter."

My heart thumped. How much did she know? How much did she know about me?

"I have seen your mother in photographs. You look like her. You were both foolish women, very foolish women, to refuse what I have—to refuse immortality."

Jealousy. I began to realize that she didn't want to be merely human—she had wanted what Mother and I had been offered, to be full members of the Conclave.

The elixir. That was something I could work with—perhaps she could be made to see how little the Conclave valued her. They gave her the elixir, but as Max had told me, they thought she had no "assets" as a human; they had never truly considered her part of their brotherhood.

"Yes, you have immortality," I said. "But what else do you possess? How many times have you left the island in the last century? Are you truly one of them, or do they merely use you?"

I could tell I hit a nerve; she bared her teeth. "You are going to die. You're going to die slowly, Arabella Sharp. I'll break your bones, tear the flesh from your muscles, and then I'll murder your friends before your eyes. Before I'm finished with you, you'll be begging for death. Begging."

She bared her teeth and lunged forward. Even with a non-fatal bite, with her venom and her teeth I would instantaneously be in her clutches. I leaped backwards, and tripped and fell.

Neil's body.

I slipped on the hard marble floor in the mess of his intestines and blood. As I struggled to stand up, fighting nausea, I tried not to think about how it was Neil's blood seeping through my trousers, tried not to think of the slippery mess that I'd fallen upon. I waited for the bite, for the sharp weight of Seraphina's teeth in my flesh.

But instead she laughed, a heartless, cruel laugh. "William said you would kill me, that you would slay me. But you are a mere fumbling girl."

Rage rushed through me as I straightened, feeling Neil's blood smeared upon my face. "You think I haven't killed before?" I spat. "I killed the Conclave. Did you know that? Did Max tell you that? They are gone, Seraphina. Only Max is alive. And I will kill him, too."

The serpent-slit eyes wavered for a moment, and I saw her human eyes, dark and deeply greenish. I suspected then that Max had not told her about their deaths. She knew I had refused the elixir, though ... did she plan to enact revenge on me, for the Conclave, since I refused to take their elixir?

I stopped and took the moment to steady my breathing, then stepped away from Neil's body, distancing myself from Seraphina.

She began shaking, trembling violently. I saw confusion, doubt on her face, and then ... finally ... rage.

She sprang at me, not as a warning this time. She meant to kill me. I could not fight her in the hall, so I turned, threw open a door behind me. The moment I slammed and bolted it, I heard her crash against it loudly, her jaws snapping together in a great clamp.

I chastised myself over what had just happened. I had been so focused on her teeth, on her claws and tail, that I had tripped over Neil's body. That mistake should have been fatal. I could not make a mistake like that again.

Monkeys shrieked behind me. The menagerie—I was in the menagerie. A lamp glowed dully against the wall on the far side of the room. Otherwise, the room was dark.

Then the door behind me burst open. Enraged, Seraphina advanced toward me. I clutched the bowie knife tighter; I had to keep the fight in here. There was at least a little light in this room; fighting her in the complete darkness of the hall was far too dangerous.

She leaped onto the grate of the empty tiger cage immediately in front of me. I saw a half-eaten deer carcass in the cage. I swiped at her with the knife, but in a single movement she knocked it aside and lifted me into the air.

I couldn't breathe; I coughed, spit. I began to see flickering sparkles in my peripheral vision—only the lingering odor of blood on her breath kept me from losing consciousness.

Her claws cut painfully into my throat. She opened her mouth, her fangs extending again.

I still had the second, short-bladed knife in my belt. With my free hand I pulled out the knife and slashed her eye. A membrane shot over it just as the blade made contact, but she screamed and hissed nonetheless. As she clutched her eye, she bit me hard in the arm and kicked me across the room with her foot.

I heard myself scream distantly, as if in a nightmare. The pain was indescribable—worse than any knife wound. I could not imagine what William had endured these past weeks. I saw a narrow gash in my arm as pain pulsed from the wound—it was like a fire searing through my veins.

I bit my lip to keep from screaming, but as I fought hysteria the tears flowed; the pain was too great. I felt my arm stiffening, quaking from the poison—I could not become immobilized. Thinking of snake venom, I sucked the wound rapidly, as hard as I could, spitting the acidic venom away. I couldn't extract it all, but I sucked and then spit out as much as possible in a few seconds, and I felt a bit of ease from the pain.

Her hissing ceased and I crouched, cowering. I knew she was stalking me now, but I didn't know where she was—she could pounce upon me at any moment and then I would be dead.

Amid the monkey shrieks and other animal howls, I

heard a softer sound near me, a soft, delicate noise, louder and more comforting than the others.

Dee-do. Dee-do.

A cool beak pecked my face. Then the bird leaned out of its enclosure, nuzzling my hand for pumpkin seeds.

A dodo!

A second dodo stepped out from behind the foliage in its enclosure. One of these dodos had to be the one I'd fed in Robert Buck's hothouse before it was transported here for safekeeping. The first dodo, unconcerned but marvelous, considered me as I crouched against the enclosure. Its marble eyes rolled downward.

I couldn't cower there any longer, waiting for her like a trapped prey.

"Seraphina," I said into the darkness. It was an invitation.

I saw her massive form step around the monkey cages near me.

She was even closer than I thought.

Pushing my terror aside, I lunged at her again with the short-bladed knife, slicing her neck.

With a great roar, she leapt at me, swiping my chest with her claws. I felt the slashes on my stomach. I had twisted my body around the second before she struck, so the slashes were not as deep as they might have been; although painful, they were infinitely less painful than the bite on my arm was.

We fought, slashing and leaping. It was an odd and grotesque dance. But I began to feel a small hope that if I could get the perfect aim in the right spot, I might survive.

Then, before I could stop her, she pinned me against the

outside bars of a huge birdcage—it was an enormous structure in the center of the menagerie, and stretched from the floor to the ceiling. I panicked, unable to push her off of me. But her weight was too much for even the thick cage wire, and it bent open, wide. Birds, dozens of birds, poured out into the room like a black cloud. In the confusion, I stabbed blindly in the direction of her chest, above the scales, but I missed with every swing. She hissed, and before I could jump away, she pushed me hard to the floor and pinned me there.

I was dead.

Although she did not have her full weight upon me, I could barely breathe. She crushed my rib cage, and I knew she was about to deliver a fatal blow. But then she roared, reared away from me in pain. I used the opportunity to roll out from under her. And it was then that I saw the sword sticking out of her back.

Simon.

The wound had not been fatal; he must have thrown the sword from the nearby doorway. She leapt off of me to pursue him out in the hall.

"Run, Simon!" I yelled. My heart dropped. He would be weakened by the blood transfusion and would not be able to flee from her or fight her. Taking a split second to retrieve my knives, I ran to the hall.

"Stop, Abbie!" Simon's voice was beside me in the darkness, and he caught my arm. He was standing immediately to the right of the door, clutching a column. His face was pale, much paler than normal.

It was then that I heard the great crash, and saw the lamia lying on the floor under a heap of canvas paintings.

The floor was smeared with blood—Neil's blood—and lamp oil. Simon had slicked down the hall and then waited near the menagerie door.

Although my arm throbbed, I could still fight. I had to keep Seraphina away from Simon. Carefully, I moved along the slicked floor of the great hall toward the doors at the far end, away from the staircase and the bedroom.

Canvases began flying in all directions as Seraphina stood, righted herself. I was tiring, and my arm was already swelling from the bite.

I continued running toward the double doors at the very end of the great hall. As I plunged through them, she turned to follow. Falling into the room, I stumbled onto a floor-to-ceiling pile of gold pieces—coins, goblets, jewelry. Stacks of money lined one entire wall. I had found the Conclave's treasury.

"Arabella Sharp!"

She was in the hall, just outside, and I hadn't yet shut and bolted the doors. I heard the click of her talons on the marble floor.

I stood up in the piles, positioning myself. Throwing the knives at her would be my best defense. I remembered how that place—that place where her heart was, near her breasts—was not so heavily scaled. I stood back, hearing the gold pieces slide around me. Two throws. That was all I had.

The next moment, I saw her form in the doorway. I heard breath flowing through her nostrils, and I smelled her venom odor. Instantly, I threw the short-bladed knife, hard.

She hissed, stared at me. Confusion, hatred in her eyes. I remembered the brief bewilderment, the seeming astonishment that had crossed her eyes for a few seconds when I had told her I had killed the Conclave. Once again, I wondered if she understood how she had been used all of these years, how they only needed her as a guard for their animals and their money.

She towered above me, and it was only then that I saw blood oozing from the wound on her neck. But it was not fatal.

Almost blindly, I plunged the bowie knife hard upwards into her chest, trying to ignore the pain and stiffness in my wounded arm. This strike had to hurt her, or she would fall upon me and kill me.

After stabbing her I rolled away through the piles of coins, seconds before she fell. I heard a great metallic rattling, a shift in the mountain of gold, as she fell heavily into it, scattering coins, jewels, goblets all around us.

I scooted away in the pile, gasping, heaving, and barely able to catch my breath. As I backed further away from her, I smelled her rancid, acidic odor.

I had pierced her heart, and it had been a fatal hit. I'd known I had to kill her to survive, and yet I felt deep remorse as I watched her collapse, clutching her chest. My heart pounded as I peered at her in the dim light. It was then that I heard a whimper, more pitiful than any death cry.

Beautiful, naked, lovely, she lay amid the gold—now in her human form, crying. She was not much taller than me. As she lay there, she turned her head toward me, fully a woman now. Her hazelnut hair covered her face. Her wounds bled, the bowie knife still protruding from her heart.

"Abbie!" Simon suddenly stood in the doorway, holding

the sword. He looked terribly pale, and clutched the doorframe for support. Nevertheless, he had a ferocity in his eyes that I had never seen before.

"No, no," I gasped, signaling him to stop where he was. I stared at her body; Simon froze, seeing that Seraphina was wounded. "It's all right," I said. "She cannot hurt us now."

I crept forward, through the coins, and then, gingerly—I'm not sure entirely of my reasons—I pushed her thick hair out of her eyes. She breathed heavily, gasping, wheezing. I knew that every breath pained her.

With a trembling hand, I pushed the hair further away from her face. A slice cut across one eye from where I had first struck her. The other eye, unblemished, pale green, rolled up at me with an expression that I could not read, that I could not understand. She tried to speak, but her voice simply gurgled in her throat.

She wanted to speak. Her lips trembled, but again, there was only that terrible gurgling. There was a desperation in her expression.

It might work, I thought, putting my hand out. The moment I touched her hand, a force came out from her, strong and vibrant as an ocean current, and my mind latched upon it. I saw what she wanted to tell me.

I saw Seraphina in the parlor of a great home, a very grand, ornate home. Silver candelabras and a mahogany clock rested upon the mantel of an enormous stone fireplace. But the parlor was in shambles, torn to pieces. The drapes had been shredded; I saw broken plates and teacup pieces scattered all over the floor. A bookshelf had been emptied, leaving books and torn pages everywhere.

Then I saw her, crouched naked in her human form, blood smeared all over her legs and arms. As the vision pulsed, initially blurry in my mind and then refocused, I saw that she crouched over the bodies of two men. The older had graying hazelnut hair. Her father. The younger dead man, I knew intuitively, was her fiancé. Their hearts had been torn out, and all that remained of their chests were great dark holes. Nonetheless, she crouched over the bodies, frenzied. Weeping.

The realization slammed over me. In in the confessional booth, Max had mentioned that she'd killed a few Bromwell natives after escaping from Robert Buck. She had returned home. She must have been hurt, terribly traumatized, to return to them and then attack them like this. Had they reacted in scorn to her monster form? With hatred? What a terrible weight killing her own father, her fiancé, must have been upon her all of these years!

In the vision, I saw a shadow cross her pale, crouched figure.

Max.

He had a blanket in his arms, a blanket he placed around her shoulders.

"Come. Come with me, my love," he said to her, wrapping the blanket around her bloodstained shoulders and lifting her into his arms. "I think we can find a better place for our pretty beast."

In this vision, this memory, Seraphina didn't say a word to him. But I saw misery, and terrible sorrow, on her face. I felt how she had nursed this, along with whatever other rages she harbored from her human past, all these decades in this place.

She wanted me to see all of this, and I knew that I was seeing her confession.

The vision swiftly left me as she coughed. She leaned to her side as the gurgling in her throat continued, and then she spit up blood. I saw that she was trying to tell me something still.

"Shhhh…" I whispered, feeling an odd sting of tears in my eyes.

I could barely hear her, but between her heaves, she said, "There is a letter…a letter that Max had dropped on the beach…" She gasped, showing her teeth, lovely human teeth now; her fangs had receded. I tried to hush her again but she continued. "Look in the photograph album…" She gasped again, and I knew that she would speak no more.

She coughed and looked up at the ceiling, her eyes focusing and then glazing over. She drew a deep, rattling breath, and then died.

Why would she tell me that? About a letter in the photograph book? Why would she give me her confession, only moments after she had tried to kill me? I felt such an onslaught of emotions in those seconds as I watched her still face.

I remained crouched in the pile of gold, clutching her hand, frozen. Tears slid down my cheeks.

Simon brought me out of my tearful reverie as he stepped forward from the doorway. I had nearly forgotten his presence; he still held the sword in his hand, and his face was stony. As my energy drained from me, I detached my hand from Seraphina's grip and took Simon's hand. My arm was stiff with shooting pain. Simon helped me as I struggled to stand, to catch my breath.

"She killed them," I murmured, croakily. "She was so sad and terrified—she returned home and killed them—her fiancé and her father."

Simon said nothing, just hushed me with an embrace.

"How is he?" I asked urgently as Simon led me from the room. I had stopped reeling from the recent battle, from what Seraphina had shown me. I paused as we entered the great hall, clutching Simon's arm again for support. When he did not answer my question, fear gripped me.

"He is still unresponsive," Simon finally said. "But his breathing has steadied a bit since the transfusion. Abbie ... I cannot say for certain whether or not he will survive. You must remember that."

When I reached William, still lying on the floor of the bedroom, I found his breathing was indeed stronger. There was a hint, a mere hint, of his old flushed color returning. After Simon found the keys to the shackles, in the menagerie, we were able to free William. I cleaned my stomach wounds while Simon attended to the wound on my arm, cleaning it and applying a healing salve. I watched his long lashes flutter as he worked, but we said very little; we were both too sobered over Neil's and Seraphina's deaths, and William's current state.

Then, as Simon built a fire in the bedroom, we heard feeble whining coming from the great hall—we rushed out and discovered, to our great relief, that Hugo was still alive.

While Simon attended to the dog's wounds, I returned to William and I knelt beside him.

"William, I am here. She is slain and cannot hurt you anymore."

I held his arm tightly. I fumbled for what to say. My rage at his past actions seemed so misplaced, so foreign here. I thought of Simon, of all that had happened between us, and of how I now felt absolutely certain of my heart's choice. I knew the nature of my love for William.

"I cannot *not* love you," I said. Bending over him, I kissed his lips.

I watched anxiously for a flutter of eyelids. For something. Anything. I was at the end of the reversed fairy tale, the princess reviving the prince, and I clung to my own foolishness, my adherence to the narrative justice that he must awake.

But nothing happened.

Simon had been cautiously optimistic, and I was desperately hoping that William would recover. But I knew how inaccurate even the best physician's guesses could be.

I laid my head on William's bare, battered chest, and I heard his heart beat far below my ear. The beat was weak, but steady.

My head still on William's chest, I felt myself crying. What if all of this was to be in vain? What if William did not awake from this?

I heard the tiger growling from the other side of the bed, softly, melodically almost. I didn't feel that his growls were such a threat, or a warning to us anymore. I felt that he sensed his mistress was gone; instinctively, he felt the loss. From out in the hall, I heard Hugo whine as Simon continued to stitch his wounds.

Then my heartbeat paused. My hair had come undone from its knot during the battle with Seraphina, and I felt William's fingers suddenly entangled in it. I lifted my tear-streaked face.

"William!" His eyes were not yet open, but I saw his lips move, as if he were trying to speak but could make no sound. His chest heaved under me at the exertion. I grasped his hands in mine.

"William!" I heard myself say. Even more tears spilled out then.

"I ... " he muttered.

I held my breath.

He paused.

"Don't speak if it hurts," I said quickly.

But he shook his head, and I realized he was pushing himself out of this, surfacing to speak to me.

His eyes remained closed, but after he had breathed hard for several seconds, and then became still again, he spoke. "I have been unjust, weak, resentful. I have behaved unforgivably. But when we were together, Abbie, I was never inconstant. Nor will I ever be. I am in love with you, Abbie. Irretrievably in love."

And then, in the dim bedroom light, with the groans of the grieving tiger in the background, I kissed William. He tasted like blood, like her venom; his skin had Seraphina's serpent-scent. But I didn't mind. I thought of how he might still hurt me, but it didn't matter—it was far too late for me to abandon him now. Indeed, my love for him was like a poison in my own blood.

I kissed his lips, then lightly kissed his jaw, his neck. William was wild. Untamed. But he was my William. I had fought this battle, but I knew that he would fight a thousand battles for me. In the firelight, with his dark curls and handsome face, he looked like a fallen hero—I thought of the mortally wounded Paris.

But there was no anguish for me now, because I knew William would heal. He would recover.

Twenty-seven

After Simon stitched up the wounds in Hugo's side, he returned to the bedroom where I remained with William. I had attended to the fire, concerned about keeping William's body temperature from dropping. Simon's salve had already eased the pain from my own bite wound, and the swelling had ceased a bit.

Simon and I now cleaned William's wounds more carefully, washed the dried blood from his forehead and hair, and placed him in Seraphina's bed. His breathing and heartbeats steadied even more after Simon gave him some laudanum, and he fell into a deep sleep.

Simon and I then tranquilized the tiger and moved him to his cage in the menagerie. We collected Seraphina's and Neil's bodies, and we buried them in a sandy part of the island. As we dug their graves, we found several bones and bone fragments in shallow graves that must have belonged to Seraphina's victims. But I think we were both too weary to discuss the matter much. As we dug into the hard sand, I felt an increasing sense of Seraphina's loneliness, of her isolation.

The morning had come on full force, yet the heavy mist that blanketed the island remained settled about us. Nature moved restlessly nearby; my eye caught several razorbills in their nests on the rocky cliffs above. A peregrine sat on a boulder near the waters, eating a fish. I still felt cocooned in this place, set apart. The isolation was almost unbearable, and I longed to return to the mainland.

As we buried Neil, I felt my heart grow even heavier. There were no circumstances under which I could consider returning his body, in its grim state, to his widow, and I did not look forward to seeing that little girl again when we went to his house to speak to his wife. I choked back a sob. A wet gust of wind blew at my hair as Simon and I packed the last bit of sand over Neil's grave.

Neil had said the child was strong; she would have to be. I tried to push away the memories of Mother's death, of Roddy's death—I carried, and would always carry, those memories with me, but they did not cripple me. The child might still be all right.

When Simon and I returned to Seraphina's home, a wave of sleepiness almost overwhelmed me, for the first time. But I could not sleep in the clothes I wore, with Seraphina's and Neil's dried blood stained across my shirt and trousers. So I went to her bedroom, hoping to find clothes and to attend again to William.

I felt my heart leap a bit as I entered—William's eyes were open. He was awake. He lay where we had left him, in bed, propped up a bit against the mound of Seraphina's pillows.

Although still very pale, with terrible bruises about his neck and wrists from the shackles, he seemed better. But he still seemed far too fragile, and I feared embracing him. He rolled to his side, wincing in great pain at the movement.

As I rushed to his bedside, he considered me with a sardonic grin. "What are you wearing?"

"Simon's clothes," I said, twirling a bit. My attempt at humor felt lovely after all that we had been through.

"That is most distasteful," he said, with a scowl and another great wince. "Speaking of the man, I believe that I'm carrying some of his blood."

"You are. The transfusion saved your life."

"That must be precisely why I'm having strange urges to fall on my knees in prayer and to wear that beastly black suit and collar that he sports so frequently. Hopefully, these religious leanings will wear off soon."

I smiled, brushing William's curls away from his forehead. "I'm glad you're feeling better." Then I kissed him. He started to pull me to him, but then pushed me away. "No, it's too bloody strange."

"What's strange?" I asked, surprised.

"Kissing you as you wear St. John's clothes."

I laughed a bit.

"I think you should inspect the lady's boudoir," William said, nodding toward a small door set into the fireplace. "She has quite an array of finery in there…"

Then his face convulsed a bit, and I felt alarmed.

"William…"

"I'm fine. I'm fine. Simon said that I might feel some

pain, some nausea during my recovery. Particularly as the venom works out of my system."

"Do you need ... "

"I need you to change out of those clothes!" he barked, closing his eyes and settling into the pillow on the bed.

I smiled a bit as I opened the boudoir door. It made me feel better that William was acting like his old self—an ass.

The boudoir was indeed extravagant. Seraphina had a large vanity with combs, pearl earbobs, gold and diamond necklaces, and sapphire rings scattered over the entire surface. I surveyed the many gowns. These were no ordinary tea dresses, the type of prim dresses that Grandmother and I wore so often. I did not see any bustles, corsets, or crinolines. These gowns were imported from the Continent—loose and free-flowing dresses of taffeta and silk gauzes, with gold and silver threading the hems. They were low-necked, with ribbons around the waists. I saw kimono robes and other gowns, shockingly low, bohemian in style. The colors showed excellent taste—no dark brown or blacks, these were all pastels, mostly the colors of the sea—greenish or light blues. There were piles upon piles of slippers, lovely slippers in pale green and plum hues.

Did Max bring her all of these?

A lump formed in my throat—all of this jewelry, these gowns, reminded me of the woman she had been. Her crumbled form in that vision ... it had been too sad, too terrible. She had also lived these years not only as a beast, but as a woman.

I washed my face and body in a porcelain tub. Then, choosing the least elaborate gown I could find, a plain rose-colored silk with red tassels falling about the waist, I put it on with a pair of her slippers. Feeling more like a china doll than myself, I left the boudoir.

When I entered the bedroom, I saw Simon standing by the bed and William asleep. Simon had turned down the lights.

"I've given him a sedative," he said quietly to me, still looking at William's face.

As I walked toward the bed, Simon's expression concerned me. "What is it?" I asked.

"We can't move him yet. Not while the venom is working out of his body. He needs to heal a bit before we return home."

"How long will that take?" I asked.

Simon shrugged a little. "Hopefully not very long. I'm quite surprised he survived this ordeal at all."

"But he'll recover completely?"

"Undoubtedly." But I saw a small shadow cross his expression.

While William slept, I sat with Simon in the library sipping brandy. Hugo slept at our feet. He would recover; his entire side had been stitched and bandaged by Simon. We discussed our plans. Apart from making the treacherous journey back to land and getting William safely returned to London, we needed to figure out what to do with all of the Conclave's animals.

"We can't just leave them here," I said, as we stared wearily at the roaring fire.

Simon took another sip of brandy. "What to do with

the animals will be a bit of a problem. Perhaps we could give some to the Zoological—"

"The photograph album!" I exclaimed, as my eye caught sight of a large album on a side table. In our concern over attending to William, Hugo, and the bodies, both Simon and I had forgotten Seraphina's last words, directing me to the album.

As I opened it, I caught my breath.

There were photographs, rows and rows of photographs.

"Max must have recorded their travels, their discoveries," Simon said as he peered over my shoulder at it. There were pictures of Julian Bartlett in Africa, of Robert Buck in India. I saw close-up photographs of Robert's shrunken heads. There were also several photographs of Seraphina, both in her monster form and in her naked human form. In one particularly stunning photograph, she sat totally nude in front of her boudoir, her back to the camera. Her long hair was pulled over her shoulders, in front of her, so that her tattoo showed boldly and clearly.

I gasped when I came to the final photograph. It was my mother, painting in our garden in Dublin. She didn't seem to know that she was being photographed, and I felt my heart freeze, wondering how many times Max had observed us there, monitored us throughout the years. He had been near us, those days before Mother's death. I recalled again her transfixed gaze as she looked into the woods on that stormy night after she had fallen ill. The argument that had ensued between her and Max after he had saved me. She had known that he was lingering near, but to then see me in his arms—I could only imagine her fear.

Then a letter fell out of a pocket on the last page of the album. Quickly, I opened it. Most of the letter had been damaged by water. I couldn't read any of the writing, even the date. I couldn't even read the signature.

Was this the letter that Seraphina wanted me to see?

Simon and I took it over to the fire, to examine it better in the light, but my eyes were tired. The exhaustion was overtaking me and I had difficulty focusing.

"The letter is written to Max," Simon said calmly.

I saw the faint shape of an "M" near the top of the page.

"There. There is one distinguishable line," I said, peering closer. The letter was so damaged, I felt as if it would crumple at any moment in my hands. I read it out loud: *"Keep him alive. You must keep him alive."*

"Keep who alive?" I asked Simon. We both tried to read the signature at the bottom, but we could not. It was impossible. "Someone wrote to Max, insisting that he keep someone alive," I concluded.

Simon drained his glass of brandy and stared hard into the fire. "Abbie, tell me again what happened to you, that night in Highgate Cemetery."

Although perplexed by the question, I quickly recalled to Simon, as best as I could, everything about that awful experience.

Simon remained thoughtful, staring ahead.

"And you saw nothing after William arrived? No more strange figures threatened you once William was there?"

"Yes. That is correct."

Simon said nothing.

Instinctively, I felt defensiveness rise within me. "William isn't responsible for this. If you think he is somehow in league with Max—"

"That's not at all what I am considering," Simon said calmly. "I am simply making some connections in my head."

My mind spun, confused.

"Are you thinking that William is the person whom the letter-writer wants Max to keep alive?"

"I'm considering it."

Simon moved his gaze from the fireplace to my face. His mouth curved into a half-amused smile. I blushed. "When was the last time you slept, Abbie?"

"When we were on the train," I said.

"Sleep now."

"But..."

"We do have more ahead of us to figure out. But nothing can be done now. William needs sleep. You need sleep."

"But Max..."

"I'll remain awake."

I started to argue, but he was already placing blankets upon the sofa.

"Shhh..." Simon said as I made a weak attempt to argue. He turned the lamps down, hushing me, and I felt my body sink onto the sofa; in spite of my anxieties, I was dead to the world before Simon even left the room.

But my sleep did not go undisturbed.

I was underwater somewhere. In the waters near here. Sunlight broke through the surface. I swam without having to breathe. It was easy, dreamlike. The waters became cloudy, and then parted. She stood in front of me, a full lamia, but kind, not threatening. She reached out and touched my fingertips with her talons. As she did this, as her image wavered, she became my mother, her long red hair rippling out—my mother as the lamia.

I heard myself whimper under the water in longing. She brushed my cheek with her scaly palm, and then swam away into the watery darkness.

The dream melted away and I found myself in a shadowed room. The smell of rot around me assaulted my nose. Spoiled meat. Then my eyes adjusted as I saw human limbs, decomposing corpses strewn everywhere. I was in some sort of underground place—a basement or a charnel house. I saw a slab table in front of me... and some sort of saw nearby.

A light approached the doorway as someone came near this room where I found myself. Then I heard a chuckle from the darkened corridor. The Ripper chuckle, the chuckle of my nightmares.

I awoke, sweating. Shaking. The library fire had died down and I hugged myself, pulling the tassels about my waist tighter. What was happening? What was Max scheming?

In horror, I thought of the graveyard murders, of our follower. Whatever was happening, I felt certain that Max was no longer alone. Was he starting a new Conclave? And why had he felt so strongly about me slaying Seraphina?

I left the library and found Simon sitting in a chair near William's bed, reading a book. William was still fast asleep. But he kept turning back and forth among his pillows.

"I think the laudanum is giving him strange dreams. He's been muttering things..." Simon said.

"What sort of things?" I asked, wondering briefly if William was having the same nightmare I had just had.

But Simon's eyes veiled a bit. "He keeps uttering your name."

I felt myself smile. In spite of everything behind and ahead of us, the fact that William and I were restored to one another was deeply gratifying to me.

"You are pale, Abbie."

I shook my head. "I had another nightmare. But I don't feel like talking about it now." I said this quickly, imploringly.

"William's fever is returning," Simon said. "This is good; at this point it means his body is fighting the infection. Nonetheless, I don't want it to get too high. We'll need to sponge him again with cool water." He stood. "But now he needs more laudanum. I'm afraid what I gave him last night will wear off soon; I will need to retrieve some more from the boat."

I felt a sudden urge to escape this place. To go outside with the wind and water.

"I'll go."

Simon frowned at me, but I was already putting on my boots—I felt certain that I looked awkward wearing my mud-stained boots under the graceful gown.

"I don't mind going upstairs," I said. "I need the fresh air."

Simon cocked his head.

"Oh truly, Simon, I just slayed a century-old lamia. I think I can take care of myself," I snapped as I walked into the boudoir to retrieve my bowie knife from where I had left it on the pile of my dirty clothes. I put the kimono robe over my gown before going outside.

After ascending the stone steps to the beach, trying not to trip over the too-long kimono robe, I noticed that there was only a little sound now in the calm night. I heard only the soft slap of waters against the island's rocks, and the small breath of wind in my ears. As I walked toward the boat, which Simon and I had checked after attending to the bodies, I was glad to see that it was still secured; fortunately it had been only a little damaged from our small crash onto the island. Carefully, I reached into the bottom of the dory and found the large laudanum bottle.

As I straightened up, I gazed out over the waters and felt a vague, prickly frustration. Seraphina's death saddened me, and Max was still alive somewhere. I felt a bit as if I were in the same place that I'd been in immediately after killing the Conclave members. I thought of what Simon had said—about the Orkney Islands being one of the settings in *Frankenstein*—and I wondered, depressed and fearful, if my dream of being a physician might evaporate in the winds. I wondered if, like Victor Frankenstein pursuing his monster, I would spend the remainder of my life hunting Max, pursuing Max, for all of my days. I sighed.

A branch cracked in the darkness somewhere behind me.

I stiffened. *Max.* I whipped around, but saw nothing except rocks and moonlight. I turned to go back inside.

But my heart paused as I heard the slough of a foot in the wet sand.

Someone was certainly behind me.

I took one more step, still holding the bottle of laudanum. I tightened my grip on the knife. I estimated the follower to be at least three feet behind me.

When I felt him step closer, I dropped the bottle in the sand and, at the same moment, whipped around, kicking my pursuer hard in the ribs. He cried out as I twisted his arm behind him and put the bowie knife to his throat; my fear and rage coursed through me so that I didn't even feel my wounded arm. But even as I surprised my follower, I knew that it was not Max; if it had been, I would not be able to subdue him so easily.

And indeed, the man wasn't Max—he was our sunburned follower. Even in the moonless night, I saw the ash-blond hair clearly.

I felt jumpy and my patience was papery thin. I kept his arm twisted behind him and, without a word, moved the knife from his throat to his back. I was a bit surprised that he didn't try to defend himself, but I seemed to have broken his rib—he was doubled over, not even trying to struggle with me.

"You! Who are you?" I demanded, pressing the knife harder into his back.

"Someone who means you no harm." He was still bent over.

"We'll see about that."

"Put your dagger down. Please," he demanded, still clutching his chest.

"No," I said firmly, pushing him in front of me as I headed down the stairs and into the great hall.

Simon was already there, alarm on his face. I didn't want to disturb William, so I led the man into the library.

Hugo, who lay before the fire unable to move due to all the bandages Simon had wrapped around his torso, lifted his head weakly as we entered and growled at the intruder.

I pushed the man into a kneeling position on the floor

and placed the knife blade against his throat again. Vaguely, I felt a twinge of guilt knowing that his ribs must hurt terribly, but I couldn't trust him for a second. I couldn't imagine that he meant well, given that he'd been following us these past few weeks.

"You have five seconds to tell me who you are, where you come from, and what you are doing here, or I'll cut your throat. Simon, tie him up, please."

Simon left and re-entered the room with the useless, water-damaged revolver and an old rope. The man still hadn't said a world.

"Three seconds!" I yelled, pressing the knife more tightly against his throat.

"Abbie," Simon said calmly, but his mouth twitched in amusement. The man's jacket flipped open as Simon tied him up, and I saw Simon's eyes focus on something on the inside flap.

"Edmund Wyatt," the man said, heaving, his chest still in pain. "I come from London. I work for Her Majesty the Queen, and I need to speak to both of you."

I hesitated and glanced at Simon. His eyes were still on the man. He cleared his throat. "I would believe him, Abbie." He reached out, tearing something from the inside of Wyatt's jacket.

I gasped—the emblem on the jacket lining was the same as the emblem on Richard's tattoo.

Simon and I looked hard at one another, over Wyatt's head.

"If you will loosen these ropes and attend to my chest, I would greatly appreciate it," Wyatt said calmly. "I know that you are a physician, young man, and I believe that she has broken my rib. I promise you, I have no ill will toward you—my concern is with the remaining Conclave member." Wyatt looked up at me, and I saw that he was perhaps older than I'd first imagined, perhaps in his early fifties. "He is doing dark deeds, dark and terrible deeds."

Epilogue

I stared out the window at the morning fog as the carriage sped through the Highlands of Caithness. William lay sleeping in the carriage seat across from me. He was wrapped in multiple blankets. He needed rest, and privacy, which we would not have on a train, so we'd decided to take the carriage all the way to London. Although his fever continued, it remained low; still, he had a long recovery ahead of him. While Simon remained on the island to care for the animals, I would take William back to Christina so that she could begin nursing him back to health.

This very morning, Simon was to go into Bromwell to speak to Neil's wife about his death. I thought of Margaret MacDiarmand and that traumatized little girl, Laura... I shuddered, relieved that Simon had decided to deliver the news himself. With his sensitivity, he would be nothing but compassionate.

The carriage took a sharp turn and we sped past an enormous loch, an expanse of dull shine under the dark morning clouds. An eagle cut gracefully through the waning fog, a silver fish in its claws.

I would return here as soon as I had delivered William safely. A tightening started in my chest—I wanted to stay with William in London to care for him. But Simon and I had too much to do with figuring out where to send the animals. Thinking through this was an enormous task. Max had often transported the animals to and from the island in small groups, but we now had, we believed, *all* of the Conclave's animals to deal with—including two dodo birds, which would cause too much of a sensation and raise too many questions if they were made public. Fortunately, money was no issue. Wyatt had told us that all of the wealth in the treasury was ours—our payment for killing the Conclave and Seraphina.

Edmund Wyatt.

"Do you trust him?" Simon had asked me, the first moment we spoke alone after meeting Wyatt.

"I'm not certain."

"Neither am I."

Simon's response had come quickly. He told me that the emblem on Wyatt's jacket—the same emblem that was tattooed upon Richard—was indeed an emblem associated with the Queen's secret service.

"How do you know this, Simon?" I asked.

He smiled coolly. "That is a whole other story. I'll tell you about Richard when we have more time. I have a bit of a history with Richard."

Although we'd said very little about it, I knew we had many of the same questions about this Edmund Wyatt.

If, as Wyatt told us, he did work for Queen Victoria, and it had been his responsibility to monitor the Conclave's actions, why hadn't he stopped them when they began killing those women last year? Why had he let Simon, William, and me deal with the Conclave both then and now? Of course, Max was a ruthless killer, evasive, with strange physical powers endowed upon him by the elixir; still, certainly the monarchy could track and control him. When Simon and I had asked Wyatt these questions, he'd given us only vague answers, telling us that he would give us more answers at a later time.

My mind spun with all that Wyatt had told us before returning to London. Once Simon and I were both back in town, we were to meet Wyatt for even more specific information.

"I am the only individual in the Queen's service who knows of the Conclave," he'd said. "This surviving Conclave member must be stopped or the very monarchy will be threatened. I assure you, he is not alone now."

Wyatt's words burned into me now. I remembered my nightmare about the charnel house, body pieces in the background. Max's cruel laugh.

I shuddered.

What was Max planning? Who else could be in league with him?

Wyatt had said "dark and terrible deeds."

After that hideous autumn last year, with the Ripper murders, I couldn't imagine what else Max could plan.

William turned a bit on the seat. Carefully, I stood and adjusted his pillows. He was in a deep sleep. As I pushed his curls away from his face and ran my finger lightly down his jaw, feeling the scratch of his dark stubble, I thought of how handsome he was even with his face flushed with fever, his cheeks hallowed, and his frame thinner.

Although I sat back down in my seat, I couldn't peel my eyes away from him. He had been raised by an unconventional adoptive father, but where he originally came from, no one, not even Christina, knew.

"William, who are you?" I asked softly.

I remembered the water-damaged letter to Max in the photo album, with the cryptic message telling him to keep someone alive. Simon had seemed to suggest that William might be the person the letter writer referred to. Why? And Simon had also made a remark about how those terrible beings had stopped pursuing me upon William's arrival at Highgate Cemetery. I'd always thought that was mere coincidence, but now I wondered.

Nothing made sense—the cannibalism, the Conclave's symbol near the bodies in the graveyard, why Max wanted me to kill Seraphina when he could have easily done it himself. I sighed and settled back into the carriage again.

There was so much ahead. So many unanswered questions, and I feared that whatever Simon, William, and I faced in the future would be far worse than what we had already seen.

I bit my lip hard and stared out the window.

A shard of sunlight broke through the sky in the distance, casting an enormous golden-brown haze upon the sides of a nearby mountain ... the color startlingly similar to the hue of Seraphina's long locks.

Photography by Roger Hutchison

About the Author

Amy Carol Reeves has a PhD in nineteenth-century British literature. She lives in Columbia, South Carolina, where she teaches at Columbia College and writes young adult books. When not teaching, writing, or spending time with her family, she likes jogging with her Labrador retriever Annie, reading Jane Austen novels, and seriously hoping that bloomers come back in style at some point. *Renegade* is her second novel.

Watch for *Resurrection*,
the thrilling conclusion to the Ripper trilogy!